DIAMOND LAKE

DAVE MEAD

Fire Mountain Press
Hillsboro, Oregon

Published by:
Fire Mountain Press
P. O. Box 3851
Hillsboro, OR 97123

Cover art from a photo by David E. Mead
Book and cover design by Andrée Shelby and Shelley Russell

ISBN: 1-929374-08-9
Printed in the U.S.A.

Books by Dave Mead:

Dead Even
Diamond Lake
Stix
Gumshoe One: A Snowball Thing
SmokeScreen
Just People Doin' the Best They Know How
Life – A Short Course

Published by:
Fire Mountain Press

Dedication & Acknowledgements

I'm dedicating my ability to write to fate,
For it is fate that I was born from
The loins of a gentle and brilliant
Woman who taught me to see life a bit differently.
It was fate that I was reared in the muddy
Footsteps of loggers.
It was fate that took me into the garbage-strewn
Night streets of Portland as a cop.
And it was again fate that I was to meet
Two women.
One, a doctor who puts me back together
When I'm broken and holds me tight at night.
The other, an editor who believes in my writing.

Prologue

They'd been in-country for close to three weeks, they being seven Navy Seals – "bubbleheads" or "frogs" to the regular Navy -- doing some clandestine thing to the Vietcong supply lines where they crossed the Perfume River just North of Dong Hoy.

The one they called "Padre" walked into the Skipper's office to report first thing when they got back. The Skipper flipped an envelope across his lucky three-legged field table, the fourth leg being an upended ammo box. A pamphlet on infectious disease acted as a shim; the pamphlet was folded in such a way that it read "In Dis" from where Padre stood. He looked at the envelope and back at the Skipper.

"Came 'bout the time you left," he said, "See you in a while."

Padre spent the next three days in transport home, the main leg over the Big Water in the canvas-sling seat of casualty transport.

There were twenty-four guys in the forward area trying not to die before they saw their folks one more time and fourteen corpses on cots aft. About halfway across they lost cabin pressure for awhile and the oxygen masks dropped down. The three overworked nurses helped their patients put the masks on, while aft, fourteen masks swung over the faces of fourteen corpses all the way to the States. It told the Padre a lot about life, but mostly about death. He wasn't sure just what he learned from the experience, but something.

When he walked into his folks' antique store in Las Vegas his mother told him that his Dad had taken his golden lab, Rex, and gone up to the cabin that they had built in the Malheur National Forest. He had only planned to be gone a week, and that was almost six weeks ago. They had been searching for him for four weeks; there was a heavy early winter snow cover but since Padre and his Dad were the only two who knew where the cabin was, the searchers hadn't found him. He drove straight through, found his father's rig, stripped, in the campground parking lot where they always left their pickup, and snow-shoed in dragging a sled of supplies.

His Dad and Rex were both dead. His father was on the bottom bunk, his hand on the back of the dog that lay on the floor at his side. He'd left him a note:

> *Son,*
>
> *This is the last time I'll put pen to paper.*
>
> *The second day here I chopped my knee with my trusty hatchet just like you said I would), and it bleeds like hell every time I try to walk. Snowed heavily for the first four days, and off and on since. We've been out of grub for over three weeks. Saw a buck yesterday. Missed him. Buck fever I guess.*
>
> *I'm leaving the door slightly ajar so Rex can go out and get water. I can't make myself eat him. After I'm dead I hope he eats*

me. It's the least I can do for him. If he does and is still alive, don't shoot him. It's what I want, and after all, he'll be part of the family then.

Get it?

Take care of your Mother; she really didn't mean what she said about you going to Vietnam.

Dad

He cussed out both his Dad and the dog. If either one of them, had been smart enough to eat the other, at least one would be alive. He rolled both of them in a tarp on the sled, gathered up his father's gear, burned the cabin, and seven days later was back with his unit.

Within two weeks of when he got back they began catching a lot of hell from the VC, and they weren't getting air support, supplies, or replacements. They were all beginning to realize that they'd been left for dead by the US Government, but didn't want to believe it.

It really hit home when Padre took a team on a Search & Rescue to try and find two fly-boys who fell out of the big blue. He led his six men through the jungle like he was equipped with a homing beacon and found the wreckage; the pilots were huddled under a wing.

Padre had a special sense about things and somehow knew that it was a trap. The guys with him didn't think it was, but had been with him enough times before and knew that they were probably alive because he had the 'feel.' The Padre told them that he figured that the VC were using the pilots as bait to see how many more they could catch. His team just got grim-faced, ran their hands over their weapons, and nodded.

Padre took Mad Dog, left the other five to cover them if shit happened and, using the cover of darkness and a heavy rain, crawled down into the swamp where the plane was and pulled the sky pilots out. They were pretty busted up, but both of them looked like they might live, if they got them to a hospital before infection killed them. Before they left Mad Dog wired the bird up real nice.

When the bird blew she took about an acre of everything with her and let the Seals know that they had about an hour's lead on the VC. A company of VC caught up with the Seals about two clicks short of the river.

The Seals were the best there was at their specialty, which was hit-and-run, sneak-and-peek, and generally raise hell. But even they couldn't fight off a whole jungle full of pissed-off VC while carrying two wounded fly boys.

Somehow they fought their way to within half a mile of the water before they were pinned down tight.

They had been screaming for air support for over an hour to no avail. Then someone radioed to ask if the pilots were still alive. They radioed an affirmative and five minutes later all hell broke loose.

Padre and Mad Dog hung back and held off the VC while the rest of his men pulled the fly boys out to the river where three Scats, the Seal version of a PT Boat, waited.

The Padre and Mad Dog fought their way to the river too, but not before Padre took two stingers, one in the left knee that left him face down in the mud and cussing. While he was feeling sorry for himself Mad Dog came back for him and it was then that Mad Dog took one in the chest. Padre dragged himself and the ungrateful bastard the last hundred feet to the lone Scat. The other two Scats were two miles down the Perfume before the crew pulled the last two Seals into the boat.

One of the two gunners was sitting behind his fifty-caliber, twin holes in the left side of his head.

"Do your thing, Padre." The boat jockey said. "It was his first fuckin' trip up the creek!"

Padre nodded, gritted his teeth against he pain from the gunshots he'd taken in his leg and levered himself over next to the dead kid.

"Go with God." He said, then asked for a first-aid pack.

"What if he don't like your God?"

"God is all encompassing."

"Well, it wasn't your God that got you air cover."

"I'm listening."

"One of the pilots is the son of a US Senator." The boat jockey laughed like a young man made old by too much death. "Of course that didn't have anything to do with finally getting air cover." He quit talking and set about squeezing the last few Rpm's out of the Scat in an effort to catch his buddies.

Mad Dog and Padre spent the last three weeks before the Tet Offensive sucking up pints of blood and trying to get the nurses to screw them. When they weren't messing with the nurses Padre had to listen to Mad Dog bitch because Padre had been too damn lazy to carry him and he got all muddy from being dragged. It seemed that Mad Dog had forgotten that Padre had taken two slugs in his leg.

Before they were flown back to the States, Mad Dog had refined his story to the point that he had also picked up a nasty sliver from not being properly transported by Padre.

Once Stateside, after spending the obligatory nine days blind drunk, Padre opted for an out and after changing his name to that of a buddy he'd watched die, took a job as a police officer in a small town in Nevada where he forgot about God.

Mad Dog decided to make a career out of "havin' frog feet."

But then, that was a long time ago.

Chapter One

Even though it didn't happen overnight, Joe went from being just another name in the long list under the heading "INVESTIGATORS" in the City of Lost Angels phone book, to becoming just another name in the long list under the heading "INVESTIGATORS" in the City of Portlandia phone book.

Her methodology had been quite simple, and he sure as hell had to commend her for the way she'd set him up.

One of her fellow welfare field agents had thrown a party and invited Gloria and several others in the office with their "significant other." It was there that a pert little redhead with a butch cut had asked Joe what he did for a living. Gloria had turned from where she was standing, across the living room, and told everyone in her beautiful, musical voice that turned to ice as she warmed to her subject, "Oh, didn't you know? My Joe is a Primate Defective. He slithers along through alleys peeping into windows. And every once in awhile, he comes lunging out of the darkness to hurt someone." She demonstrated by curling her fingers into talons and clawing the air, before continuing, "Usually financially." Then she turned her back on him and resumed her conversation with a fellow agent.

Joe had stood there with some sort of stupid grin frozen on his face, while the others in the room looked at him with a mixture of pity and apathy. It took probably a minute for the words to sink in through the scotch. And maybe another thirty seconds for him to figure out that she'd just said goodbye.

Joe had tried to save face by shrugging it off and talking shop with one of the 'significant others' who pumped gas at a local Chevron station. That conversation went nowhere pretty fast, so he'd eased over to the patio door, and stood watching her until she felt his eyes on her, then turned, smiled, and lifted her glass to him in a toast. He'd tried to nod, but really his head just gave a kind of a jerk.

Joe had drifted across the patio through the smoke from the unattended barbecue, walked around the house and down the street to where their car was parked, and driven home.

On the way home to their rented ranch, he'd pounded his fists on the steering wheel, and let the tears slide down his face. It was, he'd vowed, the last time he would ever let anyone, or any event, close enough to hurt him.

He had been surprised to find that it took only eleven minutes to put everything he wanted from living with her for three years into his one-ton surveillance van. Then he'd gone through the house methodically, looking for anything that would help him understand what had happened to their relationship. There had been nothing, which in its own way was even more disturbing.

Joe had realized that he needed to get to the bank before Gloria did the next morning, which was Friday. (Gloria and her pals worked four tens, which made Thursday their Friday. He'd asked her once what Sunday was, if Thursday was Friday, Friday was Saturday, and Saturday was Sunday? "Church," she'd said. Though she'd never gone.)

In the medicine cabinet there'd been a prescription for a knock-you-on-your-ass sleeping potion Gloria had been using periodically ever since they had been living together. Joe had smashed six of the tablets into powder, then slit the last four peppermint tea bags open just enough to insert a small long-necked funnel he fashioned from a strip of aluminum foil. Then he'd poured approximately one-and-one-half tablets worth into the center of each tea bag. He'd found a tube of household cement in a drawer by the sink, used that to seal the tea bags, then put them back into their individual envelopes. He'd left the tea box on the kitchen counter, along with the keys to their Honda and the house keys, though he kept one front door key that he'd had made the week before, planning to hide it under the flowerpot by the front door or some other equally secure location. He'd driven up the street a block, and parked behind a mom-and-pop grocery that closed at eleven. From there he'd had a straight shot at the dining room window of his former abode. He'd trained "Big E" on the window, put on earphones, turned up the volume and laid down on the cot amid his worldly possessions. When the front door of the house had slammed at two-twenty, he'd damn near clawed a hole in the van's ceiling.

Guess I had the volume up a little too high, he'd thought to himself. He'd been able to hear two women wandering around chattering about him being gone. One, naturally, had been Gloria, who said, "Well, it looks like he took the hint." The other woman had been the stoop-shouldered little brunette who Gloria spent her Sunday's with, haunting antique stores. Their Sunday; our Saturday.

When Joe had heard Gloria invite Patty to share in her nightly ritual of peppermint tea, he'd gotten worried. He'd only wanted Gloria to oversleep. He sure as hell hadn't wanted Patty to drink that and try to drive home. Both of them were already schnockered. But it'd turned out that he'd had no cause to worry. Within fifteen minutes they'd both passed out on the bed in the master bedroom. On impulse he had let himself back into the house where, after thinking about it for several minutes, he'd stripped both women and posed them in a number of career-damaging positions with one another, taking two rolls of film in the process. His intuition had paid off less than a week later when his answering service relayed a message to meet Gloria and her attorney at a cafe not far from her office.

Joe had arrived two cups of coffee and a maple bar before they had.

Without bothering to introduce herself, the attorney had informed Joe of Gloria's right to fifty percent of his gross earnings for the next five years, due to the stress his job had inflicted on her. Joe had listened politely, nodding occasionally and, when the attorney had finished her spiel, he'd given them seven of the eight-by-ten glossies to look at while he explained the ramifications of such photos being inadvertently left in various places. Gloria had risen, half out of her seat and yelled, "You stinking slimy bastard! This is a setup!" She'd turned to her attorney for verification. "Patty and I haven't ever even thought about anything like this," she'd exclaimed as she'd gestured toward the photos that now lay face down on the table.

Joe had turned and smiled at the elderly gentlemen having their lunch at the adjoining table.

Her attorney hadn't answered Gloria right away, just picked one of the photos up by the edge like she didn't want to get any on her, and looked at it. "They look authentic," she'd said with a shrug. Joe had grinned.

Gloria had gulped, then cussed some more. She was pretty good at it. And the gentlemen at the adjoining table had seemed suitably impressed, having foregone their recap of yesterday's televised golf game to listen to Gloria. She'd been aware of her audience and had increased the volume and scope of her tirade for their benefit.

After she had run out of things to call Joe and calmed down, her attorney had suggested that Gloria drop any and all requests of Joe in exchange for the photos and the negatives being destroyed. Joe had told them that he thought maybe he should consider being paid a settlement considering that he was so traumatized to learn of his wife's new lover. To the disappointment of her audience, Gloria hadn't said a word; she just turned white, then red, then kind of peachy-yellow. Joe had seen a chameleon about that color once, laying across an autumn leaf. In the end he'd shaken hands with the attorney, who'd asked for one of his cards.

Chapter Two

The morning after Joe had moved out, he had rented a storage locker for his possessions, then had spent the next two months living in his van and working too many cases. The only indulgence he'd allowed himself was a four-mile run every day, preferably in dry sand. It seemed to be the only way he could keep his knee limbered up.

Late in September he found himself with an unexpected four-day weekend. The attorneys' office that he worked for had blocked out a Thursday and Friday for court testimony on two different cases; both had been settled out of court on Wednesday afternoon, leaving him free. He, like most of the rest of the nation, had been reading the papers and watching on the tube as searchers spread out in an ever-widening half-circle trying to find two small children who had wandered away from their parents' campsite in a rugged wilderness area some two hours east of Shaky Town in the foothills of the Santa Ana Mountain Range.

On the spur of the moment, Joe decided to join the search. He gathered his gear into the back seat of a rented Monte Carlo, and by the time he pulled up to a roadblock four miles from the command center for the search, he knew by the way the wind was gusting that there wasn't much time left. He was politely informed that no one but trained search-and-rescue personnel were being allowed to participate. He flashed his official fake ID that said he was something that he wasn't and was waved through. A mile up the road he realized that he had pulled the wrong official fake ID out of his belly bag. That was a mistake that he had never made before, and God willing, never would again.

Just for drill he flipped the wallet open. Like all of his others it was well worn and contained the usual credit cards, cash, a couple of receipts for car repair, and several business cards with traceable phone numbers, all from his supposed hometown and identifying him as who he thought he was at the time.

Yep. His picture all right. The only problem was that it said that he was a research scientist with the Woods Hole Institute. Joe didn't know why in the hell a oceanographer would be on a search in a desert. But apparently neither did the State Trooper.

But that would only have been a problem if he hadn't gotten into the search area. Joe knew from the papers and TV coverage that the search was being conducted above the road only, the logic being that if the children came to a road, they would follow it, one way or the other.

Joe had grown up on a dry-land cattle ranch in Eastern Oregon and knew that there was no such thing as logical behavior when a human was lost. Be it adult or child. So he figured that if they hadn't been found with a grid search above the road, then they probably weren't there. Abduction had been pretty much ruled out. That left two terrified kids and their cocker spaniel pup out there in the broken rock, sand, and scrub pine.

Joe pulled off the road about a hundred feet short of where a puffed-up, red-faced sheriff paraded back and forth in front of the bored TV news cameras. He could feel someone watching as he shrugged into his pack. He scanned the area above the command center and found her. She had `kid's mother' written all over her. Their eyes locked. He nodded and, picking up his seven-foot walking staff that helped take the weight off his bad knee, limped across the road. Just before he dropped down out of sight behind a rock formation, he looked up. She was standing, shielding her eyes against the sun, watching him.

He paralleled the road scanning for tracks, staying just far enough below the road to be out of sight. On the ranch he had become very good at tracking everything from lost cattle and calf-killing coyotes to the pickup tracks of rustlers who didn't want to be tracked. And a few times before his Dad sold their spread, they'd helped find lost hunters.

Two hours later he caught the tracks of the children, headed downhill, away from the road. As this happened BC (Before Cell Phone), he had no way of contacting anyone. He did and he didn't want to play hero, but right now he didn't have the luxury of a choice. It was already afternoon and beginning to cloud up. Rain was forecast, with wind and falling temperatures. The general feeling, expressed via the news media, was that if the kids weren't found by nightfall, they wouldn't survive. As the weather began to deteriorate he had to agree. About twenty minutes short of having to break out a flashlight, he found them huddled under a rock outcropping.

Joe carefully wrapped them in a space blanket and talked to them while he heated water. The kids, one of each make, were in bad shape; it took him half an hour to spoon a cup of warm instant soup down the two of them. The pup drank two cups of warm water, bit Joe on the finger when he tried to feed him a scrap of jerky, and then pissed on his boot. Somehow you got to respect a pup like that.

He lengthened the straps so the top of his pack rode half way down his back, and sat the boy on the top, then wrapped an elastic bandage around himself and the boy to hold the child in place. The little girl rode against his stomach, in a sling made from his backpack hammock, with the pup curled up asleep in her lap. They were too far gone to communicate except once when the girl whispered to him that her dog's name was "Joker."

Before loading himself down with the kids Joe taped a small rock in each corner of one of the space blanket to keep the wind from blowing up under it, then slit a hole in the middle and laid it to one side until he had the children as comfortable as he could, then put it over his head, shielding the children from the coming rain and wind.

It had been a long ways down to where he'd found them. It was a hell of a lot further back up.

He caught the road a quarter of a mile above the command center at two forty-nine, about the same time that he told himself, for the fourth time, that he couldn't go any further. Tired as she was, the mother's built-in radar was working just fine. She spotted him and her children before anyone else could even make out a shape coming down the road.

The look on her face when she saw her kids changed something in Joe Greene. For the first time in a long while, he had a true purpose; something that would develop, without his consent or understanding, into a passion. He was destined to find lost people.

When a TV anchor shoved a mike in his face and demanded to know how he found the children when over three hundred trained search-and-rescue personnel couldn't, Joe smiled and said, "Because that's my specialty, finding people."

"Why weren't you here sooner?" Mister-perfect-teeth asked.

"I wasn't asked."

A month later he 'was asked.' He found that little tyke too. In a ditch. Raped and murdered.

The sheriff figured out who did it; roadblocks were set up and local ranchers were combing the area. Joe followed a hunch and a set of footprints down into a God-forsaken canyon of broken rock, buck brush and coyotes. After three days Joe made his way back up to the road alone.

The sheriff was waiting, leaning on the hood of his dusty pickup, a pair of field glasses laying on the hood beside him. He nodded at Joe and brought out a thermos of fresh coffee, didn't ask if he wanted cream, it was black and hot, that's how it had come out of the pot and that's how they drank it.

They leaned on the hood side by side drinking coffee and squinting into the sunset at four deer picking their way across a high meadow. After most of the second cup was gone, the sheriff asked in a casual sort of way if there was any reason to send his two deputies--one who was coming down with a cold, and the other, waiting on the birth of his first kid--down in that canyon after that murderin' bastard, what with winter comin' on. Joe said it probably wouldn't be necessary, especially since the one deputy was coming down with a cold. No one else much seemed to care about looking for him, either. Not once they got a look at Greene's face, anyway. Before Joe left town, the murdered child's father, Don Pringle, went down to the town's only auto dealership and sold his 4x4, and gave the money to him. Joe bought it back with orders to deliver it back to Pringle after Joe was gone. He got a nice letter from the sheriff a week later. In his letter the sheriff said that it had snowed several inches and there hadn't been any sign of the suspect. He figured that the coyotes would find him before spring.

Chapter Three

He'd only been back in Shaky Town two days and was still feeling pretty proud of what he'd done, when he ran into one of Gloria's cronies who had been at the party. She just looked him up and down with kind of a smirk on her face, said something to the two men with her, they glanced at him and laughed as they walked on through the mall. Joe had known from the night of his public disembowelment that he was leaving LA. Now he knew when. And that would be as soon as he could get out of town. The only hard part was going to be telling the firm of attorneys that he worked for. Especially Sue Studebaker. She was not only a damn fine attorney, but had become a friend. Stu, as everyone, even judges called her, was a dedicated workaholic. Her personal injury and wrongful death cases were what kept Joe on the streets at night. He called 'The Firm,' as they preferred to be known (along with every other group of attorneys in the nation), and asked Rose if Stu could be had. That was a little joke between him and Rose. It was common knowledge that the closest Stu had ever come to sex was when the taxicab she was riding in ran over two mating possums. It seemed that she could be had that very noon, and would like to buy him lunch. As he had never seen her except at either

her office, the courtroom, or eating a bagel in a taxi on the way to or from court, he was a bit stunned.

"Mr. Greene? Are you still there?"

"Yeah. I'm here. Where?"

"Where are you, or where are you meeting Stu?"

"Both."

"Well right now you are sitting across from a park, watching unsuspecting young women through a telephoto lens."

"I am not!" He paused, and added, "They are not unsuspecting."

"Stu will meet you at eleven thirty in the lobby of The Gringo."

"Do I have to wear a tie?"

"Knowing you, a clean shirt would be asking a lot."

He got there in time to hold the door open for her.

"Thanks, Joe. Is that a new shirt?"

"Yeah."

"You want me to take the price tag off the collar before we go in?"

He did and she did.

Once seated, she told him she was moving her practice to Portland, Oregon, and forming a partnership with a former college roommate.

"I'm sure you already know. I doubt there is much that goes on around you that you don't know."

He didn't have a clue, but said, "Once in a while something slips past me."

"I doubt it. And thanks for not telling anyone at The Firm."

"No problem."

"So. Will you come with me, and do what you do so well for both Barb and me?"

"What if she doesn't like my work?"

"I've had occasion where cases overlapped to allow her to see your reports. She is very impressed. And, like me, would be very pleased to have someone of your caliber on staff. Of course you'll still be an independent contractor."

"Thank you. But what's going to happen when I go look for someone?"

"As you will be a member of our team, we will handle the legal concerns, billing, and publicity."

Joe felt like he had maybe missed something someplace, but what the hell. They decided not to order right away and made small talk about what the weather would be like in Portland until their coffee came. Stu added cream, sipped, grimaced, added a packet of sugar and tried it again, apparently with satisfaction before saying, "There is only one concern that we have."

Oh, oh! he thought, here it comes. "What's that?"

"Well, I spoke with Sheriff Johnson in Montana who is quite sure, as is everyone else in the entire county, that you killed the suspect in the Pringle child rape and murder. There are apparently no negative repercussions from your actions. I just want to know. Are you positive that he was the perpetrator?"

"Yes."

"How do you know?"

"When I caught up with him he was wearin' the little girl's necklace as a bracelet. He laughed and said "Take me in, asshole. I'll get at the most seven years with three hots and a cot while remembering the pleasure she gave me. Then I'll be out again."

"So you killed him."

"Stu, he got loose and ran further down into the canyon. It was gettin' dark, and I couldn't find him. You got to remember, I'm not a cop. I'm not trained--."

"Joe. Don't try to con me. I know who you are, who you were, and what you are capable of."

"What do you mean by, `who I was?'"

"My father is with the Pentagon. Need I say more?" There wasn't any more to say as his file was classified. But he didn't need to know that.

"What are you going to have for lunch?"

They ordered, a salad for Stu and chicken pot pie for Joe. After the waitress left, Stu began again, "Do you want to tell me how you got the locket away from the suspect? The one that you gave back to the little girl's mother."

"You know, you ought to consider a career as a lawyer." He threw in a smile for luck. She wasn't buying.

"Do you know what any first-year law student could do to you on the stand?"

Joe was still smiling but his eyes had taken on an icy glint, "Show me a body with a bullet from my gun in it, or even a knife wound."

Stu watched him as he spoke, then smiled at him and said, "God but I hope he died hard." Paused to sip her coffee and continued, "Though he probably would have made a good insanity case."

"He most likely died alone, unable to crawl any further, knowing that the coyotes were waiting. So what's the next question?"

"You answered it."

"I did?"

"Well no, there is one more."

"I figured that."

"I know it's personal, but we need to know. Is your break-up with Gloria going all right?"

"Do you mean, do I have any baggage that might cause me problems?"

"Well, yes."

"No."

"Did she have an attorney?"

"Yes."

"Did you."

"No."

"Do you realize the risk you took?"

"She set me up. So I set her up."

"Joe--."

"When her attorney saw what I brought to show and tell, she dropped Gloria like she had no money."

"May I ask what you had. As if I didn't know."

"Photos. I had to agree to destroy them and the negatives."

"Did you?"

"Not yet. There was no stipulation as to when."

"I need to remember that."

The waitress brought their lunch and Stu ate two bites of sweet-and-sour chicken salad before asking, "Are you going to show me the pictures, or do I have to hurt you?" She shrugged, and gestured with her fork, "That line was used in a film I saw, to good advantage, and I always wanted to use it myself."

"You scared the hell out of me," he said as he pulled the envelope of photos out of his briefcase, and handed it to her.

"Did I really frighten you?" she asked, mock hopefully.

"It helps if you have the means to carry out your threat. In the film you saw, did the person who asked the question have the ability to back it up?"

"Well, the woman was tied to a chair in a dark, damp basement of an abandoned house. And the man had a gun." She pretended to think about it, "So I guess you could say that he had the means to carry out the threat. Why did you capitulate?"

"Charm. And money."

"Money?"

"Yeah. Here I'm makin' thirty-five an hour. What's the rate going to be up there?"

"Of course you know the cost of living is a lot less in Portland than it is here." He thought it was probably higher, but it was her spiel. "The usual rate there is thirty an hour. We hereby offer you, Joseph Greene, thirty-five dollars an hour, plus your own office."

"My own secretary, too?"

"Of course not."

"All right. I'll go."

"Good. Now let's get back to this charm business."

After Stu left, Joe stayed for dessert and more coffee. He was quite pleased with himself. He was moving to a new location, would clear more money (due to the lower cost of living) and had the opportunity to work with someone whom he respected and liked. He had, after finding out that Stu had only two steamer chests and one cardboard box to move, offered to stop by and pick them up. Half jokingly he'd offered her a ride. To his surprise, she'd accepted.

At nine a.m. a week later, he pulled up to the garden-court condominium complex where she lived. He hated trying to do surveillance on complexes with gated entrances. Like most of them, this was a nine-plex of two-story units with concrete block walls backing to the street on two sides, and a similar unit on the third side. The only way in was through the security gate that led into a common courtyard. There was no way in hell to lay doggo and watch a unit without being in another unit. The police considered that breaking and entering and frowned on the practice. Of course they would frown on a lot of things Joe did, if they knew.

Stu buzzed him in. She was wearing a jogging suit, sweat socks, and Nikes. "I'm ready, and I'm excited."

"Me too. I'm looking forward to a new town."

"I mean, I'm excited about the trip. Since I don't drive, I always go by plane." She did a little shuffle dance that ended in a Mickey Mouse bow, and added, "Thank you for offering to take me. I've always wanted to take an auto trip."

"It's not exactly going by car. More like a circus caravan." He looked out to where his white van was parked, the most recent signs painted on the sides proclaimed it to be "COLUMBIA ROOTER SERVICE." A caricature of a little fat man holding a toilet plunger, and a phone number, rounded out the image. Hooked to the rear was the obligatory bright orange U-Haul.

Stu looked at the van, frowned and asked, "What happens if someone calls that number?"

"Alice, who owns the answering service I use, always knows which con I'm running, and answers that phone number accordingly."

"You mean you change the sign on the van sometimes?"

"Oh yeah. If I'm working an extended surveillance I may have Nelly repainted two or even three times."

"I never thought about that. I guess. . ." Her voice trailed off as she led the way into the condo.

"What about the furniture?"

"The couple who are buying the condo from me bought that too."

They loaded up and headed North.

"They must think Nelly looks like a bread truck gone bad." Stu said in response to the third carload of people that passed craning their necks to see inside.

"I guess that I should have had the signs removed before we left, but it costs about two-hundred-fifty to have it painted up like it is. Since I've never worked Portland this should be good for a while. All I need to do is have the phone number changed. Besides, I want to show several different shops the quality of work I want and get bids."

They stopped for lunch in Redding, and then climbed on up I-5 to the top of the Siskiyou Pass where Joe found a side road that took them up onto a plateau overlooking the Klamath Mountains. They walked out onto a ridge for a better view and sat down.

"Okay Stu. Your turn on the hot seat."

"I guess I knew this was coming. But I can't understand why you didn't ask sooner."

"If there was anything that would cause a problem with your work, some bright attorney would have nailed you with it years ago."

"Oh. So this is personal." Stu noticeably relaxed, the waiting had been harder than having to bare her soul. She only hoped that after what she would share with Joe, he would still like her as a person.

"Why don't you go to out in public. You never have, as near as I can tell."

"Because I'm a freak."

"How so?"

"I was born without any pigmentation in my skin. I'm totally white. Can't tan, and am very susceptible to sun-burning and skin cancer."

"I'm sorry, but that doesn't make you a freak."

"There's more. I have no body hair. None."

Joe thought a few seconds. "I don't think not having to shave your legs qualifies you either."

"Joseph. You don't understand. I have no hair. No eyebrows, no eye lashes, this beautiful red hair is a wig." She paused to let that sink in. "Now do you understand?"

"Kids were pretty cruel, huh?"

He had touched her very soul with that question; she shuddered and began to cry softly. He slid across the rock to where she was sitting and put his arm around her. He didn't say anything, just held her. She started to say something a couple times only to break down. Finally in a voice so low and full of pain he had to hold his breath to hear, she began. "Even as a child I was tall and gangly. All angles. The kids called me `Ichabod.' That, I could live with. Then in the fourth grade, at lunch time on a Thursday, five seventh- and eighth-grade boys shoved me into the boys' restroom and ripped my shirt off." She paused to regain her composure, "Then the little mothers' darlings took my wig too. And of course, since it was so much fun they dragged me screaming and fighting out into the hall. I tore myself away from them and ran. They chased me, like wolves after a sick deer all the way home. Throwing rocks and jeering."

Joe didn't know what to say. It wouldn't have mattered, she wasn't listening anyway, lost as she was in her own private hell. "I never again set foot in a public school. In fact I became a recluse, until I left to go to a private women's college back east. Then I went to Lewis and Clark Law School in Portland. After graduation, Hoffman and Schleigel offered me a position in their firm. They've known my parents for forty years and are aware of my afflictions. So it was natural that I would come down here. They both agree that now I should seek a colleague of my own age and in my field. Barb was my roommate at Lewis and Clark, so there is no new ground that has to be broken there."

Joe tried to move into a more comfortable position, as his arm was starting to cramp. Stu pushed herself up straight and said, "I'm sorry. I didn't mean to--."

"You didn't do anything but show yourself to be human. Stu, have you ever watched a sunset from a mountain top?"

"No I don't think so."

"Would you like to?"

"Yes. Yes I would."

Joe brought a blanket from the van and she curled up in it.

"It sure is getting cold, isn't it?"

"We're up pretty high. Hell, they've already had several snow showers up here this season."

"No kidding! Should we leave soon?"

"No problem, my lady." Joe gave her a simulated, reproduction Medieval bow. "There is but a trace of cloud. Only enough to color the sun's rays for your pleasure. Not, I assure you, enough to produce moisture."

Joe opened the trailer and dug around in it until he found a large bag of charcoal and a can of charcoal lighter fluid that he carried over to where Stu was curled down into the blanket. "Do you realize that I can see my breath?" She blew a stream of white vapor just to prove it. Joe chuckled as he built a fire ring near her and poured about a third of the charcoal briquettes into it and lit them.

Stu watched it for a while before commenting. "That's a pathetic excuse for a fire. In the movies the hero builds a hummongous inferno with some small wilted bush and a piece of flint."

"That was one of Moses' tricks. I make it a point never to try to outdo him."

"I'm quite sure that you don't have to worry about that. And if I recall it wasn't Moses that lit the bush."

"Yeah, well I sometimes get those ancient ones mixed up."

"I think maybe you should read up on the burning bush. You can find reference to it in the Bible."

"Whatever. Now while the fire heats up--."

"It's got a ways to go." She eyed it suspiciously.

"I don't carry wood with me when I go camping. Most of the time I'm in the desert where there isn't much wood and so I just build a fire with briquettes, no smoke, no flame---."

"No heat. Mr. Woodsman, if I was to find some dry sticks could we add them to the inferno?"

By the time they got back the second time, loaded down with wood, Stu said, "This fire is really starting to put out heat. Maybe we don't need that wood after all."

"Oh we're going to use it, and more." Joe said as he added several pieces to the briquettes. "And now Counselor, for your dining pleasure, I have a loaf of French bread, a small fine imported cheese, and your choice of wine."

"You really do?"

"Yes, Ma'am. Now, as to your choice of wine. Will it be a very fine red or a modest white?"

"What do you have in a Chablis?"

"Is that white?"

"Yes."

"I don't have any white."

"But you said red or white."

"You were supposed to choose red. That I have. Good stuff too."

"Okay. What pray tell do you have in the way of a Merlot?"

"Is that a red wine?"

"Yes. A fairly common one too."

"Oh. Well how about if I bring several bottles out and you choose?"

Stu was relieved to see that none of the wines were named after a dog nor were they screw-top. One bottle of wine and some cheese later, the sun set. More blankets were procured from the van as darkness crept across the mountains. By ten o'clock that night they sought refuge in the van and cranked the propane heater up to its maximum output. Daylight found Stu naked except for the quilt that she had haphazardly wrapped around herself peering out the windshield. "Joe, is snow considered moisture?"

"What?" Came the reply from beneath two blankets and a bearskin rug that neither one of them could remember getting out of the U-haul.

She rolled the side window down enough to get a double handful of the cold stuff. After the obligatory twenty-minute early-season snow fight, they made breakfast, and ate sitting cross-legged on the bearskin.

"Do you take advantage of every woman you con into getting into this mobile den of cheap tricks?"

"I didn't take advantage of you. It was your idea."

"When I said that if I was going to lose my virginity in the wilderness it would have to be on a bearskin rug, I did not know you had one in the U-haul."

"I just told you that I had one. You're the one who dug it out of the trailer."

"Oh. Well, that was because you got me drunk."

"You were also in charge of the corkscrew."

After Stu checked both cupboards and the small refrigerator and was assured that there was enough propane and water to run the two-burner stove, heater, and hot-water heater for two or three days, she declared them snowbound.

They pulled into Portland during a wind-driven rain, having made the final five-hour leg of the journey in four days.

Stu immediately bought an umbrella, which she discarded after three weeks, having found that in Portland it can and does rain straight down and sideways at the same time and with such force as to cause the rain drops to bounce up off the pavement knee high. An umbrella only served to alert everyone within sight that you were from California. She also learned that in Oregon the word "California" is followed by spitting on the ground.

Having vented their initial lust for one another they settled down into a routine of work and an occasional one-night rendezvous at either her apartment or a sleazy motel out on Barbur Boulevard where Joe could get a room for half price, having done some probably-illegal-thing for the owner. Stu refused to stay at Joe's place. He had rented a two-car garage with an overhead storage loft and a small bathroom on the main floor. Joe converted the loft into living quarters by installing a second-hand double bed and covering part of the rough-sawn floorboards with a seventy-dollar rug he bought from a sidewalk merchant. She described his living quarters as having 'serious deficiencies.'

Joe, on the other hand, was quite pleased with his arrangement as it allowed him to lock up his van and the four-hundred-dollar Chevy beater that he used in the quick-and-dirty style of surveillance that he sometimes did.

When Stu first saw the Chevy she was visibly upset. "What is that!" she said, nearly spitting the words out.

Joe assumed the role of someone whose son had just thrown the game-losing interception at the high school homecoming. "What do you mean by that? This machine is one of a kind. Hell, it's got new tires; well almost-new tires, and the engine and transmission are rebuilt. I have spared no expense in converting this into a jewel of a surveillance vehicle."

"What do you mean by almost-new tires?"

Sometimes Stu's penchant for digging into the details of everything drove Joe nuts. But he'd learned that it was easier to tell her the truth, unless he had a foolproof fabrication figured out ahead of time (which he usually did), than to have her stir around in things she didn't need to know until she figured out what happened anyway. "I bought the tires at a garage sale. The guy had taken them off of his mother's car before they traded it in. They have hardly any wear on them."

"Mr. Greene. You spend your life driving around, sometimes in situations that require high speed, and you buy tires for your car at a garage sale?"

"Yeah. I saved like twenty-five bucks a tire."

"I rest my case."

"What case?"

"Probably insanity. Now tell me why it has to look like this? It's dirty."

"Not inside."

"It's dented and has that," she waved her hands around as though trying to erase the right front fender, if not the whole car, "and has that kind of paint on it--."

"Primer."

"Yeah, primer paint."

"Want to go for a ride in it?"

"Does the heater work?"

"Sure. And the defroster too, at least on the driver's side."

"Good. Then nobody can see me in it, with my side all fogged up."

Chapter Four

Joe had been in his new cubicle that the attorneys referred to as his `office' about a week when he noticed something funny about one of their employees. Anne was low-key and a good worker, but something bothered him about her, so without telling anyone he returned to the office after everyone else had left and installed a video camera with a motion switch on it. Three days later he took the cassette out and watched it.

Damn you're good, he told himself. She was occasionally photocopying files and taking them with her when she left. Now he had to decide what to do with the information. The next day he spent checking her out. He found that she was a single mother with a druggie for a daughter and a husband who had run out on her eight years before. Her daughter was in a private rehab center in Seattle. And so now we know, he thought. Her wages won't cover her expenses and so she's selling information. He grinned and sat back in his chair.

At seven thirty p.m. that Friday night she came home burdened down with next week's groceries. She backed through the door of her apartment and turned, setting the bags on the counter.

That's funny, she thought, I must have left the TV on this morning. As she walked toward the set, she watched her own image look around and then stuff a report into her purse. She clamped her hands over her mouth to stifle her scream as she realized that she was not alone in her apartment, and that someone knew what she was doing.

Joe snapped the living room light on and stepped out in front of her.

As she recognized him, she dropped her hands and began to plead. He slapped her across the face, knocking her to her knees, where she curled up in a fetal position, covered her head with her forearms, and began to weep.

Joe knew that her daughter had been in rehab for only six weeks, and hopefully that was when Anne started selling files. Over the next two hours she told him of every file she copied, which was six and to whom she had sold them. Joe cut her a deal. He would pay for her daughter's treatment, but she would get him anything he asked for from the office. If she ever took anything for anyone else he'd see she did jail time. From where, he told her, she could watch her daughter's body be pulled out of the river on the end of a gaff hook, after she OD'd, or maybe watch as the police picked her up in a prostitution raid out on Sandy Boulevard.

When he left Joe was certain that she would never rip off Stu and Barb again, except for him.

By spring Joe had moved across town into a small complex that housed a pest control company, a hair salon and Joe's business. His office in the law firm had been taken over by their accountant, a young woman who gave the appearance of carrying the weight of the world on her thin shoulders. In order to do all of the investigation work for the firm and for several other clients that Stu didn't know about he hired two retired Portland city cops who worked part time on commission. The "graybeards," as they called themselves, liked nothing better than digging up the dirt on potential clients for Studebaker & Rye. The only thing they seemed to like better was sturgeon fishing on the Columbia from a battered boat one of them had found half sunk along the river bank. Joe had the impression that they hadn't tried too hard to find the previous owner.

Joe's reputation for accurate reports and relatively quick turn-around times spread throughout the business community until he had to call a halt to expansion of his investigation service. He'd hired a part-time legal secretary to input all of the reports soon after he'd moved to Portland. By the time he hired the gray beards she was full-time and pregnant. The pregnant part didn't have anything to do with him other than it did mean that he was going to have to find someone else as Joan was going to quit by the seventh month of her pregnancy. And she wasn't coming back.

That someone was Janice. He met her when he was asked to get her out of a jam. She was an easily-bored little rich girl with a high IQ and the job of a secretary. So she lifted her boss's stash just to see if she could. She did a good job of it except that he had a video surveillance camera in his office. She had been given an option; jail or be his private secretary. A special kind, of private secretary. She'd chosen the latter, but after a month or so the glamour wore off of being a sex slave and she complained to her sister, who told her mother, who told her father, who called in a marker, and Joe drew the assignment. It had taken him about twenty minutes to get into the building, and nearly an hour to reprogram the boss man's camera. Two nights later he pulled the video cassette out of the camera and made two phone calls. At midnight he met a very worried boss man in an all-night diner. The meeting freed Janice from bondage and put five grand cash money in Joe's pocket; a transaction that would undoubtedly slip his mind when he made out his taxes.

A week later Janice dropped by his office to say thanks, and to ask if there was a job opening, as she was now unemployed. They established ground rules that included the knowledge that he had a video of her being a rather portly gentleman's sex toy, if she ever had the inclination to rip him off. She assured him that she would never have that inclination. Joe also suggested that they not go bump in the night, because--you know. And yes, she did know.

It turned out that she was not only a talented thief, but was, by her own description, a first-class information whore. She'd do whatever it took to get the interview or information needed, from making her eyes all big and innocent to spreading her legs. And if that didn't work, she could pick a lock with the best of them. Not that she needed to pick many locks with her innocent little sister looks and the sexual desires of a predator.

Within two months of hiring Janice, the organization included five investigators, a alarm-installation expert and a full-time legal secretary who answered to Janice. The two graybeards discovered that they had made enough extra money to buy a new-to-them twenty-foot cabin cruiser, and with the purchase of the bigger, faster boat they lost interest in investigation and drifted on down the river.

During the time Joe was building up his business Stu spent her free time in consulting numerous Realtors, acquaintances, and her banker (whom Stu later learned lived in Vancouver and had no idea of the Portland real estate market) on where to buy a condo. She decided on a new complex in John's Landing, a reclaimed community set in a basin hard against the Willamette River.

She purposely didn't tell Joe about it, wanting or maybe needing to maintain her independence. When she next saw Joe a week after making the down payment, she told him that she was going to buy a condo before her capital gains exemption ran out and asked his opinion on where she should buy.

"If I were in your shoes I'd buy one of those down in John's Landing. I'd get one of the attached units with a private view deck that looks out over the river."

"How come?"

"I met a guy about six months ago who does finish work on condos. Don't ask me why only condos cause I don't know. Got a theory, if you're interested," he paused, but she didn't seem to be interested. She just sat there cross-legged on the bed staring at him with a puzzled look on her face. So he went on. "He told me that the best buys were down there." He sat back in the rickety side chair next to the motel room desk and gave her a grin, trying to figure out why she kept looking at him like that.

"Joe, just how in hell do you meet people like that. I've spent six months trying to find the right place and here you talked to some yahoo in a coffee shop someplace and found out in five minutes what it took me six months and a lot of money to learn!"

"The guy was a client of yours. You asked me to interview him and tell you what I thought of him. In the file is his name and occupation. Where he was workin' and," Joe scratched his ear as he thought, "and you took his case. Remember? It was that air compressor with the faulty pressure-relief valve."

"Frank Johnson. Yes, I remember him." She held her glass out at arms length for him to refill. She lifted the glass to eye level and swirled it, watching his image ebb and flow through the wine. "But why would I ask him where the best condo in Portland was?"

He shrugged and took his shirt off.

Later she laid beside him in the darkness, listened to the rain pounding the motel and let her fingers find the scars that were scattered over his body and wondered how deep they went. She had seen the cross section of a tree that had a railroad spike driven into it. The tree had healed itself on the outside, but the spike was still there driven into the very heart of the tree. She could feel his eyes on her, and liked that. Looking up she said, "You are one scary son of a bitch," then rolled over and went to sleep.

Joe lay in the darkness and thought about what she'd said. Since he considered it a compliment he moved on the next aspect. Why now? Did she want something, or did she just want the pleasure of a mind fuck to keep him awake all night?

The week she moved into her condo, Ron Strick, a fellow attorney whom she's met at several recent dinner parties, convinced Stu to buy a car and learn to drive. At his suggestion she bought a Honda sedan, which he taught her to drive. She was somewhat embarrassed to find out how easy it was to learn, realizing she could have been driving for years.

Less than two months later, during which time it only quit raining twice, Joe called, "Stu. I think I left the other night without sayin' thanks for dinner. Sorry. Not for the dinner. For leavin' without sayin' thanks. But I guess it worked out okay; the little boy I went looking for got found."

"Did you find him?"

"Yep. Asleep behind the couch in the living room."

"Thank God. His parents must have been terrified to have their three-year-old son disappear after having had their daughter kidnapped."

"They were just about at the end of their ropes. I think the little fella is too, he was just tryin' to get away from the constant grief."

"Joe, I heard that the main suspect in the disappearance of their daughter committed suicide. Know anything about that?"

"Not much except what's in the papers. Her body was found buried in his garden."

"Are you going to be indicted?"

"For what?"

"If you need an attorney, call me."

"Thanks. But I'm clean."

"I hear a lot of traffic noise. Are you on your mobile?"

"No. Pay phone."

"Right. Not using your mobile or office phone, and you aren't worried about being a suspect."

"Let it ride, Doll." He paused, then went on, "Hey, I called to tell you that I bought a house up on Skyline." He needed to shut her up, just in case someone had a tap on her phone. He hadn't killed the perp, nor had he had it done. But she would always think that he had. No matter what he said now. So the best thing he could do was to get her to go on to something else. And the last thing he needed was for some enterprising cop to decide that he had.

"Honest?" She wasn't dumb. Joe had never called her "Babe" or "Doll" or "Pet" or any of the cute things guys say to keep their little women in place, so when he said, "Let it ride, Doll," it meant, Stop! Do not proceed! "You bought a house?"

"Well actually three houses and a barn. And a tavern too."

"What?"

"Well this guy I met had an uncle who wanted to sell this property that had three houses, a barn, and a tavern on it. But he hates Realtors and any kind of inspectors. You know like appraisers. So he was limited in, who he would sell to."

"So you bought it?"

"Yeah."

"Did you have an attorney?"

"He hates attorneys too."

"Do you know what kind of problems you can have with a contract, probably drawn up over a bottle of cheap whiskey, between two rednecks?"

"It wasn't cheap whiskey."

"As a friend, I would like to see what you got yourself into this time."

"Good. Do you want me to pick you up at the office or your flat?"

"It is not a `flat,' thank you. And I was referring to the contract. However I want to see what you have in the way of housing."

"I don't have a contract. Paid cash. I'll pick you up in an hour at your flat."

"Make it two hours. And if you refer to my condo one more time as a flat, I will start a rumor in the right circles that you own a pig farm."

The phone went dead. She smiled, it was nice to win one once in a while.

Stu finished a brief she was working on and took a cab home. As she changed she went over what Joe had told her. She didn't like the way he had emphasized 'barn'. After living for a year in a garage he surely wouldn't opt for the barn. Or would he? She shuddered and moved to the next point that bothered her. "Paid cash," he'd said. That's fine. So he got a personal bank loan. What did he use for collateral? She knew just about everything there was to know about Joseph Greene. Or did she? Maybe it was time to do a little investigation of her own. First, of course, she had to decide if she was considering him as her potential mate, or was he just a playmate. Her father was retired and she didn't know how to check his military records, but maybe she could do a little digging on her own.

He picked her up in a battered Bronco and headed up Burnside into the West Hills.

"Joe, where did this come from?" She gestured toward the dash.

"Oh. You haven't seen this one?" Then answered his own question. "No. I suppose not. Since this is the first day I ever drove it."

"Every time I see you lately, you have a different vehicle."

"Ride."

"What?"

"Ride. Not vehicle."

"Let's not change the subject. Why do you have so many different `rides?`"

"A couple of months ago I called a board meeting--," her sharp intake of breath made him look over at her, seeing that she was all right he continued, "And it was decided that as this is a small town and as the service now employs seven investigators, a used-car lot should be purchased, thereby allowing a constantly-changing lineup of vehicles."

"I thought the word was `ride?`"

"`Ride' is singular.  `Vehicle' should only be used as plural or pluraler."

"Thank you, Mr. English-as-a-second-language professor. What's this about a board meeting and used car lot? I thought that your corporation was a sole proprietorship?"

"It is."

"Then how did you have a board meeting?"

"There was me and a bottle of Jack Daniel's. We sat down under a big cedar tree by a pretty good fire and thought it out."

"I see. Not like the fire you built for me--."

"No. This one was hot right from the start."

She looked at him as though she didn't believe him.

So he added, "Pitch."

"Pitch?"

"Yeah. Burns real hot."

"Do you mind telling me about the car lot?"

"No. Not at all. I met this guy named Mitch." She rolled her eyes and shook her head. Joe grinned and continued, "He's an old-time car salesman with a heart problem and can't work all the time. Course he lives on coffee and junk food. He says he's got enough in the bank to take care of him for as long as he's gonna be around. But sellin' cars is in his blood. Mitch doesn't care if he makes a dime. He just loves to haggle. So I bought a little lot from a guy who was down on his luck, put in a nice clean little office trailer that I traded a car for, and fenced the lot with chain link. Then I made a deal with a detail shop next to the lot. Mitch is open Friday afternoon, Saturday, and Sunday. A kid down the street comes in and washes the cars, rakes the gravel, that sort of thing."

"Where do you get the cars for the lot?"

"A few of them are on consignment, we buy some from the auction, most come from private-party newspaper ads. And, of course, I'm always happy to take a car in trade as payment. After expenses we try to make a hundred bucks a car. Except on the trade-for-payment cars. Those I sell for cash only."

"It seems like it would be hard to keep records on that kind of transaction."

"Sometimes it's necessary to estimate the profit for tax purposes."

She nodded, seemed to buy it. Joe was surprised at how naive she sometimes was. That was good for him, usually.

"Joe this is fascinating. I don't know how you do it. So how many cars do you sell in a weekend?"

"Mitch likes to move four or five, but last weekend he went crazy. Come Monday we damn near didn't have enough rigs left for surveillance. That's why I'm driving this wreck."

"You bought this to resell?"

"Hell no! Mitch took it in on trade. No one else wanted to drive it, and since I'm the one with the brass balls, I got the call."

"You're what!"

"The Boss Man. The first in line for the shit, the last in line for pay."

"Isn't that how you want it?"

"Well. Here we are." Joe slowed the Bronco to a shuddering idle as he pointed out first one small cottage and then a second, similar dwelling. Stu didn't realize that she had been holding her breath until he pointed to a newer ranch style home set well back from the road. She caught a glimpse of a deck on the back that would insure privacy as well as take advantage of the view to the west. Joe drove them on up around a corner and into a pock-marked gravel parking lot that surrounded on three sides a squat log structure, that by virtue of a slightly-askew sign proclaimed it to be a tavern. Two battered pickup trucks and four motorcycles were haphazardly parked in front.

"You own this too?"

"Yeah. It's leased out right now. You want to go in? They make great cheeseburgers."

"I guess not. Maybe later. Right now I want to see your abode."

Joe nodded and swung the Bronco around in the lot. "I don't know why none of the crew wanted this rig. It handles pretty well." As proof he gunned the engine as he pulled out onto the pavement. The tires chirped and then there was a tremendous bang as the hapless heap bounded sideways into the ditch on the passenger's side. Stu tried not to hyperventilate as she checked herself for possible injuries. Joe looked down at her, as the Bronco was more or less laying on its side, in the ditch, and said, "We can walk from here."

By the time Joe had helped Stu out of the driver's side and onto the road, the tavern's occupants were gathered around. Two of them crawled under the Bronco to inspect the damage. They slid out oblivious to the dirt and gravel. The smaller of the two, by far the dirtiest was the spokesman. "The damn driveline pulled apart an she just pogo-sticked herself inta the ditch." He paused to wipe his forehead with his sleeve of his leather jacket, "We kin put her together fer you an you kin drive her home. If you like." The other patrons nodded agreement.

Stu didn't feel like she was in danger, but all the same felt a kind of tension among the men.

"I don't know," Joe said, "the little lady here might be a bit gun-shy about climbing back into it now."

"Shit it ain't no big deal," a bleary-eyed, skinny man in a ragged Mickey Mouse T-shirt said. He took a sharp elbow in the ribs from one of the other leather-jacket-clad men who growled at him. His eyes went round and he mouthed the word `Oh,' swallowed twice, and hastily added, "Course it coulda fucked up the brakes when the driveline gave in."

They all nodded again and relaxed some. The misspoken speaker grinned, exposing a mouth full of rotten teeth, started to say something else and was short-circuited with another well-placed elbow.

The original speaker nodded toward `rotten teeth' and said, "John ain't too bright. He's a purty good framer though." Then glared at John for several seconds before continuing, "Iffen you don't want to drive her, I might be willin' to take her off your hands."

"How much?" Joe asked.

So that's it! Stu thought. They are doing a deal for the Bronco. Okay, I can support this. "Joe honey, I don't want any part of that ride ever again!"

The leather jackets were very sympathetic and offered to buy her a pitcher of beer to ease her tension. To their surprise and delight she accepted, and they made their way across the parking lot to the tavern. Joe and the smaller man stayed behind awhile and when they came in Joe was carrying her purse, briefcase and his Nike sports bag that she knew held enough armament to take at least six countries she could think of. They pushed two tables together and Joe ordered beer, French fries, and cheeseburgers all around. The drivers of the two pickups had left at the request of the bikers before Joe came in.

Three hours later, half drunk and happy, Joe guided Stu down the road toward the big house; and then behind it to the barn. "I don't believe this," she muttered as he helped her up the ramp to the main floor. Once inside he flipped the lights on. Stu let go of his hand and wandered around. "This is beautiful, Joe." The main floor was finished like a mountain cabin. The rough-sawn walls had been sandblasted and varnished until they shone like a wooden ship's hull. There was a full bath and galley kitchen. It was maybe fifty feet to the peak. Over the kitchen and bath was a loft hung on chains.

"What's up here?" Stu asked as she climbed the stairs. "Aha, yes. The bedroom, and with its own bath." French doors led out onto a small balcony that held a hot tub and a wooden bench. "Oh my God! Joe have you seen the view from up here?"

He came out onto the balcony carrying a pitcher of ice water, two glasses and four towels. They stood drinking ice water and pointing out different groups of lights to one another until the events of the evening caught up with her and she began to shake.

"Time for the hot tub little lady."

"Would you mind if I took my hair off. I mean, my head itches when I sweat and--."

"Hold on. You don't have to make excuses. I am happy that I have earned your respect to the point that you know I will never laugh at you or take advantage of you."

"Never?"

"Never. I swear."

"Good then don't I get a percentage of the profit on the sale of the Bronco?"

"What!"

"Well, I played helpless female, and then drank beer with your friends."

"They aren't exactly friends. And you wouldn't have climbed back into that Bronco for a thousand dollars."

"Sure I would have."

"You would have?"

"Sure. You think about it while I'm in the bathroom."

When she came back, Joe was sitting in the tub gazing off into the valley.

There were three bills under her glass. She picked them up; two one-hundreds and a fifty. "First of all. Look at me."

He did, and smiled. "I like it. With those big gold hoop earrings you look like a movie star."

"Really. You don't mind?"

"Not at all. Would you really have gotten back into the Bronco?"

"Sure." She made her eyes all big and wild and got up real close to him. "But the brakes might have been all fucked up when the driveline come loose."

"Really?"

"You bet. Just ask me anything about your ride."

"Ma'am, as of right now, I ain't got a ride."

"You don't?"

"Oh. I get it. But how are your brakes?"

"I don't have any."

Sometime after daylight Stu got out of bed and went out onto the balcony and returned with her now soggy money, which she carefully laid out on Joe's chest. He didn't move, just watched, his eyes hooded, a half smile that touched only his mouth.

"Stu. Just what in hell are you doing?"

"Counting my money."

"You've counted it three times, on me, and it's wet."

"I think I like selling used cars to drunken bikers."

"They weren't drunk."

"How come they would buy the Bronco from you like that?"

"It's got a clear title, and the tags are good for another year and a half."

"I still don't understand."

"They won't transfer the title nor will they insure it. They paid for it in cash, which probably was earned 'under the table.' They won't claim the income and they now have a new ride that the cops won't know they have for a while. As for fixing it, they drove it away while you were in the bathroom last night."

"It's like they're part of an underground."

"That's why they were willin' to pay a decent price for it."

"Did you really make five hundred dollars on it?"

"Mitch gave two hundred on the trade-in, and I got seven fifty for it."

"Hey! That's five fifty profit. You owe me twenty-five dollars."

"Like hell. The tavern tab was forty and the tip made fifty even."

"You know I'm just kidding. I don't want your money. And besides, don't you have to give some of it to Mitch?"

"No. He gets paid wages, plus a commission on sales only. Normally we don't take trades". He wished that he hadn't said anything about commissions, but probably she wouldn't remember.

Nothing more was said about the money. Stu left it on the nightstand where it stayed.

Stu named the barn "The Crow's Nest." Her original choice had been "The Eagle's Nest" until her partner Barb (invited up for the weekend while Joe was in Los Angeles for a week), explained to her that the birds that inhabited the big fir trees surrounding the building were crows, not eagles. It didn't sound as good, but reality is not always what dreams are made of.

Chapter Five

Joe came back from LA with a suntan and enough raw evidence in the way of video, still shots, videoed interviews, and a defective mounting bracket (stolen off the production line she figured, but didn't ask), to allow her to settle a personal injury liability suit out of court.

She called his office less than twenty minutes after her client left.

The phone was answered on the second ring, "This is Janice."

"Janice, this is Stu. Is Joe in?"

"Nope. He's up on the hill. Did you try his mobile?"

"No, but I will." Maybe, she thought, this was a good time to do a little detective work of her own, " Uh--aren't you supposed to answer with Greene Investigations?"

"Not on the back line. If you call the front line then you get my professional voice and everything. Wow, huh?"

"How about if I call the number on the van?"

"The one that says `Eastside Antiques' or the one that says `Residential Alarm Services'?"

"Start with the Eastside."

"All right. I'd find out what you wanted while I traced the call and cross-indexed it, then if you're legit, I transfer you to our store on Belmont."

"Joe owns an antique store on Belmont?"

"Yeah. Two little grannies run the store. They are a kick-OOPS, call coming in. You want to hang?"

"Yes."

Stu scanned a paper written by one of her Law profs while she waited.

"I'm back. Where was I?"

"You were going to tell me about what I get if I call the alarm company number."

"Oh yeah. Same check, then if you're serious, Bingo we install."

"Let me guess. Joe owns an alarm installation company too."

"Uh huh. Licensed, bonded, the whole bit. Fits right in with the investigation service. Bill does all the installation. He's really a nice guy, wife, three kids. He doesn't do any investigations; his wife won't let him, says it's too dangerous."

"Can I ask one more question?"

"Sure. The Boss says to level with you. Always. And since I know the call came from your office and I recognize your voice, you ask--I answer. What's the question Counselor?"

"You just answered it."

"Phone again. Are you done with me?"

"Yes, thank you." She dialed Joe's mobile.

Joe answered with, "I hear you cut the tail off the big Bad Wolf."

"Joe, how in hell did you know it was me and how do you know about the Wolf settlement?" Her voice had an edge to it.

"It was you, and you settled favorably, right?"

"Yes and yes. Now answer my questions."

"I have a tracer hooked into my phone."

"That I buy. Now who in my office is your stoolie?"

As she spoke, Stu was glaring through the windows of her glass-enclosed office at her and Barb's six employees, trying to read deceit in the face of one.

"You really expect me to divulge my source?"

"Yes! If you ever want to work for me again!"

"I give up. It's KEX 1190 AM and FM Radio."

"What?" She sat forward in her chair.

"Wolf Enterprise's chairman walked out of your building and was approached by a newsman. He said the suit was settled and that his company had already rectified the design flaw in the mounting bracket that caused the crane to collapse and all existing brackets were in the process of being replaced at Wolf Enterprise's cost. We both know that's bullshit but the news people don't."

Stu slumped back in her chair. "I'm sorry."

"Yeah, me too. Sorry you think so little of me." He hung up.

An hour and a half later, his phone rang again. The scanner showed that it was coming from his barn. He couldn't quite get himself to think of it as "The Crows Nest'.

"Yeah?"

"Are you going to come down here so I can properly apologize or do I have to come up there and get you?"

"I won't be done for an hour or two."

"I have brandy and salmon steaks."

"An hour."

"I brought you a present."

"Half an hour."

"I'm naked."

"I'll be right down."

Before he left the tavern he made a phone call from the back room, covering his left ear to be heard above the din of the remodelers.

"Anne?"

"Yes."

"How did it go today?"

"Stu hit Wolf for 2.4 mil."

"After that?"

"She sat in her office and glared at us for an hour or so. Then before she left gave us each a hug, a dozen red roses and two tickets to the Blazers vs. Cleveland tomorrow night." Joe didn't respond so Anne added, "Sometimes she's really strange--But, we love her."

"For the next couple weeks stay away from me when I'm in."

"Oh God!" Does she suspect that I'm-"

"No. No way. Just do what I say. It's fine."

"I'm shaking. Maybe I should--."

"How's Suzy?" he asked, dragging her away from her own fears to concentrate on what she deemed as her mission in life. The one thing she would and had sacrificed everything for. Joe couldn't understand that sort of logic but was willing to take advantage of it.

"She's better. Her counselor said that she maybe can come home for a weekend pretty soon."

"Listen to me. You want Suzy off drugs and well. It costs money. A lot of it. You turn on me, and Suzy's right back out on the street. Next time I find her for you she'll either be dead from an overdose or some pimp's property."

"I know."

"Good. Now what's with Barb? How's she comin' on the Leyman case? Has that second-rate bunch of bastards she hired turned in their report yet?"

"Yes."

"Yes?! When?"

"Just before we left for the day."

"Do you have a copy for me?"

"I--I couldn't today. She has a seven p.m. client and was going to stay and go over the report until her client arrived."

"I buy that."

There was an audible sigh, "Monday evening, maybe I'll stay late and--."

"Tomorrow at 8:45 am you will be at the Eastside Antique store with a copy."

"Oh, God! I've never been there after working hours."

"If I'm late. You wait. If they aren't open, wait in front."

"I can't do it. I won't do that to her. Not again."

"It's on Belmont. Look up the address."

He hung up, leaving her to grapple with her conscience. Knowing that she would be there in the morning.

She put the phone down and drank a glass of water from shaking hands then taking her coat and keys, walked two blocks to her church. She entered the small, unlocked side chapel, dropped to her knees and prayed.

Over dessert, Joe forgave Stu for her accusations. They made love and then slept until around midnight when Stu gave Joe his gift, a box of 48 assorted fireworks. They climbed into the hot tub and threw fireworks off of the balcony to be eaten by the ground mist seventy-five feet below. At 2:47 am, a Multnomah County prowl car crept down the gravel drive and scanned the area below the barn with a searchlight.

As the prowl car was turning around a formerly dead spinner found new life and leaped several feet into the air with a brilliant display of color. The car stopped and two deputies erupted from their respective doors and took the smoldering spinner carcass into custody. After assuring the dispatcher that it was fireworks and not a house fire as reported from the community below, and that the perpetrators had left the scene, the deputies retired to their prowl car.

The perpetrators had discussed and dismissed the idea of dropping fireworks on the disgusted deputies, but not wanting the hot tub and themselves ventilated by over-enthusiastic county employees, they waited until the prowl car accelerated down the main road before lighting the last eleven pieces of pyrotechnic ingenuity.

At 8:30 a.m., Joe was parked across the street from Eastside Antiques. At 8:48, the Belmont bus let three passengers off, one of whom clutched a legal-sized manila envelope. He let her stand in front for nine minutes watching to make sure she hadn't brought a tail, before climbing out of the red Toyota pick-up he was driving and walking across the street.

"They're . . . they're not open," she stammered as he approached.

"Yeah. They don't open until noon." Joe shut the alarm off and opened the door.

"Come on," he said.

She followed him in. He locked the door behind them and led the way through the main room and up a narrow stairway to the second floor. With yet another key, he opened the third door on the left and they entered what had once been a single bedroom and had been recently converted into an efficiency apartment 16 feet deep and 10 feet wide. The window at the far end was curtained with a heavy drape. In what had been a closet next to the bathroom was a single cabinet sink and an apartment-sized refrigerator with microwave on top. Over the sink was a double cupboard; an under-shelf coffee pot hung below the cupboard. A hall tree stood next to the door across from the kitchen closet. The bathroom was 3 feet wide and 6 feet long. Past the end of the bathroom, the room widened out into its full 10-foot width.

She stood awkwardly next to the kitchen as he entered the bathroom, left the bathroom door open, urinated, then washed in a small pedestal sink before busying himself with fixing coffee.

He let the cold water run in the sink while he poured beans from a can in the cupboard into the grinder and ground them. He turned and looked at her--his eyes were cold, his body tense, like an animal watching its prey--and said, "Strip," then turned back to his task.

Maybe she had known this was coming and maybe she hadn't. She wasn't sure. She slid the envelope onto the small counter next to the sink and took off her coat. She had weighed her options while kneeling in the chapel and found that there were none, other than to obey him. As she undressed, she thought back to the morning. She had set the alarm for six, then got up at 5:30, showered, shaved her legs and put a dab of Windsong on the back of her knees, in the hollow of her throat and at each side of her pubic area. So, yes, she guessed that she had known what was to happen.

Joe leaned on the counter with his back to her and read the report, done by a competitor of his Barb. It wasn't done very well. Joe grinned.

He had an idea that it was the last time she or Stu would use the services of an agency other than his for a very long time.

Anne stood next to the hall tree that held her clothes and waited for his next command. She was wearing only three things: a small gold bracelet, a watch and a wedding ring that hadn't meant anything for a long time. She took off the watch and laid it on the counter next to her purse.

When the coffee was ready, Joe poured himself a cup and walked over and sat down on the sofa, which aside from a small dining table, two chairs and the ornate hall tree, was the only furniture.   The sofa sat across from the small gas fireplace, the room's only heat.

"You cold?" he asked. It was obvious that she was and he just as obviously enjoyed it.

She nodded, unable to speak.

He grinned, got up and turned the wall-mounted thermostat on.

"Stand in front of it." He alternately drank coffee, studied the report and watched her.

"Get dressed," he said at last. His voice was flat, all trace of either anger or caring was gone. Somehow that hurt her more than if he had raped her, for she had already relinquished all rights to her body to him.

She slid into a sitting position on the floor with her elbows on her knees, holding her head in her hands, and sobbed. He had stripped away her dignity, and what little self- esteem she had managed to retain after her divorce. She no longer had an identity. He had taken that too. How, oh how, could she have let him talk her into becoming a spy on the only people who had ever cared about her as a person. (She didn't bother to remember that she had become his "spy" only after he had caught her working for another firm, or that she had been only too willing to trade office gossip, overheard phone conversations, and more recently, occasional copies of files, in exchange for him paying for her daughter's care.) She had never, in the beginning, expected him to ask for so much. Now there was no way out. He knew it, and had just proved to her that he owned her.

"Get dressed," he repeated. He gave her a cup of coffee to drink while she dressed. At 11:47 she followed him out into the rain and waited while he locked the door and reset the alarm.

The radio was playing a series of local high school marching bands from a recent competition as the pick-up made its way downtown. Joe turned the volume down only to receive and make phone calls. Twice he used a hand-held radio to make terse short calls.

"I'm going to drop you off a block from the office and you are going to go in and get the original out of Barb's desk and bring it out to me."

Anne closed her eyes and nodded. He stopped at a Safeway and ordered her, "Stay in and keep the doors locked."

When he came back, he handed her a small paper sack with a pack of gum, her favorite brand, `Beemans,' and a bubble pack with two diaper pins in it. She looked at the pins, looked at him and looked back at the pins, a puzzled expression on her face.

He grinned at her bewilderment and said, "This time you pin the envelope to the inside of your coat, in back and act casual. My God, everyone on that bus must have thought you were either carrying a bomb or had stolen the Crown Jewels."

"I'm sorry. I'm not very good at this."

"You didn't seen to have any trouble when it was for someone else."

She gulped. "Please don't make me--."

He went on as if she hadn't said anything. "If you walk into the office and someone is there, what are you going to do?"

"What? I don't know, I guess--."

"Then is not a time to guess. You must know what you will say and what you are willing to do."

"If, say, Barb is there, you say, `Hi. I saw the lights on and stopped to check.' If she's with a client, you say, `May I fix you some coffee. Do you need anything typed?' That sort of thing." She nodded. Trying to smile.

"And if you're leaving and hear someone coming in, say, `Oh, Hi. There was a light on in Barb's office, so I stopped to see if she needed anything.' Don't say, `to make sure everything is all right'. That can make someone think that maybe everything isn't all right. Got it?"

"Yes. I've got it."

Joe drove a block past the office building that housed the attorneys' offices and parked in a lot next to a jewelry store.

"Did you notice if any lights were on in the office when we came by?"

"No. I wasn't watching."

"No problem. Cross the street, walk down a block, check and come back and tell me."

She nodded as she climbed out of the Toyota. It took her seven minutes to get back, having had to wait for the crossing lights. She stood by the driver's window trying to shield her eyes against the wind-driven rain, "They aren't on."

"Good. Now what are you after?"

"The original report submitted by Tyler Investigation Service, ordered by Barb."

"Is there a chance that she would have made a copy yet?"

"Absolutely not. She hates the copy machine. Either Joyce or I make all of her copies, do all data entry, and--."

"Okay I get it. And how are you going to bring it back?"

"Pinned inside the back of my coat."

"And how are you going to keep it dry?"

"I don't know."

"Put it in a garbage bag."

It took Anne twenty minutes to accomplish a ten-minute task, mostly due to her hands shaking so badly that she couldn't get the keys to work. Thankfully he didn't admonish her for her tardiness. Though he did instruct her to take her coat off before she got in so the report wouldn't get wrinkled.

He drove down into a residential district, turned into an overgrown alley and parked beside a ratty brown van. A hand-lettered sign in the kitchen/nook window of the house overlooking the alley said, "PRINTING & TYPING." Why wouldn't someone who was in the business of printing show off their talent and ability by at least printing their sign, Anne wondered, as Joe opened his door and climbed out? Joe took her coat, left the engine running, the heater and radio on, and snapped out instructions to honk the horn if anyone came near. She watched as he skipped the sagging steps and used the edge of a planter box to gain access to the porch. He's been here before, she surmised. He was gone thirty minutes; when she saw him come out onto the porch, she punched the button back to the station he had been listening to and unlocked the driver's door. Joe climbed in and handed her coat to her. "Don't wrinkle it." He started to back out then stopped and, looking back at the house, said: "Seems like she could at least print a sign, huh?"

They had driven several blocks before Anne had enough courage to ask, "What did you do to the report?"

Joe laughed, a dry clicking sound that sent fear racing up Anne's spine. "I'm sorry if I upset you, I just thought that if there was something that I should be watching for--."

"If I need you to think, I'll let you know."

She leaned over and looked up at the fourth floor as they drove by, "No lights."

He nodded "I know."

It was then that she realized that he had known that the office lights weren't on when they had driven by earlier.

She summoned all of her courage and said, "You're a real son of a bitch."

Again the smile, "Thanks. Now please take the report back."

Please. He said "please," she told herself and the empty elevator on the way up.

After dropping her off, Joe drove out to the car lot and let himself in through the locked chain-link gates, where he took the license plates off the car he had been driving and replaced them on the car from which they'd come. It was identical except that it was a Plain Jane and didn't have a radio or tape player. The seats were vinyl as opposed to the cloth inserts in the one Anne had been in. He checked the interior of the one they'd used and found where she'd scrawled a note on the cardboard interior saying that she had been raped and was being forced to participate in a theft of documents. It didn't surprise him to find that she was already setting him up. He ripped it out and burned it in the shop stove in the detail shop. He called Mitch and told him to sell the car he'd used that day, even if he had to give it away and not to sell the other one, but to keep it on the lot until he told him otherwise. Then he drove over to Eastside Antiques and removed the couch, hall tree and under-counter coffee maker and replaced them with the renter's articles, restoring everything to its original position, working from a photo of the room he'd taken before he had switched furniture. Just to be on the safe side he boxed up the hall tree and sent to his mother to be sold. Before he left the room the last time he used an ammonia-based cleaner to wipe down all the walls, fixtures and switches.

Three weeks later Barbara Rye, attorney at law, stormed into her office, slammed her briefcase onto her desk, opened it and threw three folders across the room, creating a minor blizzard of paper.

Stu watched the tantrum, with clinical approval, took two cups of coffee into Barb's office and sat down across from her.

"Thanks," Barb said, as she cradled the cup in her hands. It obviously wasn't a prudent time for Stu to say anything, so she didn't.   After two sips of coffee, Barb said in her most sarcastically sweet tone, "Stu, would you be so kind as to ask our staff to step in here a moment."

Stu made a little yeah-whatever kind of gesture and stepped to the door of Barb's glass cubicle. "People. Come hither, oh thy worthy group. And come now."

"You aren't funny, Stu." But in spite of herself Barb did ease up some.

When everyone was assembled, Barb leaned back in her chair--she loved theater and being on stage, whether in court or in front of her assembled subjects, as Stu had so aptly put it--and said, "I want you all to know that I had the most embarrassing court day of my life. As you all know I was in court representing a client who was injured in an automobile accident. The other party was clearly at fault. It should have been simple. But no. Using the report from the investigation service employed to obtain the facts, I, an esteemed attorney, veteran of over a hundred court battles, referred to my client's vehicle as a Ford Bronco when in fact, it was a Dodge van as was clearly pointed out to me by a gleeful attorney whom I hope burns in hell. And the defendant was not driving an old Plymouth.   No, he was driving a newer Chevrolet, again pointed out to me. Need I go on?" She looked at each in turn, sensed that her performance was top dollar, sipped more coffee, and said, "Yes, I must go on. The impoundment yard holding the defendant's vehicle was not the one I referred to. Is that not enough? No. That is not enough. In his closing argument the attorney, who shall burn in hell, suggested to the jury that perhaps I would have done better if I had prepared for the right trial, and since I did not seem to have the most obvious facts right how could they believe anything I said."

George, their "token white male" as he referred to himself, scrambled out and brought fresh coffee to both attorneys. They waited while Barb sipped her coffee, knowing they were witnessing a world-class snit.

"Now, if anyone has any questions about this case, or Tyler Investigations, please be so kind as to ask now, for if anyone in this office ever mentions Tyler Investigations after today, their employment with Studebaker and Rye will be terminated immediately."

"If I may," Stu asked, holding her hand up as though a student, her actions further defusing the situation.

"Why certainly Ms. Studebaker."

"Are we going to be sued by our former client?"

"Oh yes. You can bet on it."

"Did the jury return a verdict?" Anne asked, also holding her hand up to be recognized.

"Yes, Miss Anne, they did. Having taken pity on me they awarded a settlement of fifteen thousand five hundred dollars."

George looked around at his fellow employees, and then he to raised his hand, uncertain as to whether this was office policy in a situation like this, or if they were playing some kind of a game.

Barb nodded toward him (he almost wished he had a cap to doff) and he said cautiously, "We had hoped to obtain in the neighborhood of forty-five thousand. Since we didn't, based on an erroneous investigation report, we should be able to recover all losses plus punitive damages from Tyler Investigations. Shouldn't we?"

"To an extent yes. But what is my reputation worth, and how do we establish that?"

"Shall I begin working on that now?" Anne asked.

"No. If it's all right with Stu, I'd like to put my career in George's hands."

"Thank you. I won't let you down." He left the room with tears stinging his eyes. This was the greatest compliment and career opportunity of his life.

"Party's over, away, away, little ones." Barb said, shooing them out of her office, only to call Anne back, "Would you do me the honor of getting Tyler Investigations on the phone?"

"Yes, of course."

"Oh, by the way. I gave that assignment to George because you are too multi-talented to coop up in research for the next two months."

When she closed the door Stu said, "Your talent is wasted in the courtroom. You are one of the most talented actresses I've ever known."

"Thanks, but how many actresses have you known?"

"Just you."

"Somehow I knew that was coming."

Anne knocked as she opened the door. "Sorry, they're closed until Monday. Want I should try for a home number?"

"No. It's probably best that I wait until Monday, and cool down some."

At 10:15 on Monday, Anne interrupted the bosses' Monday morning meeting, her face lined with concern, "Tyler Investigations is no longer in business."

"What!"

"His number has been switched over to his associate's house. Tyler worked out of his house and it burned down night before last. He didn't have any backup outside his office."

"Fuck!" Barb slumped over, resting her elbows on her desk, holding her head in her hands. "Was he in the house? I hope."

"No, he's on vacation with his wife and kids in Yellowstone."

"Don't you dare say it!" Barb said, sitting up and pointing an accusing finger at Anne.

"Say what?"

"Spending the money he made working a case for Studebaker & Rye, which we paid two weeks ago." Stu grinned at her friend. "Is that what she's not supposed to say?"

"Yes. And don't think it either."

Stu left Barb's office and stopped at Anne's desk. "You look ill. Are you feeling all right?"

"No. Not really."

"Why don't you go on home, get some rest, and maybe by tomorrow you'll be feeling fine."

"Thanks. I think I will. I'm kinda woozy."

"The flu has really been going around. Don't forget to drink lots of liquids."

Anne slumped against the wall of the elevator, and wondered what she had gotten herself into. She walked two blocks to a public phone booth and called Joe's mobile number.

"May I help you?"

"You dirty bastard!" she screamed into the phone and slammed it down.

Joe immediately called Stu's office and asked for her.

"Hi Joe. What's up?"

"Thought I'd give you an update on the Bryer case."

"When will you have it for me?"

"Day after tomorrow if his nibs gets back from Seattle tonight like his wife says he will. How's things?"

"You wouldn't believe it."

"I'm listening."

"You know that Barb was unhappy with your turnaround time on the Givens case and tried one of your competitors."

"Yeah, I know, she told me."

"Before I tell you what happened today, why were you late?"

"Givens and both his brothers, who were the only witnesses, went back to New Hampshire for their father's funeral. They were gone two weeks."

"Didn't you let Barb know?"

"Of course. I left a phone message with Betty, and then followed it up with a fax."

"Umm," she said, planning to follow it up. "Well anyway your competitor, Frank Tyler screwed up the report so bad that we are probably going to get sued by our client."

"Want me to check out Tyler?"

"Probably. But here's the kicker." She loved suspense like Barb loved to be dramatic, "His home office burned down two nights ago with all of his records in it."

"Swell. So where does that leave you?"

"We don't know yet. Listen I've got to go. Barb has locked herself in her office, Betty didn't come in today, and Anne went home sick. So I get to answer the phones."

Joe was already in Portland when Anne called him and had been driving toward her apartment while talking to Stu. He arrived before she did and, rather than pick the door lock like he'd done the first time, he let himself in with a key he'd cut a month before.

Anne came in, closed and locked the door, then flipped the light on; he was sitting at the dinette table cleaning a sawed-off shotgun. She stared at him and then the shotgun for several seconds, backed against the door and slid down it to a sitting position, with her knees pulled up against her chest. He got up from the table and walked over to where she huddled on the floor.

"Remember how your husband beat you?"

"Please don't. I won't ever . . . I'm sorry."

He squatted down in front of her and took her by the throat, gently pulling her forward, tilting her face up to his. Her face had lost all color and she was panting, trying to swallow. He smiled at her and asked, his voice almost a whisper, "Do you think I burned down Tyler's home?"

Her mouth opened and closed several times, without any sound.

"Do you?" This time his voice had an edge to it.

She nodded her head up and down.

"Well, you're wrong. I didn't and neither did any of my people."

Panic can only last so long and then the human body takes steps to protect itself from further psychological harm. In this case Anne simply passed out.

When she came to, she was lying on her bed and he was gone.

She didn't hear from him or see him for three days. Friday morning she answered the phone and set an appointment for Joe with both attorneys later in the day.

When he came in she avoided eye contact with him and busied herself at the copy machine, which was at the far end of the office. When they had settled themselves in Stu's office, she began with, "Okay, Mr. Greene, here we are. What's up?" This was his clue that they were both busy and had little time to deal with lowly investigators whose time meant nothing.

"Your receptionist, Betty, has been having an affair with Frank Tyler of Tyler Investigations. When I phoned and left a message with Betty regarding the Givens case, and followed it up with a fax, neither of which were received by Ms. Rye here, it gave Betty the opportunity to suggest using Tyler instead of me."

Both women were sitting forward in their chairs, hanging on every word.

"Now, when Betty found out what a fucked-up mess Tyler had made of the case, she took it upon herself to burn down his house, either to get rid of the incriminating evidence or out of anger. And after Tyler's wife found out about the affair they were having, she threw him out. He knew his marriage and his business were both down the drain, not to mention his house on which the insurance had lapsed, so he's in hiding." Joe leaned back in the chrome-and-vinyl side chair that he had dragged into Stu's office from the reception room and grinned at them.

There was a silence that lasted nearly thirty seconds, which was quite a while for two women who had a combined earning power of three hundred dollars an hour.

Stu broke the silence, "Can you prove all of this, or is some of it speculation?"

"Proof."

"Have you notified the police?"

"No."

"How do you think we should proceed?"

"It's your call."

The two women looked at one another, Stu shrugged, Barb nodded and got and went to the door.

"Anne. Order sweet rolls. Probably two dozen, and two carafes of coffee from the deli. Then call PPD Detective Division and find out who is working the arson investigation of Tyler Investigations and get him and Detective Sergeant Brown up here. Tell them that our investigator has uncovered the arsonist." She started to close the door and added, "Have the deli send up some sandwiches too."

Then to George, "George, please bring the other arm chair out of my office for Mr. Greene." When he brought the chair in, she asked him to have one of the girls available to take notes and copy whatever the detectives needed.

When four detectives and two TV crews -- who had been anonymously alerted, possibly by a phone call from Studebaker & Rye's office -- arrived twenty minutes later, Studebaker & Rye was ready for them. At Joe's suggestion, they brought up the dismal court case and suggested that either Frank Tyler or Betty Albert had given Attorney Rye a phony or forged report. That, of course, disallowed any suit against Studebaker & Rye.

All three local TV stations as well as the next days "Metro Section" of the Oregonian gave credit to Studebaker & Rye for uncovering a phony investigation firm as well as solving an arson and burglary. There was no mention of Joe Greene or his investigation service.

Joe had been called out of town around three that afternoon and didn't return for several days. He came back to find that Betty had disappearing after leaving a handwritten confession as to the arson, but denying ever seeing or altering Frank Tyler's report. Frank Tyler had taken what Joe claimed to be the easy way out by ramming his cream-colored Dodge Dart into a concrete bridge support at well over a hundred. With Tyler dead, apparently by his own hand, and his lover missing, the police soon gave up on the case, unable to prove that the report had been altered or who would have benefited from it.

Chapter Six

I t took a first-class remodeling contractor two months after he had the permits to convert Joe's tavern into a first-class steak house with a full bar, two wood-burning fireplaces and a glass-enclosed deck overlooking the Tualatin Valley. It opened with fanfare in late June, and quickly became `the place' for the up-and-coming crowd. The bikes and battered pickups gave way to BMW's and an occasional Jeep Cherokee. Joe had built an additional room with two baths and an efficiency kitchen on the north end of the building to use as his investigation office. Before he could move in, it had been taken over as a meeting room booked a month in advance. The kitchen was now a second bar.

As much as he had looked forward to it's opening, Joe found that he didn't like being there and if he wasn't there he couldn't control the operation. In August he sold the Eagle's Nest for more than he had in the entire property, keeping the three rentals and the barn. A typical Joe deal, it was for $175,000 on contract and $185,000 cash. He rented a room at a downtown bank for the cash transfer, not trusting anyone with that kind of cash at stake. He arrived twenty minutes early and after using the restroom, took the back stairs down into the basement where he made his way over to the electrical boxes.

He checked the schematics one more time and then spent four minutes installing a radio-controlled circuit breaker in the elevator control system. He took the stairs to the third floor where the room he rented was located and put a `Caution-Wet Floor' sign on the stairway door.

When the two buyers arrived Joe was sitting at the table, his back to the wall, cleaning his fingernails with a penknife. The papers were signed and the money changed hands in less than ten minutes. The three men stood, and shook hands. Joe busied himself with his briefcase while the proud owners left.

Joe waited until they were in the elevator and between floors before activating the circuit breaker. The car they were on stopped between the second and first floors. Joe put on a long padded overcoat and longhaired gray wig, set a battered hat on his head, then wiped down the table, chairs and the door with ammonia-based window cleaner. He picked up the duffel bag and briefcase and walked down the stairs, removing the wet floor sign and sliding it into his briefcase on the way. Once in the lobby he complained about the bank's poor service to the distraught, sweating assistant manager who was clearly in charge of getting the trapped patrons out of the bank of elevators. Joe took a side door, after complaining to a second assistant manager about not having elevators for elderly patrons, and walked slowly down the sidewalk and around the corner to his car.

A few minutes after the elevators stopped, a maintenance man found what appeared to be a transistor radio on the floor near the main breaker box. The wire that should have gone to the earphones was melted off. The radio smelled of burned wiring and didn't work. "Fuck," he said to himself. "Just my luck. I find somethin' an it ain't no damn good." He had carried it some way across the basement as he fiddled with it, and was about to pry the back off and check it some more (not that he knew anything about radio's, but just out of curiosity) when he heard his supervisor's footsteps and quickly threw it in a dumpster. As the elevator repair crew was coming down the stairs at a run, the maintenance man who had tossed the `radio' was going up an internal stairway to clean up a plugged toilet in a men's restroom. By the time he was done the elevator was working again and he had forgotten about the radio.

The two men trapped in the elevator for twenty minutes were treated to a `lunch' at the Benson. After baked salmon and four drinks apiece, they were no longer concerned about the elevator. For dessert they toasted their new venture with another round of drinks, and entertained themselves by watching two young ladies in short skirts at the bar.

Joe did exactly as planned, leaving the bank and climbing into a car he had left in a two-hour slot an hour before the bank meeting, leaving the one he driven to the bank in a parking garage. He called Mitch on his cell phone and told him where the car was and to send a tow, as he couldn't get it started. He then drove across town to another bank and left the cash in a safety deposit box, using the alias under which he had obtained the box a year before.

Four days later Mitch died of a heart attack. Though it wasn't unexpected by either Mitch or Joe, it was at a rather inconvenient time.

Chapter Seven

While Joe was dealing with the car lot, detail shop and inventory, five of his seven employees left to start their own business, taking with them all of his accounts except Studebaker & Rye. He didn't find out about it until he stepped into his office at four having just returned from Mitch's funeral.

There wasn't anybody around. Janice was in Idaho taking statements from several young men concerning a wrongful death case for Attaberry's Law Firm. The message light was blinking and the supply room door was standing wide open. At first he thought that he'd been burglarized, but the more he looked the more it became apparent that a mutiny had taken place along with a theft of most of his investigative supplies and equipment. He felt like he'd run seven miles, uphill, as he went out to the Jeep wagon he'd been driving for the last few days and got a video camera. He videoed everything, scanned for bugs, found none, and called the cops. They just wanted to send him a form to fill out. He hung up and called in a marker. Lieutenant Harmon owed him, and he collected. Harmon himself and two prowl cars made an appearance, took reports, fingerprints and photos.

After they left he called Anne at home but she hung up on him as soon as she heard his voice.

"Okay," he thought, as he punched in Stu's number, only to have it answered by a man.

This time it was Joe's turn to hang up.

When Stu called the next day and asked him to come over to her condo for a drink -- not dinner, a drink -- that evening, he knew he was being set up.   Normally he would have had Shelby and probably Curtis there ahead of him, setting up their own surveillance and taking out anyone else's system.   Now he had only Janice, just back from Idaho, who wasn't trained for this kind of work, and his wits. He hadn't slept in three days and couldn't yet. So he sat in the sun on the balcony of his barn, ate a carton of cottage cheese (a holdover from Gloria), and considered his options.

There weren't any.

He was going to have to go face the music. He drove over to the car lot, let himself in through the gate, and leaving the Jeep, picked out a strong sounding, newer Olds station wagon with air shocks, a 454 engine and good tires.   Before he left the lot he went back into the office trailer and opened the safe. There was well over forty thousand dollars in cash in it. He hadn't wanted to carry it around, but he didn't want to leave it there any longer, either. He found an old briefcase that Mitch had carted around and put the cash in it, and set it on the floor behind the driver's seat. He went into the detail shop and found a gallon pickle jar that he filled two-thirds full with gasoline and placed it on the floor in front. Then he drove back across town, filling the tank and jacking the air pressure in the rear tires up to fifty pounds on the way. He parked four blocks from Stu's flat, in a pay-to-park lot, thus he would be a fashionable twenty minutes late and no one would know what he was driving.

He didn't bother to try any surveillance, if Stu had someone watching they would be good enough to keep out of sight.

As far as personal protection, Joe was wearing a Beretta .380, his trademark, for which he carried two extra clips in holders built into the webbing of the shoulder holster. A double-edged fighting knife was taped to the inside of his left forearm. A can of pepper mace, and two sets of handcuffs were in the pockets of his sport coat. The cuffs were an off-breed brand, that were very hard to open and very few people had keys for them. He'd bought them through an advertisement in a law enforcement magazine. But they hadn't cost much either.

Anne opened the door when he rang the bell. That he had expected.

"Good evening Joe," Stu said from behind Anne, "I'm glad you could make it."

He nodded, walked in, set his briefcase on the kitchen counter, and from there went directly over to the stereo system taking a tape from his jacket pocket and inserting it in the cassette player, then adjusting the volume before he spoke. The wail of a saxophone filled the room.

"There just ain't nobody like Louis Armstrong when it comes to the blues is there?" He said as he searched the condo. When he came back down stairs both women were standing in the middle of the living room. Stu had her arms crossed and was rubbing her upper arms as though she was cold.

"Cold?" Joe asked.

"No," she answered, a little too loud, "Do we have to have the stereo up so loud?"

Anne wouldn't or couldn't meet his gaze. Joe walked into the kitchen and came back with a roll of scotch tape. Anne backed away from him as he walked past her to the living room window. He ran strips of tape both vertically and horizontally across the expanse of glass, and then closed the drapes.

"What did you just do?"

"Oh that? You see a window works like a big speaker. Sound makes it vibrate. Putting tape across the glass stops the vibration, thus halts the transmission of sound waves." Joe sat down on a kitchen chair that he dragged over in front of the couch and, grinning, said, "Let's cut the crap. What is this all about?"

Stu looked at Anne who shook her head "no," and then turned to Joe and said, "Anne came to me several days ago and told me what she has been doing for you and why. Since then I've been doing a lot of checking up on you. I'm appalled at what you've done. I intend to distance myself and my business as far as I can from you."

"Sounds pretty incriminating. Just what have you found?"

"Not a damn thing I can prove. The house where you went to have Tyler's report altered was not and never has been a print shop. The woman who lives there works from nine to five and had no idea what we were talking about. The car you used is still on your lot, but it's different from the way Anne remembers it."

"I don't know what print shop you are talking about," he said smiling.

"I think that you just walked through her house out the front door and drove somewhere else using a car you had left out front for that very reason. That's why you took Anne with you, so if she ever said anything you could discredit her."

"What about this 'car?'"

"I can't divulge anything about that."

"Are you beginning to understand that nothing she's telling you really happened?"

"Your deceit caused Betty's disappearance and Frank Tyler's death."

"That's pure horseshit. Betty and Frank were lovers, she pulled a scam for or with him. When they got caught, she split and he committed suicide cause his wife found out about Betty from the cops and his business had gone up in smoke, as we in the business say."

"Aside from that, you raped Anne in a room over the Eastside Antique Store. We have decided not to pursue it, as you have an iron-tight alibi for that day, and if we did get a search warrant, the room probably wouldn't be there would it?"

"So far you have built a little fantasy world with no foundation. Would you care to try some other tack?"

"How about tax evasion? Do you like that one?"

"Before you get carried away, you damn well better have a very good reason to proceed."

"I think that the IRS would be very interested in where you got enough money to buy that property up on Skyline."

"I thought as much. You're jealous because I make more money than you do."

"Don't make me laugh. Either show me proof or I go to the IRS."

"Okay, Bitch." Joe got up and walked over to the kitchen table and opened his briefcase. He started back, then seemed to change his mind and took two rubber wedges out of his briefcase and kicked one of them in tight under the front door. When he came back from wedging the rear door Stu had a phone in her hand. He lifted it out of her grasp and held it to his ear. It rang only once before a deep male voice, that Joe would recognize anywhere, answered. Joe punched the off button.

"So my own crew is working against me."

"They aren't your crew anymore. Probably haven't been for a long time."

Anne spoke for the first time, a tremor in her voice, "Why did you wedge the doors like that?"

"Mr. Shelby and Mr. Curtis are probably going slightly nuts, having lost contact with their clients. They stole some pretty good equipment from me when they left, including several high frequency radios. Knowing those two they may become stupid via radio, and try to force their way in, one at each door. Those little wedges will cause them very large headaches. But only if they become stupid."

"Do you have something for me to read, or not."   Stu sounded tired.

"All right, here's what you asked for." He flipped a folder onto the coffee table in front of the women. "As you can see, my father died and left me a large inheritance, $210,578 to be exact." (In reality his father had left him $10,578. Joe had added the `two' in the event tonight ever happened.) "And before you get the bright idea that my ex-girlfriend is entitled to any of it, please refer to the pre-nuptial agreement."

"So that's why you weren't concerned when you met with her and her attorney."

Joe shrugged.

"You lied to me."

"No, I just told you what happened that day. It didn't have anything to do with the pre-nuptial, and you damn well know it."

"So you had enough cash to buy the Skyline property. What about the car lot, and the antique store?"

"Perhaps you've forgotten that I have worked seven days a week for several years, and with several employees, investing as I went!"

"What about the way you got paid for cars. All in cash. Like that Bronco? I was with you when you sold it. What about that?"

"Well for one thing, were you present during the transaction?"

"No. You know I wasn't. So I don't really know how much you were paid for it, do I?"

"No, you don't. But if someone were to check, they would find that sale recorded and the amount I told you documented."

"Of course. You think of everything don't you?"

"I try. God knows you've made your share off of my work."

"Yes I suppose I have. And I'm sure that I can't prove anything, but Joe, just between you and me, you're slime. And so help me God you will never work another case in this city!"

"You know Stu, we had a pretty good thing going, you and I, I don't know what your problem is, but you're way off base, and if you and your little buddy--who incidentally is lying about everything except the fact that I have been paying for her daughter's treatment--say one word to anyone, I'll hunt you down like a mad dog."

Joe had been watching Anne's eyes for about a minute. They kept straying back to the bottom of the front door. Joe smiled, the wedge under the back door was set on vinyl flooring. He had spit on the suction cups on the bottom of the wedge before kicking it into place. It wasn't going anywhere. The one under the front door was on carpet and was an entirely different matter. He hoped it was Shelby at the front door.

Joe said, "If there is nothing more, I guess I'll just put these papers back in my briefcase and mosey on out of here."

As he spoke he stood up and turned toward the table, his right hand out of sight as he pulled the pepper mace out of his sports coat. In two quick steps, he reached the front door, kicked the wedge out and pulled the door open in one fluid move. Shelby was on his knees holding a foot-long piece of wire with which he had been working the wedge loose. His mouth dropped open in an attempt to plead his case. Joe kicked him square in the face then emptied about half the can of mace into Shelby's broken, gasping face. When he turned both women were running for the back door, presumably to let Curtis in. Joe left the front door open, but instead of running, he stepped back into the condo and behind the stub wall that separated the kitchen from the living room. If there was one thing Joe had always liked about Curtis, it was his predictability. He came lumbering down the hall and into the living room followed by both women, staring at his writhing partner. Joe let him get past then yelled, "Curtis!"

The big man swung around, going into a crouch as he reached for a weapon. Joe dropped him in his tracks with a judo chop to the neck, then used a little mace on him too. He turned to point at the women, who looked like two mannequins frozen in their tracks, "Not a fucking word out of either one of you. Got it?!"

They nodded in unison.

Joe could see that the back door was closed, that was a good start. "Okay ladies, drag Boy Wonder in here beside Boy Wonder Two." Stu tried to protest but Joe raised his hand palm out toward her. "No use lying, Babe, you set me up to be hammered. It didn't work. Now you are going to join in the consequences of your behavior."

They pulled Shelby part way across the carpet before stopping. It seemed that Stu had broken a nail. For the time it took them to examine the injury and declare it fixable, they forgot about Joe and their hired guns lying unconscious at their feet. After pulling him the last eight feet, Joe had Anne remove all weapons and paraphernalia from the two men and put it all into a grocery bag he got out of the kitchen. He then handcuffed Stu to Shelby, right wrist to right wrist, and Anne to Curtis in the same fashion.

"You can't be serious!" Stu exclaimed when it became apparent what was happening.

Anne cried, begged not to be left chained to an unconscious mountain, and finally admitted to Joe that she had not been raped and had told Stu that to gain more sympathy.

Joe thanked her for her confession, Stu for her hospitality, drowned the phones in the toilet tank and, leaving the stereo wailing, left, locking the door behind him.

Once the door closed behind Joe, Stu turned to the shaking Anne and asked, "What do you mean by, `Joe, I'm sorry I said you raped me. You didn't, I just said that to get more sympathy? My God, Anne, you of all people know better than to lie to your attorney."

"I'm sorry. I really am. I went with him--."

"With him, or to him?"

"To him, knowing what was going to happen. Maybe I even wanted it. I don't know any more."

"Fuck! Fuck, Fuck, Fuck! The only thing I really thought I could prove was that he raped you. And now I find you lied about that. You know, he just may have a real nice libel case against me."

"If we don't tell anyone, maybe he'll let it slide."

"Oh sure. He'll have us doing cartwheels for his pleasure for the rest of our lives."

"Maybe we can prove something. I don't know."

"So far everything you've told me has been wrong. I'm beginning to think that maybe you did set him up. Did you?"

"Like what? Oh! No, I swear I didn't. What if we stage a rape, and videotape it. Then trade it for leaving us alone."

"And who is the victim. You?"

"If you want."

"I don't think so. He's too smart for that. Let's start by waking up the Wonder Boys and getting these cuffs off."

"I can scream real loud."

"You scream and I'll kill you. The last thing I need is for some enterprising jerk with a camera in here."

The door opened and Joe came back in. "Sorry. I forgot my briefcase. He picked it up and looked at it. "Damn. Wouldn't you know it? I forgot and left the video camera that is built into the bottom running." He pretended alarm, "And look at this. I also left the recorder on. Son of a gun, well what's a little video film among friends?"

He started for the door and then came back to crouch down in front of Stu, "I'm sorry you bet on the wrong horse."

She was sitting on the floor with tears leaking through her closed eyelids. He stood up and said, "If you roll those two over, face down, they'll come to a lot quicker."

Before he left the second time he asked Stu if he should leave his key to her `flat.' She thought it would be a good idea.

Among the things stripped from the pockets of the Wonder Boys were their keys. Joe retrieved his car and then drove around until he found their van three blocks away, where they'd had a good shot at Stu's window for their electronic eavesdropping device, which they had stolen from Joe. He stripped most of his equipment out of the van and before heading for the address on one of Shelby's new business cards, used a battery-powered drill that he found in the van to drill a small hole through each tail light lens and into each light bulb. Before he left the van he stuffed the glove box with crumpled paper towels and, taking the 9mm of his that Curtis had stolen from him, made sure that it was loaded and cocked, then laid it against the paper towels and holding it in place eased the glove box lid closed.

Their office was in a newer complex on the edge of Gresham. There wasn't anyone in the office so he parked across the street and put on a black nylon jumpsuit with removable shoulder pads to break up his silhouette, dark glasses, a long cheap wig pulled down over his forehead, shoe covers, and two pair of surgical gloves, one over the top of the others. The alarm system was one of the ones he sold. He used Curtis's keys to shut the alarm off and open the door. Once inside it took Joe ten minutes to find both remote cameras from which he removed the film. He videoed everything of his that they had stolen, displaying the serial numbers when possible. Then he took all of his good equipment and nothing of theirs, leaving the wallets, keys, Shelby's gun, and even the temporary registration of the van. Their backup disks he took as well. He was sweating from exertion and tension when he dumped the last load in the back of the station wagon, and covered his booty with a blanket. They had secured the shop in such a fashion as to be nearly impossible to break into. The only access from the outside was the main door. Joe decided to teach them something, so he took the can of epoxy glue that they had been using to build some camera mounts and sealed the steel fire door into its metal frame, then filled the three key holes, one of which deactivated the alarm, with a mixture of sand and super glue. Before he closed the door Joe turned the office thermostat up to ninety. He stripped the outer pair of surgical gloves off and dropped them in the gallon jar of gasoline that sat on the floor of the passenger side. Once he had the engine running he boosted the air shocks up to level the wagon out. The tires were six ply and inflated to fifty pounds. To a casual observer the wagon appeared to be empty. Joe drove across town to a Seven-Eleven four blocks from Janice's place and called her from a phone booth, stripping the second pair of gloves as well as the shoe covers and wig off and dropping them into the gas before getting out of the car.

When she answered with a half-awake hello he told her that her phone was probably bugged, and arranged to pick her up in ten minutes. "Damn," he thought out loud "I should have thought about her phone being bugged and had a code for a meeting place in advance."

It took Joe less than two minutes to be a block down and across the street from her apartment. The next few minutes crept by as he watched for a surveillance vehicle either present or approaching. He hadn't tried any cute stuff with her like twenty questions to confuse listeners. It didn't work and only served to give them more time to get in position. When Joe saw the streak of light shoot across the lawn from the entry door being opened and quickly closed, he moved, pulling in against the curb. Janice waited, one hand holding the entry door slightly open the other clutching a canister of pepper mace until Joe turned the dome light on light on long enough for her to see that it was him. Once she started for the station wagon he pulled the bulb out of its socket and put it in the ashtray.

As she opened the door he said, "Don't kick over the pickle jar."

Janice took one look at Joe and said, "Gee, Boss you didn't have to get all dressed up for me." She looked at him in the passing streetlights, taking in the obvious tension and fatigue, and said, "You look like hell."

"Thanks."

"What's in the pickle jar?"

"Gasoline, surgical gloves, shoe covers, and a wig."

"Sounds wonderful, shall we dump it?"

"It's about time. Probably cooked enough."

They found an overgrown vacant lot on a side street and Janice carried the jar out into the tall grass and dumped it. She went, "Blah!" and threw the jar against a broken concrete foundation, shattering it.

"That was gross!" she said as she climbed into the car. "It looked like a boiled possum, hair and all."

"You broke our toilet."

"Sorry, but there is no way in hell I'm going to squat over a jar that just contained a possum. The thought of its teeth are too vivid."

"So is your imagination."

"You want to talk about what's bothering you?"

"Yeah, I'm hungry. And I'm mad."

"That's it?"

"Yeah. I think so."

"How about wondering what happened to your crew? Why they left and stole your business?"

"I don't know why they did that."

"I think I do." She paused, unwilling to hurt him any more then he already was. "You're about as good as they come, but you've been going in a lot of different directions. Sometimes you kind of left us to fend for ourselves -- or so it seemed. I think Keith and the rest of them thought that you were making the big bucks, while they did all the work." She stared out the window at nothing for a minute, and then went on, "They didn't realize that it was your reputation that brought the work through the door. They are going to learn the hard way that it was your knowledge and instinct that sent them in the right direction and kept their asses alive. And then they started their own company, with no concept of the startup costs. Since they were already committed, they stole equipment from you rationalizing that without them you wouldn't need everything."

"Well, they are about to learn another lesson -- the hard way."

"Why don't you let it drop? You still have Studebaker & Rye. And if you want, you can spend nine thousand hours a week looking for kids that probably aren't going to ever come home again."

"I don't have Studebaker & Rye any more."

"Why not?"

"Stu hired none other than Shelby and Curtis to pin a phony rape charge on me. And I think they were to hammer me too. I can't prove that--yet."

"What! With who?"

"Anne."

"Did you?"

"No, I didn't have sex with her and I didn't rape her."

"What happened?"

"When I first started in Portland I caught her sellin' reports to the firm's competitors to pay for her daughter's drug rehab."

"You did!"

He nodded and continued, "I made her a deal. I paid for her kid and she gave me what I requested from the office. I never used it to hurt Stu or Barb but to stay one step ahead of them. Like when they'd call to have us do an investigation, I'd already have it mapped out. Gave me a better turnaround time, and made us look even better than we were. Then I caught her coverin' for Betty, I think she was helping Betty get her man, Tyler, my job so she could cut the ties with me."

"Why?"

"Her kid is due to be released from the program in about a week from now."

"How long has she been in the program?"

"It's been about two years. It's a real special place where they help the kids get their GED and then send them through a trade school. Anne's kid is going to be a veterinarian's assistant." He said it with a little pride in his voice, though he really didn't know her, he'd had quite a bit to do with her rehab and schooling.

"Is she cured?"

"I guess they think so. Anyway, I decided to set her up, which I did. But Tyler's report was so bad that it made it look like I fucked with it."

"But you didn't?"

"No, I didn't. It looked clean, and I had no way of knowin' who was drivin' what unless I'd checked . . . which I hadn't."

Janice thought about it, then asked, "What happened at Stu's condo?"

"Well, when I left, the Wonder Boys were unconscious on Stu's living room floor."

Janice had run out of words, she just shook her head.

"It gets better," he chuckled, a sound so all alone that she wanted to hold him, keep the cold away, "Stu and Anne were handcuffed to them."

"You didn't--."

"Never laid a hand on them."

"That's good. She looked out the window again and asked, "Where are we going?"

"Back to their office in Gresham. I want to set up a surveillance camera and a Big E and train them on the front door."

"Why don't you pull into this 7-11 and I'll get us some coffee. You look like you could use a cup."

She came back with two large coffees, an assortment of candy bars, four bottles of Snapple®, two sets of Twinkies® (for her), and six packets of processed cheese and crackers.

"Whatcha get?"

"All of the basic surveillance food groups."

"Good."

Janice opened a cup of coffee and handed it to her boss, then peeled the wrapper back on a Three Musketeers® candy bar and handed that across to him.

He took a bite of the candy bar, two sips of coffee, set the coffee on the dash, tilted against the windshield, and held it in place with the bitten end of his candy bar as they rounded a corner, sloshing coffee down the defroster vent.

The smell from the coffee mixing with the warm humid air of the heating system was unmistakable.

"Oh good," she said clapping her hands, "Now it even smells like a snoop-and-destroy rig."

He grinned. "Sorry."

"You are planning to destroy them, aren't you?"

"Yeah. By the way, did they ask you to join their Merry Band of Thieves?"

"No. They think I like you. I don't think they really started heisting gear until you sent me to Idaho to interview those cowboys. Man you ought to see the horses some of them have."

"Yeah, I'll bet."

"I got the information when no one else could, didn't I?"

"You sure did."

"So, how are you going to destroy them?"

"I'm going to kill them with comedy."

"Is this another one of your riddles?"

"No, not really. I had the video that is built into the bottom of my briefcase running with a wide-angle lens before I got to Stu's. Therefore I have, on video, the confession from Anne that I didn't rape her, Stu's entire bogus accusation, and the Wonder Boys in attack mode. I also have them handcuffed to their clients. Now if I can get a camera trained on the door of Star Investigation's office before they get there, it should prove interesting. Then I'll splice together a video of the Five Hapless and see that every attorney in Portland gets a copy."

"What's their front door got to do with it?"

"It's glued shut, and it's the only way in."

"Boss, I'm proud of you. You have, without a doubt, sunk to a new low." She gave him a look of total admiration and asked, "How can I help?"

"How do you figure it's low to destroy those who have stolen my business, my clients, and wrecked my reputation?"

"It was meant as a compliment. What I mean is, it's a brilliant plan. No one will go to prison, no one will get sued and nobody but nobody will ever use those clowns for anything."

"That's kind of how I figure it too."

"What about us?"

"I think my goose is cooked in this town. And I'm sure that until I get the video made and distributed we are both going to be targets, and I don't mean just physical. That's why I called you out tonight. I want to pack up and move. Since this whole mess is my fault, I'm going to give you ten grand in cash, no strings, no taxes, to help you get out of Portland and start over."

"No deal. I'm not leavin'. And thanks, but I don't need your money."

"We'll discuss it more later. Right now we're about ten blocks from there. We'll do a drive-by. If it's clear, we'll circle around and I'll drop out. I need you to crawl in back now and rig up a video with zoom telephoto lens and a motion switch. Oh yeah, and put a double battery pack on it. Then out of that box on the seat get me a roll of duct tape, two penlights and that little ear."

They rode in silence for several minutes until Janice finished, "Anything else?"

"Yeah. Test those two FM radios, those are the ones I took from those thievin' bastards at Stu's. Pick a station and set both on it."

"Where are you going to leave this?"

"There's an oak tree right across the street from their office. I'm gonna climb it and hang the stuff about fifteen or twenty feet up, so it looks right down on them. The water bureau was nice enough to put a fire hydrant in line with the tree and the door so no one can park there and block the view."

"This is the kind of thing that you always see and tell them. I don't think any of them are capable of seeing the opportunity as quickly and easily as you do. Even if you don't destroy them, they'll self-destruct."

"Feel sorry for them?"

"A little. We were friends for a long time, almost two years. Those ladies throw some outrageous parties."

"I never went to any."

"I know."

"There's the office, the parking lot is along the east side. No one's there, right? Good."

Joe pulled into the lot of a closed service station and they traded places.

He had taken the shoulder pads out of his jumpsuit while he had waited for Janice. As she drove back toward the office they were quiet; he checking gear and putting it into a padded soft-side case, she driving and thinking about the future. They met two cars on the way back, other than that there was nothing moving.   She was gripping the wheel a little too tightly; they both knew that even though what they were doing wasn't strictly illegal, there was always danger in being taken for a burglar, and neither of them, especially Janice, wanted a confrontation with any of Joe's former employees right now.

"I imagine that we are walking a pretty thin timeline here. Huh, Boss?"

He slipped on soft black leather gloves and pulled a dark blue watch cap down over his head. "I'm pretty surprised that at least some of them aren't here by now. You know the drill, four blocks up the street, face me, and other than the initial radio check don't expect me to answer. If someone shows up, I'll make my way through the backyards and meet you one block north. If I can't meet you, head for a motel, check in and wait. He dug his wallet out of his jacket pocket, pulled his right glove off with his teeth, and gave her four twenties. "Remember, no heroics."

"Got it. Do you have your pepper mace?"

"Yeah. But I better take a new one. I used about half a can on Shelby and a shot on Curtis."

He took one out of the box behind the seat and asked, "You got yours?"

"In my lap. You take care. And you know I'm good enough to do a hot pickup."

"Let's hope you don't have to. This wagon weighs too much to outrun anything faster than a bicycle."

"It acts like it has a big engine."

"It does. But we'd lose the brakes in nothing flat."

As he ran toward the tree she blew a kiss at his back and drove on down the street. She didn't know when she'd ever felt so sorry for anyone. He was kind of a bastard, but he didn't deserve this. He'd played by the rules, paid everyone well and all he expected that they do the same. She turned around and parked under a streetlight, just like he'd taught her.

She wondered if he had ever been scared, if he was scared now. He was what, forty-five, maybe. And faced with losing everything and starting over in a different city. She watched, and thought about what she knew about her boss. Not much really. Everything about him was, `I think,' or `well, I heard.' Keith had told her that no one was as good with his hands as Joe was without extensive training. The kind you get in the very cream of the military units. Lori and Pam both told her that they'd heard he moved to Portland after he killed two men in a bar fight in Texas, and that was why he wouldn't go to bars with them. She'd tried to run a trace on him one afternoon and came up with zilch. She thought that his real name was probably not Greene or even Joe for that matter. The social security number he used was for a man who'd died in the Vietnam War who happened to have the same name Joe did. Maybe she would ask him. And maybe she would sprout wings too.

Janice watched headlights come up behind her, and go on by. "Red pickup, two men, two blocks west. Headed East."

Joe stopped climbing and waited until the pickup drove past. They couldn't see him, but they might see a limb moving, and he didn't need company. He had just finished taping the camera mount down and was attaching the camera when Janice's voice froze him to the tree. He waited patiently while the old man and his leash-tugging black lab worked their way past. Joe checked his watch, noting that five minutes had been wasted. Joe was beginning to wonder why the Wonder Boys weren't there. He'd trained them better than that. He was finished and just ready to call for pickup when Janice said, "Prowl car! Headed toward you," her voice was edged with panic. "Real slow. Just shut off lights." Then a moment later she stage-whispered, "Oh my God! Two more, coming up the street from the east. No lights!"

"Stay focused. Get moving. Don't forget to use your turn signal. I'll call when clear. "

Two of the prowl cars stopped in the street, the third had pulled over with the front wheels up into the driveway of the lot where the tree and Joe were. After several minutes of consultation they pulled out and disappeared into the night.

"Let's do that pickup now."

"Coming."

"Make it one block east, south side of the street."

"Done."

Joe hadn't quite gotten the door pulled shut before Janice asked, "What happened?"

"From what I could hear someone called in a possible burglary in progress. The boys in blue were more interested in a possible pay increase than in rattling the door. Which was good. It also means that they must be loose, and probably headed this way. Let's take a shortcut. Head for Vancouver."

"Why Vancouver?"

"None of them live there. We won't cross the bridge though. Something about state lines. Let's go to the Red Lion at Jantzen Beach."

"I thought you'd never ask."

"Right. Is there any food left?"

"What? Are you accusing me of pigging out while you were up in the tree?"

"The candy wrappers are about a foot deep under my feet."

"Oh, well. Back to the camera. Why the door? Why not set up a surveillance camera inside?"

Joe was busily rummaging through the grocery sack, and when he spoke it was through a Twinkie®.

"When I left Shelby and Curtis in Stu's flat, I liberated everything they were carrying, which included two sets of keys. I found their van about three blocks away and took back most of my tools. Their business card led me to their office in Gresham. And besides if I rigged a camera inside it would prove that I had been inside which is considered disrespectful in police circles. Can you believe that those bastards even stole one of my alarm systems?"

She could, having seen the office and supply room when she got back from Idaho. "I was saving that Twinkie® for later."

He ignored her and continued, "Anyway one of the keys shut the alarm off and two others opened the door. Almost everything they stole from me is now in the back of this."

"It doesn't act like it."

"Big engine and air shocks."

"Oh."

"So anyway, while I was inside I noticed that they have the place sealed up like a vault. The only way in, when it's locked up, is through the front door. So I glued the front door shut."

"You told me that, but would you like to explain why?"

"I noticed that they were in the process of making video camera mounts and had left a full quart can of quick-dry epoxy cement on the counter. The front door is a steel fire door set in a steel frame that is in turn bolted into a concrete reinforced wall. I turned the thermostat up to help the drying process, glued the door shut, then locked it up and filled the locks with a tube of super glue I found in a desk drawer. And I added a little sand to the glue from the butt can by the door."

"Now I understand . . . we get a nice video of them trying to break into their own office. Cute."

"And one other thing. I reprogrammed the alarm to vibration from motion detection. Once they start beating on the door the alarm will go off and ring non-stop for eight hours or until they get the door open, which should take about the same length of time."

"I love it."

They rode along lost in the events of the evening until Janice asked him if he really thought that any of the group would try to do something to her. When he didn't answer, she looked over at him and smiled. He was asleep, his head against the side window, half a Twinkie® in his hand. Janice looked at the Twinkie®, looked up at the road and then carefully reached over for the Twinkie®.

"Touch my Twinkie® and I'll break your arm."

She pulled her hand back and grinned. She didn't bother him again until the Olds was backed into a head-in-only slot in front of the room she'd rented with the money he'd given her.

"Go on in. I think I'll just sleep here."

"Like hell you will. There are two queen-size beds in this room. You'll be safe, I promise."

"Hey, wait a minute. That's a guy line."

"Not anymore. There is now a thing called `Women's Lib.' -- that means women have the same rights to be jerks as men do."

Chapter Eight

I t had taken an hour for Stu and Anne to get Shelby moving. Once he seemed to understand where he was, Stu tried to help him sit up. He did, only to vomit a mixture of blood and two drive-thru cheeseburgers down the front of her blouse. She gagged and pulled as far away from him as she could, only to be pulled back when his befuddled brain registered pain associated with his eyes and he jerked his arm back to clamp his hands over them. The two women sat staring at one another until Anne, overcome by the smell of the pepper mace and the sight and smell of the raw sewage that spewed out of Shelby, began to retch.

"Anne! Don't." Stu paused to regain enough composure to continue, "For God's sake control yourself. Getting sick isn't something we have time for."

It was another forty-five minutes before Stu was able to revive Shelby enough to get him into the bathroom, where he stood wobbling and moaning in the shower with her. After ten minutes they came back into the living room, leaving a trail of water from their dripping clothes, to find Curtis up on his knees digging at his eyes and softly cursing.

"Get him into the bathroom while I take this one down to my car. I'm going to drive him to a phone booth. When I get back we'll make a plan." Her only plans were to fire Anne, and do a damage assessment, but for now she had to keep her thinking that they were still engaged in a client/attorney relationship. "For now, stay here and don't let anyone in. Knowing Mr. Greene he may have called a TV station or some crony at a paper."

Stu drove up the street six blocks to a closed service station lot where she could pull up beside a pay phone. She had to slide over into the passenger seat of her Honda (which now smelled like wet vomit) and sit with her arm out the open door while Shelby called Keith Johnson, the third male of Star Investigations, and briefed him as to what had happened and told him that they needed a set of bolt cutters. It turned out that Keith had a pair in his garage and could easily pick them up on the way from his stakeout to Stu's condo. After Shelby hung up the phone, he and Stu were able to get back into the condo without being seen, except by the pair of snickering skate-boarders who had glided past while he was talking to Keith.

They waited in uncomfortable silence for the nearly thirty minutes it took Johnson to get there. Shelby had tried small talk but found that it was hard to make conversation with a woman whom you've just puked on while handcuffed to her. At one point, Curtis asked if there was anything to eat as he had worked up an appetite. He received a cold stare in reply. Johnson arrived and was able to cut the chains and cuffs off of both men and Anne's wrist before the blade broke.

"You're kidding!" Stu said, when he told her the cutting blade was broken. "You mean I'm stuck with this on my wrist?"

"I think the fire department has cutters and . . ."

"Just get out!" she screamed at them. And slammed the door behind them.

"Think we lost her account?" Curtis asked the other two in all seriousness as they made their way down to Johnson's sedan. Shelby directed him down the street and around the corner to where they had left the van. There were sighs of relief when they saw it. They weren't quite as happy when they found that Greene had been there and taken almost everything of his and left it unlocked with the key in the ignition.

"I don't think leaving the van open was very fuckin' nice. Some son of a bitch coulda' stole it." Curtis said as he pawed through the pile of gear Greene had left in the middle of the floor.

After a hasty consultation, Keith called Pam and briefed her. He told her to find Lori and meet them at the office pronto. He then called in an anonymous tip of a burglary in progress giving their office address.

"Maybe we'll get lucky and the cops will catch Greene there." They all grinned at the thought, not believing it would ever happen, but unwilling to admit it to one another.

Johnson left first, driving as fast as he dared toward the office. The other two stayed with the van, and followed until they spotted an all-night convenience store. Curtis dug enough change out of the pocket of his slacks to buy one large coffee. "Damn it too hell," he said as Shelby pulled back out into traffic, "I forgot that bastard Greene took our wallets. I had to leave the other coffee and the aspirin too. Didn't have enough money."

Shelby nodded, too lost in his own thoughts to acknowledge or care. He shook his head 'no' when Curtis offered to share the coffee with him. They were speeding, trying to get to Gresham as fast as possible, when Shelby said, "Oh damn!"

"What?" Curtis asked, leaning over to peer at the gauges, thinking that maybe they were out of gas.

"Cops."

Curtis turned to look behind them, "This ain't cool."

"No shit. I don't have my license. I'll have to talk my way out of this."

The two night-shift PPD officers approached, one on each side. The one on the driver's side asked to see Shelby's license. He noticed the bloodshot eyes and shaking hands, thinking drugs or just coming down off a bender.

"I don't have it with me. We were robbed downtown and are just tryin' to get back to the office."

"Robbed," the officer asked? He thought it was more likely they had picked up a couple of hookers and had been rolled by either them or their pimp. "Did you report it?"

The second officer, hearing his partner's voice take on an edge, backed up one step and pulled his pistol while keying his mike, "We need a cover car right away."

The terse request was like a straight shot of adrenaline to all the units that heard it. Four units swung toward what had been a routine traffic stop, urged on by the dispatcher who fed them the location.

"No, not yet. We want to get to our office first. You see, we're private investigators. We got jumped and maced."

"Who else is in the van with you?" Come on use your head, keep 'em talkin' until cover arrives, the officer told himself, having heard the exchange between his partner and the dispatcher in his earpiece.

"Just my partner here."

"This your van?"

"Well, it's owned by our agency. How come you stopped us?"

"No taillights, sir."

"What the fuck!" Shelby stopped there, realization beginning to dawn.

"The registration comes back for a Howard Higgs. Either one of you Mr. Higgs?"

"No, but we just bought it last week. The registration probably hasn't been changed yet in DMV's computer." Shelby by now had a pretty good idea as to why they didn't have taillights, and as much as he was beginning to hate Joe Greene, he had to respect his thoughtfulness. Oh fuck! he thought. Now I know why he didn't take all of his stuff. I'll bet he filed a burglary report and named us as suspects.

Curtis was starting to get mad. Shelby realized that somehow he had to let Curtis know what was happening and cool him down before he did something stupid. He reached for Curtis's arm, hoping to convey the message to just sit still and keep quiet. Curtis pushed his hand away and sat forward in his seat so he could look out at the officer who was asking the questions.

"We got the temporary registration right here," Curtis said, irritation creeping into his voice. "What the fuck is this, some kind of shakedown?" He threw the empty coffee cup on the floor and punched the glove box release. To his surprise, a 9mm Smith & Wesson, one that they had taken from Greene, flopped down on the glove box door as though spring loaded. Through bloodshot eyes he saw that it was on full cock. He grabbed the gun, intending to put it back in the glove box, but it wouldn't go. The glove box was stuffed with paper, which was oozing out onto the glove box door and leaving no place to put the gun.

Neither man was working with a full deck after the events of the evening and before they could fully grasp what was happening, there were screaming sirens, searchlights, and far too many commands. As they sat there, stunned by lights and sound, Curtis still holding the 9mm, the interior of the van was flooded with pepper mace. Staggering out of the van they were met with batons, lights, and the hard surface of the pavement. For the second time that night, they were handcuffed. Semiconscious, bleeding and sick, they were transported, separated and questioned.

During the time Curtis and Shelby were being arrested, the police were again called concerning an attempted break-in of

Star Investigations in Gresham. This time, rather than an anonymous tip, there were numerous area residents willing to give their names. When the same three cars arrived silently on the scene they found two women prying at a door with a crow bar and a man beating frantically on it with a pair of bolt-cutters, while the alarm blared.

The three were held at gunpoint while being searched. When it was found that all three were armed, and that the two women's weapons had been reported stolen in a burglary in Portland, they were handcuffed and transported to Gresham Police Headquarters for further questioning. The two women spent most of their time impressing the officers with their command of American slang insults. When that didn't work, they dissolved into tears and crotch shots. That didn't work either. It took them four hours to make bail and they arrived back at their office just in time to hear the last gasp of the alarm as the battery finally gave up, much to the relief of the neighbors.

"What the fuck is going on?" Lori demanded of no one in particular. "What I want to know is where are Curtis and Shelby?"

Pam turned to Johnson and asked, "I thought you said that they were right behind you?"

"They were."

"Where the hell could they have gone? They better have one damn good reason why they aren't here."

"Who cares where they are," Lori said, "What in hell happened to the door and what did we get charged with?"

"Somebody, guess who, sealed the door shut and we got charged with carrying concealed weapons, resisting arrest, and being in possession of stolen property. It seems that the esteemed police of Gresham do not choose to recognize our Portland City Concealed Weapons Permits," Johnson said, his voice losing enthusiasm as he began to see his world falling apart.

"And the guns you two were carrying belong to a Joseph Greene, who filed a burglary report and give the police a list of all the items missing from his office, including your guns, and the one Curtis carried, which might explain why they aren't here."

"Oh God! You think they might have been picked up too?"

"That would explain why they didn't show up."

"If we all get charged with felonies, we're out of business, aren't we?"

"Only if convicted. I think that right now we need to try and find some way to open this fucking door. If I'm not mistaken the door would have had to be open before the sealant could be put around it." Both women stared at the door, realizing what Keith was implying.

"Oh God!" Pam exclaimed. "You mean that Joe was in `our' office?"

"Who in the hell does he think he is?"

"Maybe he took his stuff back."

"Fuck him! He used us for two years. We are entitled to something."

"I guess he thought that training us and paying us was enough," Pam said.

"If you are so fuckin' enthralled with him why did you leave?" Lori's voice was dripping with sarcasm. "Maybe you should go crawling back."

"Quit it, Lori. Right now isn't the time to argue. We have to get this door open and find out what kind of a mess is inside."

"You're right Keith." Lori leaned her head against the door. "Hey, this door is hot."

Keith put his hand on the door, "Geeze you're right."

"Do you think he set a fire inside?"

"No, I think maybe he jacked the heat up."

"Why?"

"Make the sealant set up faster," Pam finished.

"I bet you're right," Keith said. "It sounds like something Joe would think of."

Pam walked over to her car and came back dialing her cell phone. The other two, like her, were still in a state of shock after the morning's problems. They were content to stand and watch as she talked to someone for several minutes. She hung up and sighed, "Well I found them." Her comrades didn't say anything, so she went on, "You were right, Keith, they're in jail. We can have them back for seventy-four thousand apiece."

Lori's jaw dropped and her eyes bugged out. "How much?"

"What are the charges?" Keith asked.

"Curtis pulled a loaded 9mm on a cop in a routine traffic stop, also resisting arrest, no drivers license or proof of insurance, no taillights, speeding, concealed weapons, possession of stolen property -- which included the 9mm -- and being assholes in possession of human bodies."

"I love it." Lori said. "I fuckin' love it. We work our asses off to start this business and then those two clowns screw it for everybody."

"Let me have that phone a minute," Keith said.

"Who are you callin'?" Pam asked, trying to get a smile out of someone, even herself, "The airline?"

"More like the bus line," Lori said, not amused.

A few minutes later he handed the phone back to Pam. "I got a guy comin' with a torch and two big hydraulic jacks."

"Oh, that's all we need, torch a hole in the door and start a fuckin' fire inside," Lori said.

Before Keith had a chance to blow up at Lori, Pam said, "I'm going to go get us some burgers and cokes."

"Coke hell, bring a half case of beer. And get me a large order of fries, too."

"Any special requests Keith?"

"What? Oh, no, nothing special."

A ratty-looking shop truck arrived while Pam was gone. A huge black man, the sleeves of his shirt missing his wrists by several inches, slid out from behind the wheel and sauntered over to stand beside Keith. "What ya got?"

"Somebody glued our office door shut."

Lori stepped up and stuck her hand out, "My name is Lori."

"Fine by me," he said and turned back to the door. He ran his hands all around the door where it joined the frame. "And . . . he done a good job of it."

"Can you get it open?"

"See as to how I'm here, don't see why not." He paused to run his fingers along the bottom of the door, whistled and winced, "How much you offerin?"

"Forty bucks."

"That be cash?"

"Yeah."

"Gonna need a receipt?"

"No."

The big man took a worn red bandanna out of his right hip pocket and wiped his forehead. "I'ma thinkin a little more'n that."

"I can go fifty. That taps me."

"Up front?"

"Done."

He didn't move until Keith pulled two twenties and a ten out of his wallet and handed them over. He took the money, carefully folded it into a small square and slid in into a front pocket of his bib overalls, and snapped the pocket shut. He then turned around toward his shop truck and went, "Yo."

The passenger door opened on dry hinges and a small, wizened man of indeterminate age climbed out and walked over to confer with the large man. They spoke in muted tones for about two minutes, until finally the small man nodded, went over and climbed slowly up into the back of the truck. After several minutes of banging and moving things around he slowly climbed out carrying the largest sledgehammer either Keith or Lori had ever seen. He walked without haste over to where the big man was standing in front of the door, seemingly in a trance. The old man set the hammer on its head, handle up, between the door and the big man, then walked back and climbed into the shop truck. The door creaked shut as the big man shook himself awake and looked at the hammer. He nodded, spit on his hands and rubbed them together. He looked at the door, picked up the hammer as though it was made of balsa wood, and swung it with blinding speed at the door, hitting it squarely on the main deadbolt locking mechanism. The single blow sounded like a sonic boom and left the door hanging by only the bottom hinge. The big man nodded, apparently pleased with himself, and walked back to his shop truck, tossing the hammer over the side on his way to the cab. Keith and Lori were left standing, wordless, in an acid cloud of exhaust.

Pam came back to find them in the office, the door as the man had left it.

"Did I miss something?"

"Not really. Greene was here. He took most of his equipment, and we need to gather up the rest of his shit and get it the hell out of here. It would be just our luck to have the cops show up again."

Lori, perched on the edge of a desk, asked, "You don't really think the cops would bother to come back today, do you?"

"Once they get the report from Portland regarding the stolen property found in the van, even these small town boys will figure it out."

"Maybe, but I doubt it," she said, not bothering to help, seemingly content to watch the way the sunlight played against her legs.

Johnson was proven right two minutes later when a detective and two uniformed officers of the Gresham Police Department walked in with a search warrant. For the second time that day the three were handcuffed and taken to the Gresham City Police Station.

A week later a video appeared in Portland-area law offices, and became almost a cult hit among attorneys who sent copies to one another and colleagues in other cities. The video opened with a voice that sounded almost too much like Walter Cronkite announcing the opening of Star Investigation Service, a new company in Portland, just as soon as they could get their door open. The video showed two women and a man beating on a door that proudly displayed their company name. The women were dressed more like hookers than anything else; there was some talk among attorneys about the distinct correlation between the two professions. The longer they beat on the door the more profane they became. The video went on to show their arrest and return, excerpts from the discussion of their right to Greene's property, the opening of the door, supplies being stocked (the beer and burgers) and then the second arrest for stolen property, while the announcer explained that they were so anxious to begin serving all their customers that rather than using the time-consuming method of shopping -- and paying for -- supplies, they simply stole them from a former employer. The video showed a re-enactment of the arrest of the other two members of the group based on the police report. The actor playing Curtis in the video may have been quite a bit more aggressive than what actually happened. The arresting officers, after seeing the video and knowing their case of assault with a deadly weapon was a little weak, tried to have it entered as evidence in court;

it was denied, but served to give further credence to the video's authenticity. At the end of the nine-minute video was this statement intoned in a Cronkite-like voice while the camera showed the mug shots of the five: "Wouldn't you like to go to court knowing that the other firm used the services of this group? For a complete client list of Star Investigation Service call the 900 number displayed on the screen. Please be advised that the call will cost two dollars ninety-five cents a minute. Thank you and good night."

The entire list cost a caller nearly nine dollars, and netted Joe Greene enough to pay for making the video.

Chapter Nine

I t had taken Janice several minutes to convince Joe and convey him into the room. She came out of the bathroom to find him asleep, his clothes in a heap on the floor. She slid into bed beside him and propped herself up on one elbow. "You know, my sleeping beast, this is the first time I've ever been in bed with a man," she thought a minute and added, "or woman, when they didn't want something other than sleep." She eased the covers back enough to see that he was naked except for his gun in its shoulder holster and an ugly-looking knife strapped to the inside of his left forearm. After a few seconds she got out of his bed and climbed into the other one. Somehow she felt safer that way.

Joe woke suddenly at 3:15 a.m., slipped silently out of bed with the .380 cradled in his right hand, and watched through the blinds until he was sure that the sounds he had heard were those of an elderly couple as they moved their suitcases into the adjoining room. He then spent several minutes lying in bed planning the next few weeks and listening to the little sleep noises that Janice made.

When Janice crawled out of her bed at around ten, she found a note from Joe in the bathroom asking her to call his mobile before she left. There were three twenties beside the note to cover breakfast and a taxi. The tension was gone, leaving her with sore muscles and what felt like a hangover.

As instructed she called her boss.

When he answered she said, "Love 'em and leave 'em, huh?"

"Good morning, Janice. I went by your place; they didn't break in last night, and having thought about it, I don't think they will now."

"Why?"

"Well, for one thing, they all were arrested on varying felony charges during the night. I think that they will be occupied with dealing with the consequences of their behavior for some time to come."

"Somehow that doesn't surprise me. Want me to come to the office? Or should I just loll around in this motel room until you come for me?"

"They will throw you out at noon."

"Does that mean you're not coming back?"

"There are about thirty-five messages on the machine. I will not be available to return calls for several days."

"Okay. Okay. I'm on my way. Are you going out of town?"

"As far as anyone other than you is concerned, yes."

Joe spent the next week tying up loose ends, selling surplus equipment, and covering his tracks. By the following Friday he was satisfied that no one -- including the IRS -- could touch him. He was feeling pretty good about life in general when he called his office.

"Boss, I think everything is in order. Bill came by and picked up the van you left for him and all the rest of the alarm systems. You know, you really are a nice guy. Bill couldn't believe the deal you gave him. The van alone is worth more than you sold him the entire business for."

"Well, he and you are the only two who didn't try to screw me."

"I tried to screw you, just the other night, but you wouldn't wake up."

"That's not what I'm talkin' about. I'm referring to business."

"It would have been business if you'd screwed me and then left sixty bucks on the sink."

"Would you please lock up and go find something to rub up against."

"Sure, where are you?"

"Not me, damn it."

"What about Stu?"

"I don't think she likes you."

"I mean for you."

"Me?"

"She's called about twenty times again today. She's been home since noon."

"What's she want?"

"I don't know. She doesn't like me."

"Why not?"

"I guess I'm not her type. That and she knows that you are in town."

"How does she know that?"

"She's had a tail on you for a week. Didn't you know?"

"Of course I knew." He hadn't had a clue. He wondered, going back over the last few days, if anyone could have seen anything out of line.

"Hello. Earth to Boss. Are you there?"

"Yeah, I'll see you Monday." He hung up before she could continue her game. He should have seen any tail. He'd even bought a car off a lot out on 82nd to make sure he wasn't draggin' a bug. Then he grinned, knowing that was something Stu would say, to make him curious enough to call. It worked.

She answered with a "Yes?"

"What do you want?"

"Dinner in a neutral zone."

"I don't think so."

"I'll buy."

"Where do you want to meet?"

"You pick."

"Turkey Shoot."

"Where's that?"

"Tennessee."

"I have to work tomorrow."

"Oh sure. Tell me to pick the restaurant, and when I do, you say 'no.'"

"Try someplace in Portland."

"The Hilton."

"You'll have to wear a tie."

"How about pizza?"

"How about the Hilton. I'll bring you a tie."

"Ron leave a tie there?"

"No. Ron has never removed his tie in my presence, thank you."

Joe had a mental image of a tall skinny man naked except for a black silk tie sipping cocktails with Stu.

"How do you know about Ron?"

"I thought you'd figure it out by now.   Any and all information regarding your office and clients is available to the highest bidder."

"Anne," Stu paused, trying to sort out what she knew from what she felt, "You mean Anne is selling--?"

"I was in the process of setting her up when she conned you into thinking that I was a loose cannon.   She's a lot smarter than I gave her credit for.   So in the commotion of having five of my employees steal my equipment and business, plus having Mitch croak at the most inopportune time, I stepped on my dick."

"Meet me at the Hilton in an hour, please?"

"I'll be there.   And I'll bring my own tie."

They made small talk over a couple of drinks until their table was ready.   Once seated, Stu took a deep breath and said, "I want to start by apologizing for doubting you, and I want to thank you for not putting me, handcuffed to one of the Wonder Boys as you so aptly called them, in your video.   I further want to thank you for not including our firm in the 900-number list."

"You called my 900 number?" Joe sat back in his chair and grinned.

"Actually we are into your scam for nearly forty-five dollars. It seems that five of us in the office called to check, not knowing that anyone else in the office had done so."

"Scam?" The grin was replaced by a frown.

"What would you call it?"

"Slow death." He grinned again.

It made Stu think of an animal about to dine on a fellow beast.

"I wouldn't call it slow.   Not only will no one use them, no one will even represent them in court."

"Will they do time?"

"If you don't drop the charges, they will probably cop a plea. I'd guess no jail time, two years probation and they will definitely each have a felony record."

"Which will prevent their ever being able to hang out a shingle as an investigator again."

She nodded and smiled, more to align herself with him than out of any feeling of mirth. "If you don't drop the charges."

"I heard you the first time. Why would I drop the charges?"

"Let's just say that I've seen both Pam and Lori. They are in some respects similar to you. They're both predators. That's why you hired them in the first place. And like you, they are willing to do or sacrifice whatever is necessary to accomplish the task at hand." She stopped talking, raised her hands up in a kind of I'm-sorry-but-that's-the-way-it-is gesture, and when he didn't respond, continued, "Their problem is that they aren't as smart as you are, and worse for them, they have human emotions."

"I don't have emotions?"

"No, you don't. It's taken me five years to figure that out about you, but it's true, isn't it?"

"Describe emotion."

"Case closed."

"Okay, fine. But how are they going to get me to drop the charges?"

"You tell me? Sex? I doubt it."

"I like sex."

"Yes, of course you do. But you don't ever pay for it."

"You mean like, sex for dropping the charges?"

"Of course. I imagine that they are capable of being pretty much whatever you'd want."

"That sounds good."

"But it will cost you," she paused for emphasis, "Big time."

"You mean like a video of me and one of them doing whatever."

"I imagine whips, chains, begging and then the next day, presto, a rape charge with video to back it up, or, drop the charges."

"I liked part of it."

"I thought you would." She took a sip of ice water, and asked over the rim of her glass, "What part?"

"Making videos. I'm thinking about starting a production company--." The waiter came for their order before Joe could finish.

When the waiter left, Stu continued, "Or they might try to buy you out." She shook her head at him, "But you don't need money, do you?"

"I'm not destitute, if that's what you mean."

"I know what you have in the bank. And I know what you have in the way of investments." Joe smiled at her, and thought, you don't have a clue, Babe. "I don't know how much you have in a hole in the ground, but I think it's more than you have showing."

Joe loved this. She was female, and she was on a roll, soon she would tell him everything she knew about him and how she had found out. It would take hours of torture, well not hours, minutes (if he really wanted to know and wasn't just enjoying the job), but she would like to think it would take hours, to get the information she was about to give him to prove that she was a worthy adversary.

Over the last few days he had tried to understand why he continued the relationship with Stu. He realized that it was like swinging across a pool of quicksand on a rotten vine. Sometimes it was the only way to get across and sometimes it was for the adrenaline rush.

Sooner or later, he was going to fall in. Then the question would be -- could he get out, and at what cost? The waiter brought bread, salad, and a decent red wine. They ate in silence for awhile before Stu picked up where she had left off. "I hired one of your competitors, though no doubt you're aware of it, to run a check on you and tail you."

"Who did he use for a tail?" And then he knew, remembered her fumbling in her purse at a stop light out on Sandy Boulevard and then again an hour later when he came out of a Fred Meyer store on 122nd. He knew he didn't have anything to worry about.

"You tell me. Then I'll know if I have to pay her for her time."

"The little redhead? She's probably trainable."

"I'm sure she will be happy to hear that."

"I was a little worried about her a couple times. She could have gotten into a lot of trouble when she ducked into that tavern out in North Portland."

"Poor little thing. She told me that she did the best she could, but a least half the time she was climbing through parts of Portland that she didn't even know existed, wondering if she was even on the same side of the river that you were."

"I kept an eye out for her. When you see her, ask if she remembers the big black man that kept that bunch of bikers off of her out on Lombard?" He didn't know anything about bikers, a black savior, nor had he even driven down Lombard all week, but her imagination would kick in, and she would remember.

"You did that for her?"

"Yeah. Why not? She's out there tryin' to make a buck, and she sure as hell gives it her best shot. I'd use her if I were you. She's got gumption." Having seen her only twice, both times sitting in a car, fumbling in her purse, he didn't really know if she even had legs. But, what the hell, everyone starts at the bottom and can use a little help.

"No, wait! We still want to use you. Barb doesn't have a clue that I ever doubted you. She thinks you walk on water."

"I'm tainted, Stu. You know it. I know it. What happened wasn't my fault, but it reflects on me. So I'm gone and you're off the hook."

"Joe, I only had you checked out because I believe in you."

Bullshit, Joe thought, but it meant that they hadn't found so much as a shred of an impropriety. This was a good thing.

"Joe, there's more to this than just this thing with your former employees. You aren't 'tainted.' And even if you were you are tough enough to withstand it. Hell, every firm in town would love to have your name on their surveillance reports." She thought about what she had just said, "Oh, so that's it. Someone offered you more money per hour. I'm sorry, I should have known. I can't offer you anything extra until I talk to Barb, but we'll compete."

"It's not money."

"Then what is it?"

"That's a good question. One I don't have an answer to right now."

"I know you're upset with me, but you operate in such a fashion as to make everyone suspicious of everything you do. So I feel that I was within my rights to check you out."

"Checking out and accusing are two entirely different things. You asked me over to your flat just to set me up. Not to ask me my side of anything; just to set me up for a fall."

"I admit, I was wrong. Anne snowed me, just like your employees snowed you. At least I didn't lose my business too."

"And why was that? Could it have been that even after everything you did to me, I still protected you?" Joe was beginning to get mad, he mentally gave himself a "Cool It" command, no use playing into her hands. So far, instead of getting information out of her, he was giving her everything she wanted. Who, he wondered, was conning who? Somehow he had to get her back on track. "So you know I own a couple houses up on Skyline, and an antique store, that's not a crime. How does that make me a potential criminal?"

"It doesn't. Nor does the used car lot that just happens to have, on the same property, an old service station that you lease out to a detail shop. Not to mention the two houses which have been converted into four commercial rental units each."

"Hey, your man did his deed well." Not real well, for there was a furnished apartment in the attic of one of the houses, accessed from an outside stairwell in the back yard. The stairwell was hidden from view by a large ornamental pine that grew next to the stairway. This was one of Joe's safe houses, if he ever needed it.

"That's not all, Mr. Greene, is it?"

"Pretty close."

"On that lot, there are sixteen vehicles that you have clear title to."

She was gloating. Joe pretended to be slightly shocked. There were another twenty-one vehicles, the good ones, all four-wheel drive pickups, in a leased warehouse in the town of Newberg, two counties west. Each and every rig in that warehouse had the title signed, there was no recorded owner, and nothing owing on any of them – and none of them were stolen. He'd paid cash for each of them, buying them one at a time from private parties, always wearing a disguise, and always arriving on foot. He'd picked Newberg for two reasons; one, it was in a different county, and two, it was a large enough town that no one cared what anybody else did. Each vehicle had been through the detail shop before it was put into storage.

"Damn, sounds like Lowery did a bang-up job on me."

"See, I knew you would know who was working your back -- as we in the trade say."

"Thanks for clarifying that for me. But," Joe paused as though considering whether or not to tell her, "Didn't he find the two rentals out on the Eastside?"

"No, he didn't." Which wasn't surprising, since he didn't have any rentals on the Eastside, except those next to the car lot.

Good, seeds of doubt sown about a new investigator would only sprout to become cause for concern. It was the least he could do for Stu. Maybe she would watch her back a little more.

"Is he sloppy?"

"No, not really. Lowery is limited in his abilities. You remember when you went up against Moore and Associates last year?"

"Yes. I kicked some butt, thanks in part to your in-depth report."

"Lowery was, and probably still is, Moore's investigator."

"Oh good, just what I need, second rate."

"I'd watch that little redhead. If I were you, I'd think about putting her on staff, that way you'll have some control over her."

"You won't stay?"

"Nope. I'm outta here."

"Will you at least help her if she needs advice, or backup?"

"My price for consultation is fifty dollars an hour, plus expenses. Back up is out of the question."

"Maybe that rape charge wasn't wholly unfounded."

Joe grinned and went on, "Lowery found 'bout everything, all right."

"Except the two rentals out on the Eastside."

And Joe thought, the eighteen containers of antiques in a warehouse in Las Vegas, all bought and paid for with cash. Most people other than attorneys didn't want any trail of having hired a PI to lead up to their door, and were most happy to pay in cash, cars and antiques--if they had any-- rather than by check, and they didn't want a receipt. The problem with cash is that if you leave it lying around it becomes nearly worthless with inflation. Can't put it in the bank, Uncle Sam would want a cut; can't spend it openly, Uncle Sam would smell money.

Joe's folks had bought an antique store in Las Vegas after they'd sold the ranch. Joe had always wondered whether his Dad had been happy there or not; but he'd never asked and his Dad had never said. He had intended to get to know his ol' man better but he'd died of exposure while Joe was upcountry in 'Nam. He hadn't heard about it until two weeks after the funeral. Somehow he pretty much lost his interest in God after that. And then there was his mom. She didn't seem to be any more bitter than she had been. As near as Joe could tell, she didn't like him any less than she had since the night he'd told them that he had enlisted and was going to Nam. After his Dad died, she had kept the store and had done quite well. Over the years they had developed a casual business relationship that revolved around their shared love of antiques.

After Joe had started his career as what his mom termed a `paid asshole,' he took her any spare cash that came his way and she bought antiques for him, keeping a piece now and then for herself, as was their agreement. Joe had purchased a small warehouse near her shop, where his inventory and her overrun were stored. With no property taxes and a dry climate, it was working out quite well.

Joe had taken the equity in a rundown building on Belmont in exchange for a very dicey piece of locate-and-return involving two rather rare paintings that the owner didn't want Uncle or the authorities to know he possessed. Rather than let it sit empty, Joe called his Mom and asked her if she knew

anyone in the trade who lived in Portland.   She did, and Joe
hired both of them, thus Eastside Antiques was born.

The second floor had been set up for call girls years before
Joe bought it. Joe had put in an exterior stairway from the
rear parking lot to the second floor, and added a bath and
efficiency kitchen in each of the eight rooms, which were then
leased out to executives who `needed a place to unwind.'
Again most payments were in cash, which in turn bought more
antiques. The basement was damp and unfit for storage; that
bothered Joe.   He liked to see everything being used for
something.

Joe realized that Stu had been speaking for some time, "--
can't spend your cash."

"Who says that I have a stash?"

"Did you hear anything I said?"

"You didn't give me a name."

"Let's change the subject. Two days ago I went over to
your shop looking for you, and fell in love with a red leather
living room set. I had intended to negotiate with the saleslady,
I still think thirty-eight hundred was too much for the set." Joe
had to agree, his mother had paid twelve for it, and apologized
for spending so much.   "Anyway, this bitch, I'm sorry, but
that's what she was -- she had Lake Oswego old money written
all over her -- came in." Stu waved her hands around to show
what a bitch the lady had been, "She looked at me like I had
just crawled out of the sewer, and asked the saleslady how
much the set was. Joe, I have to tell you, your sales clerk tried
to tell her that I was considering the set, but the bitch said,
`Well has she (she said `she' like I was a cur dog), paid for it?'
She didn't even have the courtesy to speak directly to me. The
clerk told her that I hadn't but I was considering a full price
offer. `Which is?' she sneered. And the clerk told her thirty-
eight hundred. So Miss-way-past-Lake-Oswego says, `I'll take
it for thirty nine.' Again the clerk tells her that I'm first in line.
`So tell your boss that you turned down a full-price offer plus a

hundred, because some `lady' thinks she might want it, even though she probably can't afford it."

"Joe, I nearly slapped her. I've never been so mad in my life, so I said four thousand. She smirked and went forty-three. I got the set for forty-four hundred. After that bitch left, I probably shouldn't tell you this, the clerk gave me a set of beautiful end tables that match the set perfectly."

"Gave them to you?"

"Listen, I've told you this in confidence. Please don't get upset with her."

Joe wasn't. For one reason the end tables had come with the set, and for another, the Lake Oswego Old Money Bitch was the single mom with two kids who ran the coffee cart two doors down from the shop. Her take was twenty percent of anything over sales price. It was sleazy, but it paid her rent. Joe wondered if he should tell Stu that she had been had. Naw, this gave her good break-the-ice small talk for client dinners at her flat for years to come. A small price to pay for that, considering some he'd suffered through.

"My Mom bought that set from an old Russian couple two years ago. She wouldn't sell it because she fell in love with it herself. I think it's probably pretty valuable." He wondered if his Mom had ever even seen it, having bought it from one of the finders who worked the Midwest for her and Joe. "I don't think you got hurt on the deal."

"Your Mom is still living?" Stu leaned forward on her elbows.

Damn you Greene! he told himself. When in hell are you going to learn to keep your mouth shut?

"Yeah." Here goes, might as well 'fess up, cause she's gonna find out, one way or another. "She has a little antique store in Vegas. That's where I picked up the bug."

"You've never told me anything about your parents. Is your father living?"

"No. He died some years back."

"I'm sorry. Were you close?"

"No. Several thousand miles apart when he tipped over."

"Cute. But that's not what I mean."

"I know. I'm trying to tell you politely that it's none of your business."   'That's the right thing to say, you idiot!' He admonished himself. 'That's like pouring gas on a grease fire.'

"Why? Why don't you want to talk about your father? It's okay to feel grief at the loss of your Dad."

"But is it all right to feel nothing at all?"

"No, that's not allowed. You are probably angry at him for leaving you and your mother. That's a form of love, don't hide it." She stopped to consider her next move in the role of therapist. "Why don't we go back to my place, where it's quiet, and we'll talk?"

And that, he knew, was what she meant. Most of the time a woman would rather get into your head than into your pants.

"Thanks, but I'm flyin' out in about two hours."

"Show me your ticket, or come with me."

Why did God make women want to fix everything in a male, when it wasn't broken, Joe wondered. If it was some kind of a test, he wished he could buy a cheat sheet for it. He'd always been able to get his hands on one in school, why not now, when it really counted?

"Stu, it's a private job. I'm leavin' on a private plane from the Hillsboro Airport bound for trouble, return not guaranteed." He didn't have any place to go except to bed, but he needed to get away from Stu before he drowned in the quicksand. He didn't know why he said that stupid thing about not comin' back. It just came into his head.

"For some reason, I believe you."

"I better go. I've still got to go by what's left of my office and throw a pack together."

They shook hands under the restaurant awning, and stepped out into the rain, she into a cab and he down the street to his pickup, if he could remember which one he was driving tonight.

He had left his phone in the glove box, and it was ringing when he climbed in.

"Yeah?"

Janice didn't scold or ask why he hadn't answered his phone for the last three hours, she just said, "Boss, I think you're gonna want to think about this one."

"What is it?" He could already feel the adrenaline start to flow.

"Three girls, one eleven and two twelve, are missing from a resort lake in northern Montana."

"How long?"

"Three days. They aren't in the lake and they weren't taken."

"What's the drill?"

"There's a Leer waiting for you at the Hillsboro Airport. If you can get there in two hours they can have you to the lake by noon."

The hair was beginning to stand up on the back of Joe's neck. "Why not till noon?"

"The last leg is by float plane. What do I tell them?"

"I'll be at the airport in one hour." He tried to rub the hair back down. It wouldn't go. "Will you take a taxi out to the airport and pick this rig up sometime tomorrow?"

"Of course. What is it?"

"A red Ford pickup. I'll leave the keys on top of the left rear tire."

"Right." She mulled over what to say, "Boss?"

"Yeah?"

"There's something about this one."

"I know. I feel it too."

"I almost didn't call you."

"Yeah, I know. Want to hear something funny?"

"Not really. What?"

"I was having a meeting with Stu and about twenty minutes ago I told her that I was leavin' in a private plane from Hillsboro Airport in less than two hours. I admit, I was just trying for an excuse to leave, but I guess I knew then."

"What else did you tell her?"

There was a knot in his gut and a chill was sliding up and down his spine, "I told her, `return trip not guaranteed.'"

"You sure you want to do this?"

"I don't have choice, do I?"

She didn't answer, just hung up.

Joe drove by his office, put his pack together, and was starting out the door when he remembered something he had to do and went back to his safe. He twisted the dial in the right sequence and pulled the door open. From a small hand-carved wooden box he took two wrinkled one-hundred-dollar bills and a fifty in the same condition. He addressed an envelope to: "Studebaker & Rye, Attention: Stu," added the address and put the money in the envelope. He locked the empty box back in the safe and turned out the lights.

When he dropped the envelope in a mailbox in front of the Hillsboro Airport he knew he couldn't ever come back.

Chapter Ten

Rori Tomlin was leaning back, eyes closed, in the co-pilot seat of an older, six-passenger jet, waiting for their client. She hadn't felt good for two days and had gone to bed early the night before. Her husband, Mark, was on a four-day run to southern California, and since he wouldn't be back until tomorrow, there wasn't any reason not to. She'd just snuggled down with her two cats, a People magazine, and a small dish of low-fat strawberry ice cream, when the phone rang.

Now here she was, made up, suited up, the preflight done and waiting. She looked at her `official pilot's watch' her father had given her when she got her wings. (Those `wings' were earned the summer she turned seventeen and allowed her to solo a single-engine Piper around, and around, and around that little Kansas air strip with its dusty asphalt runway.) Two hours and twenty minutes she'd been here, most of that time waiting. Which was really what this job was about, waiting. The glamour of flight had turned into a mundane way to make a buck.

She'd been flying for Exec-Air for almost four years and was qualified for left seat, but most of the time she ended up as co-pilot and flight engineer or flight attendant for groups of better-than-you-are skiers and gamblers, flying on Exec-Air's group rate packages. They were a six-bird outfit, and everyone, except the `Captains,' did whatever was necessary to keep them in the air and keep their passengers happy. Within reason, of course.

Martin came up the two-step ramp and hollered from the doorway, "You know who we're waiting for?"

"Not a clue."

"Guy named Joe Greene. Ever hear of him?"

"Yeah. He's some sort of wizard. Lives here in Portland."

"Wizard!" Martin had moved up to stand behind her, "Let me guess. You bought another copy of National Enquirer."

"That's not where I read that."

"But you do admit that you buy National Enquirer?"

Martin knew damn well that she read magazines usually found at supermarket checkout counters. And he knew that she knew that he couldn't wait for her to put them down so he could pick them up. She shrugged and changed the subject back to Joe Greene, "I've read that he can find people, especially kids, lost in remote areas even after everyone else has given up on finding them. No one knows how he does it. "

"Just for the hell of it, why don't you go call Carol? She was flight attendant on a haul that took him down into Arizona about three or four months ago. It's always nice to know what the cargo is."

"Martin, it's almost midnight."

"What? You think her phone doesn't ring after ten?" He stood up, pulled his shoulders back, and in his version of Star Ship Commander, began, "Tomlin. As your captain--."

"Martin, don't start that crap with me. I'll go call Carol, but you know how she likes to be awakened."

"Yeah. By being poked by some dweeb she found in bar."

The phone was answered after the fourth ring by a throaty rasp that could only belong to Carol.

Rori assumed a high hysterical identity and screamed into the phone, "Is my husband there?"

There was a pause during which time Rori figured that Carol was checking her king-size bed for other occupants, "Not tonight dearie, why don't you check with Rori Tomlin, she'll screw anything, even you."

"Carol!"

"Got you, you pervert." Carol laughed and said, "If you're going to keep on using that same voice, at least change the line."

"Those guys you pick up use the same line on you every time, so why should I change."

"For as much as you've knocked about the world, you are still one naive little wench." Rori was treated to the sound of Carol's tobacco-damaged lungs trying to clear themselves, and then the sound of her lighter in action. "Okay. Now I'm all better." She blew smoke and continued, "I've been rudely awakened, so how may I be of service? Something that does not involve getting out of bed, I hope."

"You hauled a cargo by the name of Joe Greene across the country awhile back. Martin and I are waiting for his arrival, actually we've been waiting nearly three hours for his arrival, and we want to know something about him."

"You called me at midnight to ask about somebody I hauled three months ago?"

"Yeah, we're bored."

"Why don't you call Suicide Hotline next time. There are people there who might be able to help you."

"Come on, Carol, talk or I'm sick next time you want me to baby-sit one of these prima donnas whom we must call `Captain' in front of clients so that you can do whatever it is you do with one of those guys you pick up in a bar."

"Do you want me to tell you what I do with them?"

"No, tell me about Greene."

"He's okay-looking if you like the outdoor type." Carol didn't. "He's about forty five, two hundred, lots of muscle, not much hair, a nasty scar on his face, just in front of his left ear and he walks with a limp."

"You are good . . . if you aren't making it up."

"I didn't have anything to do for three hours except sit and watch him."

"Did he talk much?"

"He mostly sat and read maps, fiddled with his gear, and drank tea. He didn't want to talk, but there was something about him," she took another drag on her cigarette while she thought about it, "It was like it was cold around him."

"What?"

"Yeah. I've thought about it before, and couldn't place what was different about him. Cold I think is what it was."

"Like a force field?"

"Sorry, Rori, but I don't buy into your sci-fi logic."

"Well, maybe I'll go back and chat him up once we get in the air."

"Who's your hostess?"

"Glen is our flight attendant tonight."

"Oh yeah, we can't call anyone a hostess any more can we? Oh, by the way, he's armed, got some kind of a waiver I guess."

"Well he'll be better than what we've been hauling lately."

"You mean those felons?"

"Yeah."

"At least they make a pass at you once in a while, and say `thank you' when you serve them a paper cup of that lukewarm coffee the Fed's bring on with them."

"Is that why you didn't like him? He wouldn't come on to you?"

"I told you there's something weird about him."

Carol began to cough again and after several seconds when the coughing hadn't quit, she hung up.

"Thank you, Carol." Rori said into the dead phone.

She stopped off in the ladies room and used the toilet and checked her makeup. She was okay with the image looking back at her. Nothing special, but it was good enough to have caught her a long-haul truck driver. And she was pregnant! She turned sideways and checked herself in the mirror. Five months along and she didn't show yet. With luck she could work another two months before the powers-that-be took her out of the friendly skies and stuck her behind a desk for six months. Six months behind a desk for a child was a fair tradeoff.

She did some stretching exercises and then ran the hundred feet to the jet and up the ramp, flopping down in her seat.

"Well now that you've won the airport marathon, what's next, Ms. Tomlin?"

"Carol doesn't know anything. I think she's alone in bed, and she should give up the cigarettes."

"It took you twenty minutes to find that out?"

"Uh-huh."

"I'm going to go in and see if our Mr. Greene is coming any time soon."

Rori closed her eyes again and took several deep breaths of the stale cabin air. She sat up, and was stretching again when something caught her attention. A man, or at least a person was walking down along the outside of the main terminal building. He was loaded down with bags, but still seemed to move with the easy grace of an athlete. She hit the wiper button, clearing off the windscreen and sat forward, watching. She had nothing better to do and maybe this was Greene. Though why he didn't come in through the terminal she didn't know. Unless . . . unless this was his 'special waiver' for bringing guns aboard. She looked down at the radio, trying to decide whether she should call the tower or not. If he did have a permit, and she got security involved, and pissed him off. . . she let her hand drop away from the mike, No, it wasn't worth it. When she looked up, he was gone. She scanned the area along the building trying to see where he had gone, and then there he was in the shadow of a light pole, staring at her.

As their eyes locked, her baby kicked for the first time. She sat back in her seat, only to find that she was sweating. She felt her stomach. This was supposed to be a happy occasion, the first kick. But it was nearly a month too early. God! She needed to see her doctor. Martin could find someone to take her place. She got up, grabbed her flight bag and when she turned around Joe Greene was standing there in the cabin watching her.

"Are you the captain?"

"No. He just went to check on your whereabouts."

"I must have passed him in the lounge."

"Oh, probably." And then she knew that he came around the building on purpose, and was telling her to keep her mouth shut. She set her bag down and said, "I'll go get him."

"Not necessary." Greene was looking out through one of the porthole-style windows in the cabin, "He's coming across the lot now."

Rori stepped back to where she could look out the windscreen. "So he is." She watched Martin for a few seconds then asked Greene, "If you thought I was the captain, how did you know he was coming, if you didn't even know who he was."

"Inside he was acting more like what I perceive a junior officer to act like," he gestured with his hands, "A complete jerk."

She pushed her flight bag back in behind her seat with her foot, and went to meet Martin.

"He's on board, Captain."

"Walked right past me, I guess."

Greene stepped forward and stuck his hand out, "Like ships in the night. Hello, I'm Joe. And you're?"

"Captain Finley. Welcome aboard. If you are ready we'll take off."

"That's better than the other option." They all laughed and as `the captain' strode off toward the cockpit, Joe smiled at Rori and shook his head.

Before Rori could introduce herself, Martin called her to the cockpit, where he told her that Glen had the flu, and that she would have to see to their guest's needs as well as the duties of co-pilot and flight engineer.

They took off, swung wide of Hillsboro, curled around and headed up the Columbia Gorge. As they passed the tip of Mt. Hood, shining in the moonlight and wreathed in clouds, Rori shut off the seatbelt light and, slipping out of her seat, went aft.

Their passenger was sitting at the table across from the seats, reading a fax and looking at a map. It appeared to her that Mr. Greene had been there for some time; could he, she wondered, possibly not believe in seatbelt signs? She ignored his indiscretion and gave him a smile. It looked like Mr. Greene was one of those people to whom rules did not apply. She would normally have called him on it, but if he complained, and if the company found out that she was pregnant, they could very easily put her on maternity leave and not have a job for her when she came back. So as fate would have it, he could do just about as he pleased. She had the feeling he knew it, too.

"Hi, I'm Rori. Can I get you something?"

He looked up from the map he was studying, "Rori. I like the name. But let me guess. Your father wanted a boy, got a girl instead, gave her a boy's name and she grew up having to prove she was as good as a boy. So to please him she became a pilot. Her father had been one in what--the Korean War?"

"Bravo. My whole life in twenty seconds."

"That's not quite all. You are married and pregnant."

Rori sat down suddenly on the bench across from him.

"How do you know?"

"The wedding ring, for starts."

"That's a given, how do you know I'm pregnant?"

"You're walking legs spread, elbows out like you're trying to protect something fragile, and you smell like all women do when they are cookin' up a kid."

She closed her eyes and shook her head. "No one except my husband and our doctor know."

"I get the message. If you wouldn't mind fixing me some peppermint tea," he stopped talking to look at her again, "does that jerk up front know the way to Butte, Montana, or should you go back up there?"

"He's never killed himself in a plane crash that I know of."

"That's encouraging."

She rose and went to the galley located just behind the cockpit and was reaching for the tea bags stored over the sink when the plane hit a down draft.

They dropped two hundred and fifty feet like a rock before the jet -- that went instantly to full power -- carried them out of it.

When she came to, she was laying strapped in on the bench seat behind the table.

"Are we okay?" She asked Mr. Greene, who was sitting where she had last seen him.

"No damage, except for you. Do you want to land and be taken to a hospital? Your head hit the sink pretty hard. He's got clearance in to Boise."

"No, I guess not." She opened the seat belt holding her in and sat up, hoping she wouldn't faint. She didn't. If she went to the hospital they would want to X-ray her and then she would have to tell them she was pregnant.

Greene stood up and went forward to the cockpit and was gone for several minutes.

When he came back, he stopped off at the galley and brought her a glass of water.

"Thanks. How's Martin, er, the captain?"

"He did real well. Laid on the power, banked down and around, and flew us right out of it. I'll write a letter of commendation when I get back."

A strange look came over his face for a second, then he smiled.

"What's the matter? Were you hurt?"

He didn't answer for the space of several breathes, "I got a premonition about this job."

"What kind of premonition?"

He looked at her for a moment, "I don't think I'm coming back."

The way he said it chilled Rori to the bone. She sat there clutching her glass and thinking, then said, "I'll fix that tea now."

"The baby okay?"

"I don't know. I think so." She was feeling the lump on her forehead.

"He's only kicked once. Right?"

She turned to stare at him, and in a voice tinged with fear said, "Just what in hell are you! Some kind of alien?"

"No, just observant."

She got him his tea and then went into the cockpit where she stayed until they landed, coming in on instruments through a heavy cloud cover. After they saw Mr. Greene off and began the return flight Rori began to experience chills and nausea. An hour after landing in Portland, Rori Tomlin miscarried a dead male fetus. Two days later she was placed on indefinite medical leave.

Chapter Eleven

Joe spent the first thirty minutes after landing trying to find someone who would fly him into Diamond Lake. He was politely informed that it was a pothole lake with limited clearance in good weather. The only way there was by car. He ended up with a mid-sized Ford and a road map.

He bought a cheap thermos bottle that he filled with coffee at a full-service gas station, along with two sandwiches made with stale bread and a meat type substance. He left lucky that that neither sandwich's life had exceeded the expiration date. Thus armed with food, he headed northeast.

Once out of town there wasn't much to do but wonder how he had gotten to where he was and why.

He began to go back over his life, trying to decide if anything he'd done caused him to come to the point of knowing he was going into trouble and being unable to turn away.

He guessed that his present life had really started some ten years before when, after getting out of the service and spending eight years on two different small-town police departments, he'd hung out his shingle as a private detective.

It had proven lucrative right from the start, but for the most part it didn't create the high he'd learned to live for when he was a Navy Seal in Nam.

Whether it had been luck or fate, when he'd found those first two kids, and carried them out into the bright lights of a TV camera, his life had changed. Sense then he'd gone, at first of his own accord, and then because quite often he was asked, to help look for people lost in wilderness situations. Sometimes he found them and sometimes he didn't. Though successful searches were becoming more frequent. There had been several articles written about him, mostly in the vein of the supernatural. To him that just meant that no one wanted to believe that he did his homework, used his head and wasn't bogged down with regulations that governed most search operations. He'd tried to explain it to a reporter, that he felt more alive and sure of himself when he was looking for someone than any other time of his life. That wasn't necessarily true, but he'd learned to tell reporters what they wanted to hear, because they would write what they wanted to have heard anyway.

For some reason, his thoughts turned to Gloria. Until he'd met her, he'd been more interested in a weekend rendezvous than a relationship.

He found her one night sitting on the hood of her Honda in a pullout on Beach Road. He'd stopped and asked if she was all right. She'd said yes except that her car was dead. He'd called a tow truck, waited with her until it came, and then had taken her home. She'd said that he was welcome to stay for dinner. He'd accepted. She'd set a six- pack of cheap beer and two cartons of cottage cheese on the table.

Since he'd been a guest, he'd gotten the unopened carton and a clean spoon.

It's hard to forget someone like that. It was then that he realized that he hadn't forgotten her. He wondered if she was okay. He grinned remembering how much she loved stray anythings. From birds to cats, "Hell." He said aloud, realizing that was probably why she'd been attracted to him. He was pretty much a stray.

He was still thinking about her, beginning to understand now that his feeling for her was that for someone he'd once known, and hoped life had turned out all right for, when he saw a wooden sign pointing off to his left.

It said 'Diamond Lake Lodge'.

A small 'Open' sign hung under the main sign, slightly askew.

Chapter Twelve

Joe parked his rented ride as far from the lodge as the parking lot would allow, and climbed up and out. He was muttering to himself about how much he hated little tin boxes that rental companies in small airports pawned off on people in a hurry, as he dragged his backpack and duffel bag out of the back seat, pausing to do several-- well, really three--deep knee bends. The parking lot had appeared suddenly, a half-acre graveled area carved out of the timber. He had planned to stop and limber up before arriving in Diamond Lake.

Now it was too late. Three men were striding across the parking lot toward him. A big ruddy-faced man was two strides ahead of the other two and had worry written all over him. Must be my employer, Joe said to himself.

"You Greene?" He demanded from twenty feet away.

"Yep."

"Glad you're here." He came to a halt in front of Greene, thrusting a wrinkled envelope with the Diamond Lake logo on it at him. "We agreed on twenty-five thousand, right? Plus expenses, of course."

"You are Tom Bradley, right?"

The big man nodded. "There is a boat tied to the dock. She can have you over to the girls' camp before dark."

"Mind if I piss first?"

Joe swung his left pack strap and fanny pack over his left shoulder, picked up his duffel bag and followed Bradley, leaving the trunk open and the rest of his gear in it.

Without a word the other two men fell in behind him.

Joe wasn't surprised or upset by Bradley's actions. He'd seen what he thought to be all possible combinations of grief, anger, resentment, sorrow and occasionally happiness in the ten years since he'd hung out his shingle.

It was the occasional happiness, that and the money, that kept him looking for lost people. Too damn many of them were kids. Kids who weren't ever coming back. But somehow he had been given the gift of finding them. For most of the time, the investigation service had supported him and contributed to the expense of locating people. Now though, he was financially secure enough to pursue his desire to find lost people, but mostly kids. Kids that couldn't find their way back from being lost or stolen. He realized as he followed Bradley toward the lodge that he did know what he was going to do with the rest of his life. He shuddered, still bedeviled by the notion that maybe this was it. Maybe there wouldn't be a next time. And yet here he was, unable to leave even if he wanted to.

"It's like some damn curse, or spell," he mumbled to himself.

"What?" Bradley said.

"I said, `It's a long trip by car.'"

Bradley didn't respond, probably didn't care. Joe couldn't blame him. Time was the problem now.

Greene watched the group of men and women standing around the entrance to the lodge, steeling himself for the who-in-the-hell-does-he-think-he-is stares and verbal assessments. There were none. These people were exhausted, mentally and physically. They were ready to except any help, as long as it didn't involve them.

"Place I can change?" he asked no one in particular.

A small man with a bad back and blue eyes stepped to the edge of the porch and gestured with his thumb toward the front door of the lodge, "Second door on the left past the fireplace. Leave what you want and I'll put it in a room for you."

Joe dropped his duffel bag and the fanny pack on a log bench and stepped through the door. It was rustic lake lodge. The dark smoke-stained two-story great room was dominated by a river-rock fireplace and surrounded by padded half-log furniture. A small desk against the east wall appeared to serve as a check-in counter and mail drop for guests. The first door past the fireplace was probably the office, as there was a small brass plate affixed to it that said "OFFICE." Once a cop and so forth, Joe thought as he opened the indicated door, which led into a bathroom. There wasn't a lock on the door and no indication of whether it was for men or women. He didn't like not having his privacy, but it did tell him something about the people. He didn't know what it told him, but something.

He changed, pissed; there wasn't a urinal, just a single toilet next to a cracked pedestal sink. The toilet was out of adjustment, and it was necessary to hold the handle down for the full cycle in order to get it to flush.

Five minutes later he paused at the top of the steps next to Blue Eyes, "Toilet needs adjusting."

As Joe went down the steps Blue Eyes said, "Ayup."

Leaning against a pole at the end of the dock that held a hand-lettered sign expounding the evils and dangers of diving from said dock was a large, very large woman. Tied to the dock was an eighteen-foot flat-bottomed skiff with an ungodly large outboard lashed the stern. As he approached, the woman, who he assumed was his guide since she was the only one there, stepped into the skiff (which tilted dangerously) and pulled the starter rope once, the engine spat into the lake with a steady rhythm. She then settled down onto the center seat and picked up the extension handle. By the time Joe had untied the skiff, tossed his packs into the bow and stepped into the boat, they were moving. About halfway across the lake the cloud cover lifted.

His guide cut the engine and let the skiff drift. "You do this."

"What do you mean?" he asked.

"They say you're a psychic. They say you do things," her voice trailed off.

He didn't answer. He wasn't a psychic. Mostly just lucky, plus he did his homework. But she didn't want to hear that. So he just sat and looked around. He'd spent five hours on a Leer jet studying charts and maps and three hours in a redesigned Coke can thinking about this lake and the surrounding basin. The lodge and village were where they were supposed to be. The timbered slopes ran a scant one hundred yards to an imposing rimrock. Joe let his eyes travel around the basin twice, and then sighed.

"There weren't no place for them to go."

"Did you try to track them?"

"We got Harry Two Finger up from down river. He can flat track a mouse across dry rock." She chewed the stub of a dead cigar awhile and went on, "And tell you where it stopped to scratch fleas."

"Then why am I here?"

She chewed her cigar some more, Joe expected her to spit over the side before she answered, but she didn't, "Cause Bradley's got all the money in California and we is flat out of ideas."

"Let's go on over to where they were camped."

"I knowed a medicine man once. Could do things like you done with the clouds. He weren't from my tribe, but I knowed him purty good."

"It quite often clears up just before it snows."

"It quite often don't, too."

She moved to the stern, lifting the bow and Joe a good three feet out of the water. The outboard started on the first pull, she pointed the bow toward the far shoreline as the first flakes drifted down.

By the time the bow scraped up onto the sliver of beach, it was snowing hard.

"Ain't gonna see much."

Joe pulled his moccasins and socks off and shrugged out of his coveralls. Underneath he wore a tattered wet suit. He pulled flippers and a facemask out of his duffel bag and put them on. Then he put a weight belt on, tied a canvas bag onto it and, taking a waterproof flashlight, slipped over the side, careful not to stir up the sediment.

He pulled himself up out of the water and asked, "You got a name?"

She worked the cigar to the corner of her mouth before answering.

"Sally. Sally Springwater. Most folks call me Sally."

He spent an hour working his way back and forth along the shoreline stopping once to replace the batteries in his flashlight.

When at last he was finished, Sally had to help him into the boat.

Joe looked up at her from where he huddled against the bow seat. He tried to speak but his teeth were chattering too much, so he held the canvas sack up and nodded. He couldn't get his hands to work well enough to put his coveralls on, but was able to slip his feet into the moccasins. He dug the watch cap out of his duffel bag and pulled it down over his ears.

It was pitch dark and still snowing when Sally eased the skiff up against the dock. Two men materialized out of the snow and helped Joe up to the lodge and into the sauna, where after several minutes he was able to peel off his wetsuit. When he came out of the sauna his clothes and a new pair of fur-lined boots with moccasin soles, were sitting on a bench.

He could hear dishes rattling and muted conversation from the direction of the dining room. He limped into the dining room. His duffel bag and the canvas sack sat on a table near the fireplace that backed up against the fireplace in the greatroom.

By the time he made it to the table a young woman wearing a dark green floor-length skirt and white peasant blouse had poured a cup of steaming coffee and set it beside the canvas sack. Joe looked at Bradley, then at the group of people who crowded around the table, and then back at Bradley, who shrugged.

There were ten pair of eyes on him when he pulled what he considered to be the most telling item out of the bag. A woman gasped. Joe looked up and reassessed his count to eleven. An attractive woman, fine boned and dressed in new-money rustic camp, was being held up by Tom Bradley.

"Those are Susie's glasses," she whispered.

Bradley nodded, he had aged about ten years in about ten seconds. The front door opened and a man clomped in and over to the group. He had cop written all over him; he was wearing the uniform of a County Mountie, but Joe knew that he would have known he was a cop even if the guy hadn't been wearing a uniform. The chef -- yeah he was wearing a chef's hat, and yeah Joe would have known anyway -- moved to the side so the County Mountie (he didn't have a name tag) could squeeze in.

Sally spoke to the new arrival. "This here's a psychic. Come all the way from Oregon to help out. Course he didn't come fer free."

"I'm Charlie Walker." He held out his hand to Joe.

"Joe Greene."

"Yeah I know. Checked you out. Very impressive. What did you find?"

"Susie's glasses." He glanced over at Bradley for verification.

Bradley nodded.

"Where?"

Before he could speak Sally said, "Off the lake bottom. He dove in and swam right to where this stuff was throwed." She waved an arm at the table.

Joe looked at the deputy who said, "Go ahead."

In answer Joe dumped the contents of the canvas bag onto the table. The deputy began separating items by shoving them around with the tip of his pen, pausing to look up at the Bradleys as each piece was moved away from the others.

The first, a rusted tin coffee cup, received a negative shake of the head. The second was a clear plastic rain bonnet, opaque from days or months washing along the lake bottom. Again a negative. The next, a large button shaped like a miniature anchor, brought a conference between parents and a probable yes. Jennifer Lang had been wearing a coat with buttons at least similar to that one. The deputy asked where the other two girls' parents were. Joe figured this was done for his benefit.

"They are on their way up from California," Bradley replied. "This damn snow storm has them waiting in Cheyenne, of all places."

There were five more items, none of which were deemed to have any bearing on the case, except one, which meant something to Greene and the deputy who exchanged glances.

Greene picked up his coffee cup and moved off toward the fireplace. Walker tagged each item and placed them in individual plastic bags that he took out of his briefcase, before coming over to join Greene.

"I wasn't trying to make a public affair out of what I found."

"We do things a little different up here. Everyone expects to be involved in everything. If you try to cut someone out, no one cooperates."

Greene nodded, "So I gathered. The Bradleys seem comfortable with it."

"Bradley has been bringing his family and clients up here for ten years. The other two girls are daughters of two of his biggest accounts."

"So this will hurt both Bradley and Diamond Lake Lodge."

"If you're fishing for a motive, the whole damn village will suffer."

"What do you make of that?" Greene pointed at the only bag that Walker hadn't put in his briefcase.

"I was waiting for you to tell me. But since you asked, I'd guess that it is a pin out of a fire extinguisher. Which brings me to a question for you." Walker paused, wondering if this high-priced private detective would share everything or if he was on a power trip.

"Wondering if I'll tell you everything I know?"

"Yeah."

"I was hired to find the girls. The more help I have the faster I get done," he paused, to give the illusion that he had to think of how to phrase the rest of the sentence, "and the faster those folks get their kids back."

Greene had no intention of telling anybody anything, unless it helped him. Walker had to stay within the bounds of the law, Greene didn't. Probably Walker knew that, but he had to ask.

"Where did the fire extinguisher pin come from?"

"I noticed Sally's boat didn't have a fire extinguisher on board. Do any of boats on the lake carry them?"

"No. The local theory is that if you're sitting in a lake of water, why do you need more?" Walker was used to evasive answers, and knew that this was an exchange of information. To get an answer, give one. He paused, waiting.

"I don't know where it could have come from. Maybe it isn't from a fire extinguisher. Could have been on a backpack or camera bag. You know how all the in-crowd has accessories that look like anything but what they are."

Walker wasn't too happy. So far he hadn't gotten anything. Well, except the Bradley girl's glasses. But he hadn't found them, Greene had. "I'll be back in the morning. Most likely the Sheriff will be along. We'll go back over to where you found the stuff. Finding the girl's glasses and that button off of one of the other's coat makes it pretty obvious they were taken against their will."

"Yeah. But I got a question."

Walker liked this. To get an answer, Greene was going to have to answer one. Trouble was, right now Walker didn't have a question.

"How can you be sure they aren't floatin' on the bottom of the lake?"

"At the deepest the lake is only twenty feet deep, most of it is six- to eight-feet deep. And Diamond Lake gets its name for its purity. When the sun is out, you can see a coin laying on the bottom. We grid searched it -- twice. And both days the sun was out." Walker paused for emphasis, and added, "Frankly, it would have been a lot better for the lodge and town if we had found them drowned, than to have to put up with the stigma of having had them kidnapped. That's pretty harsh but I want you to know we looked real good." Walker's stance was becoming aggressive. But Greene still wanted more information and Walker was liable to give the most unbiased answers. He wished he'd been able to bring Janice with him. But she was in Portland, watching his back. Here he was, needing information, and no Janice. So he did what he had to do; leaned back against the wall and let himself shrink down, so Walker could look down at him.

"How do we know that someone from town didn't grab 'em? Got 'em in a shed or a basement?"

"We've been through every building and every house."

"Even yours?"

"My folks' place. And yes theirs too." Walker relaxed a little.

"Where would you suggest I start looking?"

"That's why you're here." Walker turned to leave, then turned back. "Keep me posted of everything you turn up."

"Will do." Not that it was necessary. Greene wondered who had called Walker. "Ah, thanks for the help."

"The sooner the girls are found, the sooner I get done, the sooner Bradleys get their daughter back and the sooner you get paid."

He didn't add "more than I make in six months," but it was implied.

After Walker left, Joe got a refill and walked out onto the front porch. It was snowing hard. Already the tracks from Walker's Blazer were losing their form.

He had to wait nearly five minutes before Sally came out. With her was Blue Eyes. "Mr. Greene, this here's my husband, Bob."

Greene stuck out his hand, "We've met." The thought of them in bed crossed his mind.

"Ayup."

"Can I ask you a few questions?"

"That's why we're here."

"Are there any boats on the lake that aren't flat bottomed sleds? Like a tri-hull or a catamaran?"

"A-nope. Got rules about that." Bob used the railing to push himself up straight. Obviously he'd played a major role in the restrictions. "Them kind of boats drag the bottom, stir up mud. Got rules on outboards, too. Nothin' over three-and-a-half horse." He thought a minute then added, "Except for two that is used for haulin' freight and the like."

Apparently Joe fell in the "And the like" category. "Okay, so what leaves marks like these?" Joe pulled a notebook out of his shirt pocket and drew two inverted V's on the paper, "About six feet apart in two feet of water, maybe less?"

"Float plane." Sally was letting Bob do all the talking. She nodded in agreement with his answers. "But there weren't none here Friday when the girls come up missin."

"Take a crazy to fly in here at night." Sally spoke for the first time.

"Has it ever been done?"

"Course. It's done alla time. Just you gotta be crazy to do it."

Joe was watching Sally. Her knuckles were turning white on the railing. Joe wondered, do I ask her directly, or keep on asking questions until it's so apparent that she has to speak up to keep from implicating herself. As whoever was involved would probably be related to at least some of the people here, Joe figured that it was best to keep on with the questions. "If some crazy flew in here Friday night--."

Bob shook his head from side to side, "Woulda seen his lights. Heard him."

"It wouldn't be hard to pull the fuse on the running lights. And come in without landing lights."

"Nope. Wouldn't work. Gotta see where you're gonna put down. You can't set it on the ground or on the water without some way of tellin' where you're gonna touch, or else you'll be doin' cartwheels. And that ain't fun, not more'n once er twice anyhow."

Joe figured that was how Bob had hurt his back since he'd more or less said so. "What about a couple of portable lanterns. That work?"

"Yeah, specially if they was aimed out over the lake. They'd make a couple streaks of light. That could do it."

"What happened here Friday night that could mask the landing and take-off of a small plane?"

"Landin' wouldn't be no trouble. You could come in purty much dead-stick."

"Suppose a crazy flies in, grabs the girls and is ready to take off. What happened Friday night that could mask his take-off?"

"Just before dark the power went off. Happens all the time in the winter. Not usually in the summer and fall."

"Know why?"

"Yeah. Neil come by Saturday an said that some asshole fell a tree on the power line. I'd a figured someone cuttin' dead pine for firewood. Neil said `no, it was a green tree and in a bitch of a place to get to.`"

"So it was done on purpose."

"I hadn't thought of it, but yeah looks that way. Don't it?"

"Does Walker know about it?"

"Don't know. Didn't think to mention it, what with lookin' for them kids."

"I'm bettin' the power outage has something to do with the girls."

"I see that now."

"After the power went out, what happened?"

"Most everyone started their generators."

"Some pretty loud?"

"Not usually. We got rules about that. But Friday night, the one that runs this here place sounded purty bad. Muffler's shot."

"Did you check it?"

"A-yep. That be my job. I checked it an ordered a new one, but it hasn't come in yet."

"Jerry was out there." Sally said. Her voice was soft, flat, like she was speaking either of the dead, or to the dead. Joe felt the chills slide up his spine again.

"Who's Jerry?"

"My brother." Both men turned to look a Sally, as she almost spit the words out. "I'll get a flashlight."

She came out wearing a coat and carrying two blanket coats with the Diamond Lake logo on the back and two flashlights. She handed them the coats and kept both flashlights. They walked around the lodge and back into the stand of pine that screened the lodge from the village until they came to a small locked building. Bob unlocked the door and they entered. The west wall was one-inch square hardware cloth. The generator, powered by a large Briggs and Stratton engine, took up about half of the building's floor space. The four-inch exhaust pipe that screwed onto the end of the muffler protruded through the hardware cloth.

Joe took one of the two flashlights from Sally and went outside. He couldn't see anything by shining the light up the exhaust pipe and said so. Bob rummaged through two tool boxes before finding a pipe wrench, which he handed to Sally. She unscrewed the muffler and handed it to Bob who handed it to Joe.

"Looks to me like someone drove a chisel or small pipe up through the fins." He handed the muffler back to Bob who in turn peered down into it.

"All right, Sally, what do you know?"

"I don't know nothin'. It's what I think that's botherin' me."

"Which is?"

"When you started askin' about how someone must of helped, if a plane took 'em, I started thinkin' who round here that might be."

She stopped to wipe the sweat off her face with the sleeve of her shirt, even though it was only about thirty degrees, if that. Then went on, "Jerry, he's been real moody lately. He ain't got no money, won't work, you see. An he drinks, when he can get it. Cuts just enough firewood to keep from starvin.'" She swallowed twice, pushed the muffler around with the toe of her boot from where Bob had laid it. Joe knew that what she was saying was hard for her and he had sense enough to keep his mouth shut and let her pick her way through it. "Jerry didn't come help look for the girls, which ain't like him. You know, he'd a picked up free food and Mr. Bradley was offerin' to pay anyone what wanted to get paid for lookin'. No one else would take his money, but Jerry sure as hell woulda." She looked at Joe, wondering if she should say anything about his fee, but decided to let it pass, see how he did before she passed judgment. "I didn't think nothin' of it, 'cept to figure he was layin' drunk somewheres. Then two days ago he comes in, been to town he told me. He was wearin' new boots. An he had a box near to full of supplies in the back of his truck. Most of which was al-coe-hal."

Both men waited until they were sure she was done before Bob said real slow, almost a snarl, which surprised Joe, "You're thinkin' he got paid to fall the tree on the power line and wreck this here muffler?"

"Yeah, that's about it. I figure. But that don't mean he knew the girls was gonna be snatched."

"Woman, if a plane landed, then someone had to put lights out. Meanin' he'd a knowed all right. Maybe helped load 'em."

She nodded, head down. It wasn't sweat dripping off her cheeks. "Go find out, please."

"I'll go with you. Know right where he holes up."

"No, I don't think that's a good idea. If he didn't do anything, I don't want him comin' back on you. And if he did have anything to do with the girls' disappearance, he's gonna tell me all about it."

Sally shook her head then in almost a whisper began, "Oh he done it all right. Now that I thinks about it. But he won't tell you nothin'. Maybe shoot you, if he thinks you're comin' for him."

They walked back to the lodge in silence. Joe Greene had a feeling that at all hell was about to break loose.

When he walked into the lodge he was aware of the heat and of Bradley's eyes on him. He made eye contact and nodded his head toward the hall. When Bradley caught up with him, Joe was standing in front of the office door.

"It's not locked, we can go in, if you like."

Once inside Joe began to pace and Bradley sat on the edge of the desk. Joe told Bradley what he knew and what he thought. Well, most of what he knew, and some of what he thought.

"I wish I'd called you three days ago."

"The preliminary would still have had to be done. It's not too hard to come in at this point in an investigation and look good. Are you with me, or do I go alone?"

"We'll take Bob's Jeep and I'll drive. I know the way, and am familiar with the way he drives. Hopefully we can get in the door before he realizes it's not Bob."

"Okay by me. But I go through the door first."

"I would certainly hope so." Bradley's quick smile told Joe something about the man. He wasn't sure what, but something.

On the way up to Jerry's cabin there wasn't much to do but hang on as the road was really just a trail. The snow-laden branches kept slapping against the windshield, reducing visibility to something close to nothing.

"This isn't really a road," Bradley yelled to be heard above the whine of the ancient rig, "It's a Forest Service pack trail."

"Did anyone think to check Jerry's cabin for the girls?"

"Bob drove up this way with Two Fingers, the tracker. Bob stuck his head into Jerry's, said that he wasn't home, and hadn't been for awhile. Stove was cold, or some such thing."

"Let me know when we're about two minutes from his cabin."

They rode in bone-jarring silence for several minutes until Bradley said, "We're about there."

"If I go down, fire that shotgun into the cabin and then run. Don't worry about me. I'll either be dead or I won't."

"I understand, but I don't like it."

"What's the inside like? Is it just one room?"

"Yeah, he's got a combination heating/cook stove in the far left corner, with a sink and a table straight ahead, his bed takes up the right-hand side. It looks like he spends most of his time there."

"In the bed?"

"Yeah. It's one of those single beds with the curved pipe head-and-foot-boards. There's a metal shelf unit with locking doors, keeps the mice out, I guess. It's just to the right of the door and an old rocker to the left. And that's it."

"Guns."

"Oh, sorry. A .30-.30 on pegs over his bed. I think he can reach it without even sitting up. He has a .38 revolver but I don't know where he keeps it. Probably in bed with him."

"What about the door? Does it have a regular knob and latch, or is it some kind of a homemade arrangement?"

"Let's see, it's a single arm that fits into a U-bracket on the inside of the door. There's a peg through the door that you lift up to open. He doesn't have a lock on it."

"How come you remember it so well?"

"I own a reproduction blacksmith shop as well as my other interests. I reproduced several door latches and hinges that I found still in use up here."

A glow up ahead caught Joe's attention. "That it?"

"Yep."

"Park with my side as close to the cabin's door as you can."

Joe was out of the Jeep before it came to a stop. He took the three steps and threw himself against the door as he lifted the latch.

Jerry, who was laying on his bed in his black wool longjohns, was already swinging the .30-.30 toward the door as Joe came through it, going instantly into a crouch, the Beretta held in both hands and trained on Jerry's chest.

"Give me a reason, asshole."

They stared at one another for several seconds before Jerry lowered the rifle and licked his lips, "Who the hell 'er you, come bustin' in my place." He shook his long matted hair out of his eyes (which showed no fear), licked his lips again, and continued, "I should shoot your fuckin' ass."

Greene never let his concentration waver as he heard Bradley come up the steps and into the room.

Jerry recognized Bradley and his face formed a terrified grin, "Hey, Mr. Bradley, what you come up my place for?"

Bradley didn't answer, he just stepped past Greene and slammed the butt of the shotgun into Jerry's face. "Where's my daughter, you piece of shit?!"

Jerry slumped back onto his cot, his left hand sliding up under the wad of clothing that served as a pillow. Greene had to step around Bradley, and as he did so Bradley brought the shotgun butt down on Jerry's left forearm with all of his strength. Jerry grunted, grabbed his left arm with his right hand and rolled into a ball. Before Greene could get involved, Bradley took Jerry by the hair and pulled him off the cot and out into the middle of the room.

"This is the last time I'm going to ask nice. Where is my daughter?"

Greene was sure that Jerry wouldn't survive it if Bradley didn't ask nice. He pulled Bradley back and stepped between them.

"Jerry, I'm going to look around a little. If I find anything that makes me think you had anything to do with the kidnapping, I'm going to let Mr. Bradley ask you again. Unless you want to tell me about it right now."

In answer, Jerry tried to spit at him. A combination of blood and teeth slid down his broken face. His eyes were pools of hatred. There wasn't a trace of fear. Greene walked over to the stove and opened the damper. He gave a satisfied grunt as he lifted the lid on a two-gallon canner to find it nearly full of hot water. Next he began a systematic search of the metal cabinet. Inside he found three new orange plastic lanterns. Beside them lay a partial roll of duct tape. On the top shelf was a three-pound coffee can. He lifted it off the shelf and turned around. While watching Jerry he pried the plastic lid off and dumped the contents on the floor, his eyes never leaving Jerry's face.

"Okay you pathetic little bastard, who paid you and how much did he give you to help steal the girls?"

Jerry swallowed, tried to lick the blood off of his mouth and said, "Thas mine! All mine!"

He rolled over and crawled to where the money lay on the floor. Moaning, he scooped it up only to have it slide out of his shaking hands and fall back on the floor. Bradley was moving toward him, raising the shotgun as he came. Greene stepped in front of Bradley, reaching for the shotgun. Obviously Bradley was past listening.

Jerry was slight, fast, and fighting for his life. He dove for the cot and rolled with his back to the wall as his right hand closed around the butt of his .38.

Joe Greene had been in his share of scraps and if he knew anything, it was to never count anyone down and out, unless they were three times dead. So it was that as he reached for the shotgun, he sensed movement and, guessing where Jerry was headed, threw himself at the cot. Even then luck played a part in his catching Jerry by the wrist as he pulled the revolver out from under the clothes. Jerry still managed to get two rounds off before he was subdued. Both rounds pierced the stove, which seemed to like it and began burning with renewed enthusiasm.

Gulping for air, Greene instructed, "Get that roll of duct tape and tape this bastard's wrists to the top of this cot."

That done Bradley asked, "The feet?"

"Yeah." When Jerry kicked Bradley away from the bed, Greene, who was standing right foot on the floor and left knee in Jerry's abdomen, struck him with the side of his right hand in the groin. Jerry screamed and his legs shot straight out. Bradley had no trouble taping the bare ankles to the metal foot-board.

Greene was still panting when he stood up, "Okay, Mr. Bradley, this is where you go wait in the Jeep."

Jerry rolled his head toward Greene. For the first time his eyes showed something other than contempt and anger. "Fuck you. I don't got nothin' to say. You might just as well go."

Bradley shook his head and glaring at Jerry said, "No. I'm going to enjoy this."

He didn't, Greene figured, know what was going to happen.

There was a small sink next to the stove that drained into a bucket. Laying on its side in the sink was an aluminum coffee pot. Joe took the lid off and pulled the basket out. He took the lid off the now boiling canner and dipped the coffee pot full. He sighed and walked over to the cot. "Last chance," he offered. Hoping Jerry would take it, knowing he wouldn't. Without hesitating further he stepped to the end of the bed and began pouring a thin stream of boiling water onto the man's right foot. Jerry screamed, thrashed, and eyes bulging, cursed. By the end of the third pot of water, the toe nails on his right foot had lifted from their beds and the calluses on the bottom of his foot had peeled off, leaving steaming, cooked meat underneath.

Joe let him rest several minutes then began on his left foot.

Joe glanced at Bradley, his face was ashen and he was sweating.

Halfway through the second pot of water poured onto his left foot, Jerry began to talk.

They took both guns, the money and the keys and distributor cap to Jerry's old 4X4 Chev, cut the tape on his wrists and left him.

They didn't speak all the way back.

When Bradley shut the engine off in front of the lodge, they sat watching the snow hit the windshield.

Greene broke the silence, "Times this job makes me feel dirty. Real dirty."

"He had it comin'. And more. I wanted to kill him."

"Yeah, I noticed. And then we'd have never found out where they are."

"Tell me. In all honesty. Do you think they are still alive?"

"Yeah I do. We're not close enough to them for me to pick up any what you might call vibes, or impulses from them. But someone went to a lot of trouble to heist three teenagers, when let's face it, for what he paid Jerry alone he could have bought the services of several young girls for a week. So based on that, I'd say, yes they're alive. Probably not for much longer though."

"Why?"

"Why didn't he rent girls? Probably because it's a one-way trip. Porno and torture. It sells for a lot in Asia and parts of Europe."

"Aren't you jumping to conclusions? They're only little girls. They aren't even - Hell they won't even understand what is happening to them."

"I think that's what appeals to the sickos who buy videos of that kind of entertainment. I also found some things that I didn't bring to show and tell." Bradley didn't say anything. He must have known that Greene wouldn't have said that unless he had a damn good reason. "I found a video cassette wrapper and box. As high quality as you can buy. I slipped it inside my wetsuit, because it wouldn't fit in the canvas sack and then when I saw how what I found was to be presented, I kept it to myself."

"Why didn't you tell me sooner? Or Walker at least."

"Walker is bound by law. I'm not quite so picky. And because then I probably couldn't have kept you from killing that little bastard. We needed information, and we don't need to be charged with murder."

"You could have fixed it to look like a fight."

"Maybe. Maybe not. But we don't have the time to waste."

"You've done what I paid you to do. And more. So I guess this is where we part company. I'll go in and call the police. They'll take it from here."

"That's your wife on the porch isn't it?" He couldn't see much of her, the way she was bundled up; but her stance told him a lot.

"By the way. You said something about being able to tell that they are alive if you get close enough."

"Yeah."

"Well as far as that woman up there is concerned, you are close enough and can sense that they are alive and not in pain. Got it?"

"There's no harm in that."

Chapter Thirteen

Agnes Bradley had walked out on the porch with the two men, then watched them drive away and went back in, bypassing the lobby and going up to her room. Her room was connected to her husband's by a pass-through door that was seldom opened by either of them.

She had met her husband three days into her first job as a nurse. She had graduated from nursing school and had taken a job working for a general practitioner at a remote desert town, wanting to get as far away from the city and her past as she could.

Funny, now that she thought back on it, Tom never once had asked her how she financed school. He had known that her mother was a single-mom-waitress and didn't have the funds to help her. The thought occurred to her that maybe he did know, and was keeping the information in case he ever needed it to slander and shame her.

"Oh God!" she said aloud, "I'll bet he does know."

She had met him when the sheriff brought him and his companion in to the clinic after their sports car took a flying lesson and ended up in a dry streambed.

Panic-stricken, she had done her best to remember everything she'd been taught about shock, bleeding, and sanitation, doing by-the-book procedures until Doctor Wallace arrived nearly two hours later, covered with deer hair and blood. He'd washed his hands, put on a lab coat over his filthy clothes, poured himself and the two men cups of coffee (much to the dismay of Nurse Radcliff) and spent the next hour drinking coffee and verbally hunting the area with the two men while she worried about everything.

Three days later a courier had delivered two dozen yellow roses for her and a case of premium wines for Doctor Wallace.

Forty-six dozen roses later she'd married Tom Bradley and quit the nursing profession to become a rich man's wife. She had soon discovered that to be Tom's wife was to be just another well-tanned and turned out bauble bouncing around on the tennis court of his country club.

The only bright spots in her life were her daughter and her painting. One was missing and the other packed away for the return trip to California.

The windows that overlooked the lake and normally gave her the best light of any room in the lodge for her painting were tonight covered with snow.

She'd stood in the dark for several minutes before flipping on the lights and unpacking her painting supplies. For years she had turned to her easel when being "Mrs. Bradley" had become almost too much. Now she needed to retreat from reality long enough to recharge her batteries, and be able to cope with whatever came next.

Many painters used photos as visionary aides, and line drawing to get the proportions right. Or better yet, they painted while looking at the subject, be it a mountain or a human. Agnes used only her memory and her watercolors; the fruits of her labors now gracing the better homes and galleries in the West.

She had set up her easel, and carefully mixed her paints in preparation for duplicating Mr. Greene. She'd been distracted momentarily by someone's heavy tread in the hall, and when she'd turned her eyes back to the easel, she found that she had, without realizing it, painted a single bold line down the left hand side of the paper, angling from left to right. As she'd watched, the line had begun to dry a deep purple almost black, with bluish highlights. She'd looked from the line to her paints and back again, wondering how and what she had accidentally mixed to come up with that color.

With her foot, she'd pulled a chair out and sat down on it, staring at what she had done.

She knew that a random vertical line drawn by a right-handed person, which she was, would slant from the top to the left of center at the bottom. So the line she had drawn was not random, but an action that was preceded by forethought.

The color was a combination of hues that would normally take six to eight brush strokes, each from a different combination of pigments; and she couldn't even remember having made one brush stroke.

She'd remained in the chair, legs spread, forearms across her knees, hands hanging down between her legs trying to fathom what she had done.

Twice she'd lifted her brush and tried to force herself to add to what she had done, but she couldn't remember what Greene looked like, or even how he moved. Of course she was under stress, but some of her most fascinating works were done when her painting had seemed to be the only way she could cope. She needed Marilyn.

She had met her mentor and teacher, Marilyn, when she had stopped to watch her recreate a cactus that grew along their driveway, the summer after Jeani was born. Two weeks later she again saw the dusty Volkswagen bug pulled off the road near the country club. After watching Marilyn for a while she'd asked her if she gave lessons.

"No, I don't. I have commitments to three galleries, and besides, most people can't paint no matter how many lessons they have."

After watching a while longer Agnes had asked where she might take lessons.

Marilyn had ignored her for the several minutes it took her to finish the painting she was working on, before answering.

"Tell you what. I can tell in ten minutes if you have any talent. I'm going to mix the paint for you, give you the proper brush, and you paint that hill over there. If you've got what it takes, I'll help you from time to time, if you don't, then keep going the next time you see me."

For some reason Agnes hadn't been intimidated in the least, and her first watercolor attempt, though crude, was judged acceptable. Over the next three years her work began to take on life and then one day she received the ultimate compliment from her teacher.

"Honey, I've been workin' at paintin' for twenty years, and I think I'm good. Hell I know I'm good! But you're better than I can ever hope to be."

They had continued to work together; though their shows were separate, they were always well attended and all their works sold, usually in the first day of weekend events.

The only difference was price. Agnes' works sold for around ten times what Marilyn's brought.

And now it was Agnes who turned away would-be students.

"Oh what a tangled web we mortals spin," she said aloud, thinking what if Marilyn was here.   She would say in her high, cracked reed voice, "What is it you are trying to say?"

And that was the question, what was she trying to create?

A man she had seen only half an hour ago.

A man in whose hands her daughter's life lay.

And she couldn't even remember anything about him?

Maybe if she went over what she knew about him she could recall his face, and then his hands and that would be enough to start with. She had read the file an investigation service had faxed Tom. From that she knew that he had been in a Spec 4 unit in Vietnam and had worked on two different police agencies before going out on his own as an investigator. The report had gone on to say that the name Joe Greene was a legal business name and not his real name. The real Joseph Greene had been killed in action on the Perfume River in Vietnam. The man who called himself Joe Greene was reputed to have been the platoon leader when Joseph Greene was killed. His name was classified. As were the circumstances under which Greene was killed. The report further stated that the corporation named Joe Greene had extensive investments in Portland, Oregon, and Las Vegas, Nevada. The net worth of Joe Greene was in excess of two million dollars.

Sally had said something about him earlier that day, before he arrived--something about him being a shaman, someone like a medicine man, only different.

When she and Marilyn had traveled down to the Pueblo ruins to paint, they had hired a guide who on several occasions refused to accompany them up into canyons where he said that the spirit gods lived.

"Yes," he'd said, he'd seen spirit gods, but, "No," he couldn't remember what they looked like.

The Anglos had a name for people who seemed to be able to accomplish things ordinary people couldn't. They were called spellbinders, and were usually known for their oratory skills. And like the spirit gods, they were often seen through their accomplishments and not so much as a human. Hitler was one, remembered for his ability to summon people to do his will, no matter how horrid. When asked to describe him even those who knew him personally commented on his mustache, brown shirt and little else. Churchill was remembered for his girth and cigar, though he summoned England's strength and courage, long after there was nothing left, so they overcame all the odds.

Too often though, oratory ability leads to power; power that can only be fed by crisis. When the crisis is over, the spellbinder fades or creates a new crisis to perpetuate his skill, which becomes ambition, the desire to be the center of attention. How well she knew that being `the artist' at a show was worth more than the money her paintings brought. This type of ambition or power could be dangerous and yet became almost a craving.

From what she knew about Greene, he was not of that type; he was more like the spirit gods, driven not by ambition nor greed, but one who blossomed in individual times of need and then faded into the night, taking with him nothing but the knowledge that he had done what was right (and perhaps several pieces of silver).

The report stated that at times Greene was paid handsomely, and just as often he took nothing; in many cases, reuniting those who had been given up for dead with their loved ones. She dropped to her knees and prayed:

"Oh God, please grant him the power to find our girls.

Let him fly with the ravens, walk with the spirits.

Please let him find them and bring them home safe.

Amen."

She realized that she was holding the paintbrush between her clasped hands. She looked down at the bristles. She closed her eyes and then opened them again to stare at the brush.

There was no paint on it!

She was still on her knees trying to comprehend what had happened when she heard the old Jeep coming down toward the lodge. She stood up, put on a coat and fur hat, then ran down the stairs to the porch.

Chapter Fourteen

They climbed stiffly out of the unheated relic and while Bradley was talking to his wife, Joe went in, found his room, showered, put on clean clothes and went down to the dining room where he forced himself to eat a large dinner from the banquet table.

No one said a word to him, treating him like he had the plague. It was to be expected, even if Bradley didn't tell anyone how Greene had made Jerry talk, they had to know it hadn't been pretty. And no matter how much they might despise and even hate Jerry, he was of the village, and Joe was an outsider, one who was moving far too fast for their comfort. He knew that they would think he had made them look like fools, or that someone might think that they were covering up for Jerry.

They would change their mind when the backlash hit them in the pocketbook.

Once back in his room he dressed for what lay ahead, went through his pack and gear, then sat down in the overstuffed chair next to the bed, waiting.

Twenty minutes later someone tapped lightly on his bedroom door.

"Come on in, Sally."

"You knowed I was comin?"

"Yes."

"When did you know?"

"Before I got back from your brother Jerry's cabin."

"But I didn't even know then."

"Yeah but I did. Cause you're the only one I know who can find your way to the upper lake in a blizzard, and you are the only one that I can trust."

"Did you kill him?"

"You know I didn't."

"You shoulda kilt him."

"He's not going any place. Except to prison."

"He'll make trouble."

"I don't see how. And besides, I'm not an executioner."

"I'm atellin' you, you shoulda kilt him."

"We better move, the police will be here any time now."

"You got a rifle?"

"No. I had enough trouble getting my .380 through the gate, even though I was on a private plane."

He didn't tell her about his other pistol, The less she knew about him and what he had in the way of tools, the better.

"What kind do you want?"

"Do you have a 30-06 with a scope and a box of 200-grain hollow points?"

"Waitin' fer you in the boat. But you knowed that, didn't you?"

He didn't, but he had seen two of them in Bob's gun case in his office, and figured that was what would be offered.

Joe had been aware of someone standing just outside the door since shortly after Sally had come in. He motioned Sally to wait, walked silently to the door, and pulled it open.

"Mrs. Bradley, I presume." He stepped to the side so she could walk past him, "Won't you join us?" He didn't smile, he didn't like being spied on.

"I was waiting for the right time to knock."

"It's usually before listening to someone else's conversation."

"Granted. But it's my daughter out there." She turned to Sally and said, "May I please have a word alone with Mr. Greene?"

"I'll be on the dock. If the cops get here before we get gone, we won't be going." She looked pointedly at Mrs. Bradley.

"My husband thinks you are done. But I knew better. When you walked up to the lodge, right then--."

"It's not necessary Mrs. Bradley. I'm going, not because of praise, glory, or the thirty pieces of silver you are about to offer me, but because I am who I am."

"On most people that line would sound corny. On you it fits."

"Why are you here?"

"To offer you thirty pieces of silver, and to give you Susie's spare glasses. The policeman took her others as evidence. Like she won't ever need them again."

She fought to control herself. While she stood, head down, fists clenched, Joe took the opportunity to study her. She was maybe forty-five, one twenty-five to one-thirty and obviously took care of herself. She carried herself well and had a certain presence about her, the kind that couldn't be bought. He liked and respected that in a person.

She looked up suddenly and said, "I would go with you, if I could be of any service."

"I know that. I'll give the Kid her glasses. Anything else?"

"I shall spend the rest of the night praying for you and the girls."

"Don't bother about me."

She smiled for the first time, "I assure you, it won't be a bother."

He picked up his pack, unhappy with the weight, but knowing that later he most likely would be damn glad he had it.

She stopped him as he crossed the threshold, "Mr. Greene, are you. . . are you. . .do you have special power?"

"I don't know for sure. Sometimes I can sense things, but mostly I think it's just recognizing that I have a sixth sense and that I react to it."

She nodded, still trying to find meaning in the painting. "I think you are a Spirit God, or maybe a spellbinder."

"Is that good?" he asked, giving her a lopsided grin.

"Only if you don't abuse the power."

Good, he thought as he made his way down to the dock. I've been called a alien, a medicine man, a money-hungry bastard, a troublemaker, and now a spellbinder; whatever in hell that was.

They were a hundred yards from shore and moving fast when headlights, three sets, came across the parking lot and up to the lodge.

"Timed that about close."

Joe nodded as they disappeared into the storm. Ten minutes later the shoreline appeared suddenly.

"Hold on!" Sally yelled as the sled slammed into the beach and slid some twenty-five feet up the bank, coming to rest between two small pines.

They sat there for nearly a minute before Joe spoke, "Well she shouldn't wash back into the lake while we're gone."

When Sally didn't speak he turned, following her gaze to where the transom and outboard lay some ten feet behind the rest of the boat.

She began to laugh, at first just a low chuckle that built until she was whooping. Sally laughed until tears slid down her cheeks. She wiped them away with the back of her hand and said, "I ain't never done that before."

Then they both laughed, rocking back and forth in the broken boat.

They were still chuckling as they started up the trail. All too soon though, all their energy was being used to keep climbing at a steady pace up through the storm. Already the snow was three inches deep, making walking difficult. An hour into the climb, Sally stopped for the third time shortly after choosing a fork in the trail.

"This here snow throws me off kilter sometimes. Had to look twice to see the right fork. Ifin' we took the right trail we'll be comin' up onto a flat 'bout now."

It was, he knew, her way of showing off a bit.

Ten minutes later the terrain leveled out onto a windswept mesa, and almost immediately they started down the other side. They found a place to catch their breath behind some broken slabs of rock where the rimrock had collapsed and they were out of the wind.

"Well, I see what you mean about not bein' able to use snowmobiles around here."

"Yeah, them things don't handle broken rim rock and heavy brush. Bob an the village folk bin thinkin' bout tryin to put some trails in that people can hike on in the summer an ride them damn things on in the winter. That would give us some winter guests, which is good for everybody."

"What did people around here do for income before you and Bob built the lodge?"

"Oh it ain't that bigga deal. Most of the men who live around here either log or work for the Forest Service. The lodge gives some of the women work and side pocket money for whoever of the men what wants a little extra."

Another hour of slipping, falling only to rise and fall again brought them to level ground. It was here that Sally called a halt. They found shelter under the sweeping limbs of what Joe thought was a cedar of some kind. She shrugged out of her pack and began the process of making tea. Joe took his pack off and sat on it. Sally pulled two thick sandwiches out of a side pocket of her pack and handed Joe one. They both watched the quart saucepan, their mouths watering at the prospect of hot tea. When at last the water boiled, they moved their packs over against the base of the tree, leaned back, stretched their legs out and, cupping their mugs in their hands, sipped the tea.

"I guess you know, I ain't comin' back."

"What in hell are you talkin' about?"

"This here is gonna taint the lodge and town. Specially what with my brother bein' up to his ass in it."

"Sally for cryin' . . ."

"Let me finish." She sipped at her tea, took a bite of sandwich and spoke around a mouthful of meatloaf, "Me an Bob built the lodge most with our own hands. 'Cept for the electricity which Dale come up on weekends and did." She swallowed, took another bite and continued, "Just last year we got to where we don't owe nobody, then Bob fell off the roof an broke his back."

"I thought that he did that in a plane crash."

"Hah. There ain't been a plane built can hurt Bob. Sure he's rolled them up till they look like a wad of toilet paper, then walked away without a scratch."

She chased the second bite of meatloaf with more tea before she went on, "Cost us big time. We got a rock on the lodge bigger then when we started. I ain't been feelin' too hot the last year or so, I didn't tell no one what with Bob bein' so worried about how we was gonna pay back the bank. But I got to hurtin' so bad that I went an told Betty, she runs the store in the village, and has got some herbs and minerals in the back that she traded off of one of the Far Walkers that come through last summer. I thought maybe she might would have somethin' for the pain. She toll her old man who toll my Bob. Bob took me in to the sawbones right quick. I got the cancer; and I done waited bout a year or more too long. They can't fix it, you see. Last week we done ask Doc straight out. "How bad is it?" He said I got maybe two months, maybe less." She dug a bottle out of her shirt pocket and took four pills. "These here are for the pain."

"If you think that I'm going to let you kill yourself--."

"You don't have to worry about that. Jerry he's a comin'. I can feel it, an so can you. He's gonna have to go around, and cross the creek down about three miles below where we'll cross with the canoes. When he comes along he's gonna hafta kill me to get past. And he will, I'll see to that." Tears where running down her face as she asked, "I only got one request from you. Mr. Bradley said you could feel that the little girls ain't been hurt. You save 'em. You gotta do that! An what with me gitten kilt helpin' you, I think that will save the lodge. You see, Bob ain't got nothin' else."

Joe couldn't think of anything to say. He pulled a couple paper towels out of his jacket pocket and handed them to Sally. She thanked him, wiped her eyes and then blew her nose.

"What does Bob think about this?"

"He's okay with it."

"Did you tell him straight out?"

"No. Cause he wouldn't have let me come. I done wrote him a letter an left it on his piller. Mister you can't let us down! You gotta promise that you will git them girls and keep 'em safe." She was leaning forward, pleading with him.

So much for `no harm in that,' he thought as he sipped his tea and tried to think of some way to take Sally home alive. "Yeah, you've got my word on gettin' the girls out."

"Safe. You gotta promise they'll be alive and not hurt."

"You've got my word on it." There wasn't much else he could say.

She nodded, seemingly okay with it.

They packed up, and an hour later came to the lake. The two canoes were upside down on a rack about fifty feet from the shore.

Sally leaned against a tree and waited for Joe to pull them down to the water. "Sorry I can't help, but I'm plum tuckered."

Joe didn't know if she was as tired as she appeared to be or if she was acting to prove how sick she was.

"Sally, we need to talk."

"Let's git movin', then I'll tell you everything I know bout this lake. That murderin' bastard of a brother ain't fer behind."

"I thought you said he has to cross two miles downstream?"

"I did, but he knows how sick I is, an that I ain't got much push."

Joe thought that if she'd had any more 'push' he would have had to have a jetpack to keep up.

"I'ma thinkin' he may figure that he can catch us afore we get out on the water."

"That's a helluva gamble."

"Not really. This here bitch of a trail is faster than the other one, 'specially in the snow. There's a good flat trail all along this shoreline. Most down to where he'll have to cross. Comin' this way, he'd lose maybe thirty minutes."

"Sally, there isn't any way he can walk. I burned his feet pretty bad."

"Won't stop him. He can, and always could, set to doin' a task an' go off in his head somewheres else."

"The aborigines call that 'go walk-about.'"

"I s'pose it's the same thing. It's why he don't do much. You know, he does some little thing then lays up an thinks about it for a time."

"You mean relives it?"

"Yep. An like now, once he sets out after us he most likely will be thinkin' about what happened, an' he won't feel no pain. That's why you shoulda kilt him. All you done was shame him, an most likely make him killin' mad."

"Damn!"

"You know he's comin'. You can feel it too. Can't chu?"

Yeah he could sense something. But he thought it was probably brought on by Sally's insistence; nevertheless Joe-- who wouldn't have any second thoughts about taking a rubber boat out into rough seas, but had never used or trusted canoes--managed to get the both of them in the lake and himself and Sally aboard without mishap.

And he did it pretty quickly too.

The second canoe containing their packs and the two extra paddles was being pulled along behind.

The hair on the back of Joe's neck was standing up again. He was beginning to feel like a kenneled cur that was cornered by three other dogs; that and the proverbial sitting duck. Only one that was afraid of getting wet as well as being shot.

He turned part way around on the stern seat and peered through the darkness at the receding shoreline, as he did his paddle bumped the canoe with a hollow 'thonk'.

"Duck!" He stage whispered, fell onto his knees and began unhooking the rubber tie-downs that held the 30:06 to the center seat. "I think I saw someone standing on the shore."

Chapter Fifteen

Jerry squinted into the darkness. He couldn't see anything as the snow was coming out of the North riding a small breeze and blinding him. But he could hear a faint splash as the white man dug his paddle into the water. Sally would of course paddle silently, as one should. He brought his rifle up to his shoulder and waited until he heard a wooden paddle bump against the aluminum canoe. He smiled, adjusted for it and fired. He heard the distinct sound of the slug striking the aluminum canoe, raised the tip of the muzzle one inch and fired three times in rapid succession. There was no indication that he had hit anything with the last three shots.

He only had five rounds left, and as there was nothing to be gained by standing, staring off into the darkness, he turned south along the shoreline. The trail was easy to follow, Jerry began to go over the events again that had led to this, and except when he stumbled, which was often, he stayed out of body, so as to not feel the pain.

A week ago he'd been down in the village, trying to bum cigarettes from Betty Floyd. She'd told him that if he'd unload the cord of wood from the back of her old man's pickup and stack it in the shed behind the store she'd give him ten dollars. He'd argued for fifteen. No deal.

He'd headed up the road, walkin' cause his old pickup was half way between his cabin and the lodge, out of gas. He was mad at Betty--she could of gone fifteen--then he'd have had enough for smokes, a box of pancake mix, and a bag of apples. He wasn't worried about the gas, Sally would always give him a jug of gas, but she wouldn't front him cash, not any more. She was gittin' too damn uppity.

He'd stopped to watch a float plane drop in and waddle over to the town dock. He hung around, if the pilot left it, maybe he could hook something that the pawn shop man in town would buy.

He wouldn't take nothin except people hadn't been treatin' him right, an he had some good times comin'.

If the Boss was with the pilot then Jerry stood to make some easy pocket money runnin' errands and the like.

They were both in the plane. Jerry had smiled at them, and started to move off, hoping they would call him back.

Just like he'd hoped, the pilot had called out to him to wait. The pilot and his boss had stood around talkin to him for a while, Jerry didn't like either of them, but it smelled like there might be some money in it, so he'd stayed. The boss man sent the pilot up to the store for beer and chips.

They'd walked separately until they were out of sight below the village where they set on a windfall and made a plan.

The boss man had flown down to the lodge a week before and seen three little girls that he wanted. Jerry didn't understand why he'd want them, when for forty dollars he could drive to town and lay up with a "cut" all night, but he never knew what these whites were thinkin'.

When the Man told Jerry what he wanted him to do, and offered him twenty-five hundred dollars, Jerry couldn't believe his luck. He'd stayed behind and got drunk on the rest of the beer, while the other two, rented one of the two beaters the lodge kept and went into town.

At some point Jerry had passed out.

When he came to the next morning he found a swallow left in two or three of the bottles that were lying around and headed up toward the lodge hoping his good fortune hadn't been a dream.

Sally gave him a two-gallon can of gas and a lecture.

His head was pounding and her chatter hadn't helped. He tried not to think too much about what was supposed to be at his cabin for fear of jinxing it, as he guided the old pickup up the trail to his cabin.

When he opened the door, there, on the table, had been three lanterns, a roll of duct tape, and an envelope with five hundred dollars in it.

He'd gone into town that afternoon and bought a new pair of mustard-yellow high-top work shoes and then spent the rest of the day looking at buying a new-to-him four-wheel-drive pickup.

He'd eaten two orders of deep-fried oysters chased with Jack Daniel's and driven home.

The next day he noticed that the right front fender of his pick up had a new ding in it. He wondered idly what he'd hit to take half the fender off like that. Then he remembered he was gittin' a new rig and it didn't matter.

He'd gone into the village the next day and hung out, something he was very good at. It was when he was hangin' that most everything good that had ever happened to him, happened. Though nothing came of the day, except when he 'found' a bag of store bought cookies in the seat of an unlocked car.

After dark he'd taken an iron bar out of his pickup and poked the baffles out of two generators in town. One of them being the one that ran the store--let that uppity bitch see how she liked payin' for a new one--and besides she kept the store open till eight and would need the juice.

Then, not quite blind drunk from two or was it three bottles of Mad Dog he'd bought off a timber faller he knew, he drove up to the lodge and stumbled out into the brush to the lodge's generator house where he realized that he'd forgotten the iron bar.

On the way back to his pickup, he'd run into Sally, who'd wanted to know what he was doing. The shit would have been in the fryin' pan if he'd had the iron bar then. He told her he'd had to piss and knowing that she didn't like him in her fuckin' lodge when he was drunk, had pissed outside like a dog.

She'd gone off in a huff.

He'd driven part way up the track toward his cabin, left the pickup and walked back through the timber to the generator house, and poked the baffles out of the generator.

On the way back to his pickup he remembered that his chain saw wasn't running and he'd have to make a quick trip to town the next morning. Jeff down in the village could fix it, but he'd thrown him out of his shop three weeks ago for stealing a box of saw files.

It had been a pretty good business while it lasted. He'd walk off with a box of files and sell them to Pete for half of what Jeff sold them for. Pete had been stayin' on a job site for a week and so he'd tried to sell them to Ol' Johnson. That fuckin' Johnson had grabbed him by the arm and marched him right down to Jeff's.

Jerry still couldn't believe it. After all, Johnson had two in grade school and one in the oven; you'd think the guy would be happy to get a deal.

He shook his head, thinking back on it, stumbled and fell headfirst into a clump of buck brush growing along the shoreline.

He was momentarily stunned. Not from the fall, but from the fact that even blind drunk, one of his favorite states of mind, he never fell. Never.

He fought his way out of the bush, losing his cap in the process, and climbed to his feet only to fall again. This time landing on his butt. He sat there a minute then grabbed his right pant leg and pulled his foot up for a close examination.

"No wonder." He chuckled and dropped his foot. There was no pain, and no longer any blood seeping out through his shoe. "You're fuckin' froze solid." He told his foot. After glaring at the offending appendage for a few seconds he turned his gaze to his left foot. "So er you."

He tried to move his toes. There was no response. He attempted to rotate his ankles with limited success. Then, digging a bottle of whiskey out of his jacket, he hefted it, figuring it to be a little less than half full. He tipped his head back and let the heat run down his throat and fire up in his belly, careful not to let the bottle touch his broken mouth.

Jerry sat there until the snow melted under him and soaked through his pants. He rolled over onto his hands and knees then, using the 30-30 as a crutch, levered himself onto his feet.

The first twenty feet were nearly more than he could bear. He hobbled down the trail until he came to a patch of small pine interlaced with vine maple where he cut a six-foot vine maple staff, then carefully cleaned the snow off of the 30-30, made a sling for it from a piece of nylon rope taken from the small pack he carried, and slung it over his back--barrel down.

Taking the nearly empty whiskey bottle out of his jacket, he filled his mouth and swirled it around. The pain of the alcohol in the empty tooth sockets and smashed gums made tears stream down his cheeks. He worked the whiskey around in his mouth some more, then spit.

His lips were swollen and split to the point that the bloody mess dribbled down the front of his jacket, embarrassing him.

He felt no animosity toward Bradley even though he was the one who had broken his mouth. His was one of the girls the Man had wanted; so he had a right to do whatever he felt was needed in an effort to make the situation right. But the other one. The one Bradley called Greene. Him Jerry planned to kill. It wouldn't be quick, and he wouldn't die easy.

A smoldering rage had begun when Greene had burst into his cabin and got the down on him. Coupled with the shame that was his for allowing Greene to make him talk, for that he must die. And he must die by Jerry's hand, so that the shame would be erased from his ancestor's name.

So now he had to follow Greene to the old hunting lodge where the Man was staying. There he knew he would find Greene. He would kill him, in front of the Man. Then the shame would be lifted and he would stand tall in the eyes of the Man. So it was better that he had not caught them before they launched the canoes. His father would have been proud, if he had lived.

Once he killed Greene he planned to take enough supplies to last the winter and hole up in one of two abandoned mine shafts he knew of.

Come spring he'd drift back.

Oh, he knew that the police would throw him jail for a while. But they'd have to let him go, he hadn't done anything they could prove.

He wasn't sure what to do about Sally. She was his sister and bound by tribal law never to turn on him, but she had been corrupted by her husband. He might have to deal roughly with her. It was time she started treating him with the respect he deserved as her older brother.

Jerry had been pushing through snow-laden brush for some twenty minutes before he realized that he had passed the walk log across the creek.

Rather than blame himself, he cursed Greene as he retraced the quarter mile to the walk log. He had to crawl across, which further infuriated and embarrassed him. Once across the trail led north, and was easier going.

Again he lapsed into his dream world, reliving the events of the past several days.

Chapter Sixteen

Joe waited for nearly a minute before sitting up. The canoe was tilted dangerously to starboard and the sound of bullets striking flesh had been unmistakable.

"Sally. Are you with me?"

There was no answer and Joe couldn't slide far enough ahead in the fragile craft to grab her coat without sinking them.

"Sally. Can you hear me?"

The wind-driven waves slapping against the aluminum canoe masked her breathing if, in fact, she was still breathing.

"Sally, you can't leave yet. I still need your help to find the girls. Come on, Sally, for Bob's sake and the village. You care about them don't you?" There was no answer and Joe couldn't risk using a flashlight to see her. Dead or alive he was going to have to move her into the center of the canoe, or abandon her; the waves, even though they rose only four to six inches, were starting to splash into the canoe. He couldn't roll her over the side, her weight would instantly swamp the canoe.

He pulled the other canoe along side and felt for the bullet hole.

"Oh damn," he said. The bullet had ripped a gash over two feet long just above the waterline on the starboard side. It wasn't sinking but it couldn't take on any more weight either.

It was beginning to look like his only option was to stuff the gash in the other canoe with his spare socks, roll into it, let the one they were in now, flip, dumping Sally into the lake and then right it, bail it out and somehow get back into it before the one he would be in sank.

The water temperature in the deep, spring-fed lake was probably just above freezing. If he fell in, he would lose all sensation and drown before he could pull himself back into the canoe.

He didn't like the odds, and even if he succeeded, the time wasted would allow Jerry to get around the lake to alert the kidnappers. There wouldn't be a trace of the girls by the time he got there.

And then Sally groaned.

It was one of the most beautiful sounds Joe had ever heard.

"Sally! Sally, push yourself back toward the center of the canoe."

Slowly the canoe began to level out. Joe reached forward as far as he dared and touched, then grabbed, her coat collar. Carefully he pulled her back into a sitting position against the center seat.

He had to lean forward to hear what she was saying.

"See. I told you he would kill me."

"You aren't dead, and I don't think you're hit too bad, even though it hurts like hell." He hated saying that. There wasn't, he knew from experience, any such thing as being hit good. "Now Sally, tell me all about where we're goin'."

"I can't talk much. Hurts."

"I know, but we have to save the girls, and I can't do it without you."

"Quarter into the wind."

She was silent for maybe thirty seconds, "How long. . . how long was I out?"

"Maybe five minutes. Not more than that."

"You must paddle like the wind itself."

"I'm gettin' the hang of it. I used to be able to paddle a rubber boat all night long, fight all day and paddle all night again."

"You in Army?"

"Marines. Years ago. I was in what they call `Seal Teams.^"

"You dig your paddle too deep. Take long shallow strokes. Don't hit the side of canoe again. Sounds like a drum from the shore."

"Yeah. I figured that was how he knew where to shoot. I'm sorry he got you."

"Don't matter. Just means you gotta do all the paddling. You should take the other canoe and leave me. Without the second canoe and my weight you will maybe make it in time. The spirits will find me, wherever I am."

"Can't. The other ones got a two foot gash just above the waterline."

She didn't answer, preparing to die, he supposed. He envied those like Sally who had a god, or spirit, or even a stone idol to turn to in death. For dying is not easy, nor is it fun. He hated to interrupt this most sacred time, but to have any chance of saving the kids, providing they actually were still alive, he needed information.

"Tell me what I'm looking for," he gasped.

"If I could move my bulk, I would go into the lake."

"Sally, don't leave me. I need to know things. Talk. I'll listen."

When she began to speak it was with someone else's voice, it was soft, and yet even with the wind, his gasping for air and the sound of the waves splashing against the hull, he heard every word clearly. Part way through the instructions and descriptions he realized that the voice he was hearing was not spoken, but was being produced inside his head. For the third time in as many days the hair stood up on the back of his neck, and even though he was sweating the chills bumped down his spine.

He had lost all track of time and when he sighted the shore, a scant four yards away through the swirling snow he was not surprised, he was just there.

The canoe ground to a halt against a rocky shelf that sloped from the waterline up to a stand of stunted juniper.

It took awhile for Joe to regain his strength enough to climb out. He stumbled and fell when he tried to put weight on his bum knee, catching himself by using the rifle butt as a cane. He knew that he would have been easy pickings for anyone for the first three or four minutes that he was ashore. As soon as he could he pulled the second canoe up onto the gravel beach and carried the packs up into the juniper. He pushed the canoe with Sally in it out away from shore and using the bow line walked it down a ways to where the juniper grew almost to the water's edge. He was surprised at how easy it was to pull the canoe with Sally in it, up through the snow and into the shelter of the juniper.

He jogged back, forcing his legs to work and picked up their packs, and took them back to where he'd left Sally. He covered her with two blankets, and gave her four of the pain pills from her jacket pocket, then before he left he kissed her on the forehead, and propped her rifle up beside her.

There were no tracks of anyone ahead of him. The trick would be to avoid getting caught in a crossfire between Sally's brother and the kidnappers. He had no idea how many of them there would be. Six probably, that was the capacity of the plane that two of them had flown down to the lodge several times before the abduction.

Joe knew that if it was just a matter of taking out six men, it would be no particular problem. He would probably just set fire to the building and take them when they came out. But to go in alone and find three little terrified girls, get them out alive and keep them that way, was going to be close to impossible. Especially with a kill-crazy son-of-a-bitch coming up behind him.

He didn't bother to try to hide his tracks, it would be a waste of time. Time that he didn't have.

He came around a point and up to the old lodge before he expected to. The lake probably wasn't as big as Diamond Lake which was only a mile long and about two thirds of that wide.

There are precautions that a man can take, and there are chances that a man must take, in a situation like this. Nam was a long time ago, but Joe was pleased to feel the same kind of euphoria that he'd always felt just before his team hit a target.

When he'd stopped at his office on the way to the plane, he'd taken something out of his safe and put it, disassembled, into the bottom of his pack, never intending to use it. He'd only brought it because some strange feeling had told him to. He squatted in the snow next to a clump of buck brush and reassembled it. When he was done, he held a stainless steel .22 automatic with a silencer screwed onto the muzzle and a twelve-round clip in its butt. It was a Seal Team assassination tool; one he'd forgotten to turn in when he left. He and most of the other Seals' had found it more effective than the televised version of the knife-fighting commandos. He levered a round into the chamber and stood up.

There was the sound of a radio or TV from inside the lodge. The sound was somehow alien and out of place here. He knew from listening to the voice on the way over that the only way in from the shore was up the ramp, as the building was set on pilings some five feet above the water. Each piling had a rat guard around the top to keep critters out. They would also keep him from climbing them. There was also a deck on the lake side that they tied float planes and boats to. The door from the dock opened directly into the great room and it would be suicide to try to enter from there.

Joe didn't stand around waiting to be seen or caught from behind. He simply walked up to the ramp.

He had one foot on the ramp when the door opened and a short balding man stepped out, already unbuttoning his pants in preparation for pissing over the railing that surrounded the porch. When he saw Joe, he stopped, perplexed, and then realization dawned. His eyes bugged out and his mouth opened to scream.

The .22 spit twice and the man died, his hands still obeying his now-defunct brain's command to open his fly. His body jackknifed down the snow-covered ramp to end up at Joe's feet.

Joe eased the corpse over the edge with his foot, where it bounced off the bank and slid into the lake.

A stain spread over the surface, but there was no one there to see it. Joe had already stepped inside. He knew that a hallway led straight ahead to the great room. To his left was a stub hall from which opened the lodge's four bedrooms.

He could hear an argument raging in the great room as he closed the door.

"We woulda been done and gone two days ago if this frickin' bitch hadn't fixed us rotten chicken!"

"Now just hold on. Who are you to call anyone names?"

"All right! That's enough!" The deep authoritative voice could belong to no one other than the one who had come with the pilot to the lodge. The one the pilot called 'sir'. "Now gentlemen, are we all well enough to perform?"

"Yeah. I can make them scream."

"Good. Now were in hell is Bailey?"

"He stepped out to take a leak."

"When he gets back in, have him set up the cameras. John, you and Patrick get into your costumes."

Joe stepped back against the wall, waiting for the two men to come to him. Maybe this would be easy. It was then that he heard the boss man demanding to know why his two actors-cum-rapists were going up the loft ladder instead of to their bedroom.

"It's too cold back there. We've been sleeping up here where it's warm."

Three of the doors were standing slightly ajar, probably to let heat into the otherwise unheated rooms, the building's only heat coming from the fireplace in the great room.

Only the first door on the left was closed. There were no locks on the doors, but this one was held closed by a plank notched to fit down behind the doorknob. Joe lifted the plank away from the door and pushed it open to find the three girls huddled in a terrified ball in the corner furthest from the door. He put his finger to his lips, then whispered, "Susie, your father sent me to rescue you three. You must come quietly and quickly. Understand?"

They nodded, but didn't move.

He motioned for them to hurry. Again, they nodded, but didn't move. He left them to check the hall, only to hear the boss asking again where Bailey was. Someone Joe hadn't heard before said that he was probably smoking to settle his nerves, and would be in a few minutes.

Joe stepped back to the door. The girls were at least standing, looking uncertainly at him. He tried a new tack, "Susie, Sally came with me, but she got shot by her brother Jerry, who helped these bastards kidnap you. She's laying down on the beach, bleeding. I have to get back to her. Are you coming or not?"

Then he remembered and unbuttoned a shirt pocket. "Susie, your Mom sent you your spare glasses."

That did it. They came at a rush.

"Each of you, grab a blanket."

There were six down parkas hanging on pegs in the hall, across from the room the girls had been held in. Joe pulled three of them down and handed each girl one. Then he eased around the corner into the main hall. So far his luck was holding. He motioned the girls out the door and followed, backing out. The door into the lodge opened in, so it could be opened in case of heavy snow, but had a forged iron loop handle on the outside to pull it shut with. Joe picked up a small piece of firewood from the pile on the porch and jammed it through the iron loop and across the door frame. It would maybe gain them a few minutes.

He led his tiny ragamuffin band out into the timber and behind a windfall, where he took the jackets and, using a jackknife, cut the sleeves off to fit each girl, then made sure that each jacket was zipped up, and the hoods tied tight under their chins. He was explaining to them how he wanted them to follow, and was showing them the hand signals that they would use when he heard four gun shots down where he'd left Sally.

And then four more, from a different rifle.

Grim-faced and sick, he and the three girls began what was to become an odyssey in human courage and survival.

Behind them the sound of men cursing and beating on the door faded. He picked his way toward the canoes, knowing that a killer was waiting for them.

Behind them a door splintered.

When he looked back to check on his charges, he discovered that they were not only leaving tracks, but also a trail of goose down as it worked its way out of the cut off sleeves. For some reason it made him smile.

"Where are you, Jerry," he said under his breath. "Come on, let's get this over quickly."

He was almost to where he'd left Sally, visually searching every available hiding place for her brother. And then he saw him. Face down in the snow, in a pool of freezing blood.

He had no choice but to take his troops with him when he crossed the open space between the timber and the patch of scrub spruce where to he'd left Sally.

She was still sitting in the canoe, which was now also riddled with bullet holes. It looked like she'd taken at least one more slug in her left leg. Hopefully she was far enough gone that it hadn't hurt much.

There were fresh tracks all around the canoe, made by one man. Joe wasn't certain, but he thought that they were Bob's tracks.

Joe knelt down beside her and said, "Sally, I kept my promise. They're here. Safe and sound."

She opened her eyes, but it took her a while to focus on first Joe and then the girls. She looked at them for several long seconds, then smiled.

"Bob say to wait. He went for their plane."

"How long ago?"

Her eyes closed and she took several shuddering breaths before saying, "Bob say wait."

The girls knelt around Sally, tears streaming down their faces. Joe stepped to the edge of the lake and looked toward the lodge. The other canoe was gone. Either he hadn't pulled it up far enough onto the shore or Bob had taken it.

He would wait.

Joe took one of the blankets and cut it into strips, from which he fashioned leggings for each of the girls. He had just tied the last legging in place on the smallest girl when something made him turn around.

He turned back to the kids and said, "Girls, all of our lives depend on you not letting those men sneak up on us. I want all three of you to watch. If you see one of them, whistle." He started off then came back, "You can whistle, can't you?"

"Sally taught me." It was the first time any one of them had spoken.   Up to now they had communicated with him by nodding and shrugging.

Joe ran down along the shore to where Bob was poling a floatplane toward them, helped along by the wind. Bob's chest was heaving and he was near collapse. He nodded at Joe and threw him a mooring line. Joe pulled the plane the rest of the way while Bob squatted on the near float trying to catch his breath. They swung the plane around, nose into the wind and tied it to a root that had been exposed by the wave action.

Maybe it was adrenaline or maybe it was because Sally's Gods were calling her, but Joe was able to lift her out of the canoe and set her in the copilot seat without help.

Joe had a pretty good idea what Bob had planned; it wasn't something they could discuss.

"You be all right with them girls until the County Mounties get here?"

"Yep. What about patchin' the canoe. Takin' them across in it?"

"Too much wind now. She'd sink. Guess you know, you upset them kid stealers somethin' fierce." Bob grinned and Joe grinned back. "You might want to get them kids up in the timber afore I light her off, cause they're gonna be double pissed now."

Joe untied the plane and pushed it out into the lake where the wind caught it and took it out of sight. He wanted to stay here, where he could lay down a covering fire for Bob, but he couldn't take the chance of getting caught and surrounded. He knew it and Bob knew it.

Joe took a long look at the timberline some hundred feet away and told the girls, "When I nod, you run like deer for the woods."

They nodded, he nodded and they ran, though not very well. He was sure that they should be able to outrun just about anything, but they weren't showing any signs of it.

As he passed Jerry's body he thought he saw Jerry's right hand move. He had the desire to dump a couple rounds into him. But he didn't want to horrify the kids any more than they already were. And besides if he wasn't dead, he soon would be.

They made it into the timber as the plane's engine turned over somewhere out on the lake.

From a hundred yards up the shoreline rifle fire began. Joe made sure the girls were down behind a windfall, and stepped out into the edge of the clearing. Bob would never get off the water if he didn't help. Joe emptied the rifle, keying on the gunshots, and drawing most of their fire, reloaded and emptied it again, all the while listening but never hearing the distinctive sound of slugs tearing into the plane.

Bob had spent little if any time letting the plane warm up before he gunned it into the wind.

Joe smiled when he heard the plane lift off the lake and drone off into the storm.

He hoped that the girls hadn't been able to run because of fear or being cooped up to long. Joe really didn't want to ask three preteens or whatever they were, if they had been raped. He didn't want to know. It wasn't any of his business to know.

"Why didn't Bob take us with him?" The smallest one asked, when he got back to where he'd left them.

"He's taking Sally to see a medicine man someplace north of here."

"Is she going to die?"

"In the sense we know death, yes, I suppose she will."

"Then why is he taking her to a doctor?"

"Not a doctor, Jeani." This must be Susie, she was wearing the glasses Mrs. Bradley had sent. Once a cop and so on he told himself. "A medicine man is like a witch doctor. He will take her spirit from her body and give it life in another body."

"I hope they make it in time."

"Listen, kids. These bastards behind us only have one chance to keep from being charged with kidnapping and stuff, and that is to kill all of us and hide the bodies where they won't ever be found. So we are going to play a game of hide-and-seek with them." He looked a each of them in turn, "If we lose, we die. Now let's go."

Joe had hoped to outrun the men to the walk log some three miles downstream. Probably four from here he thought. After a short hundred yards it was apparent that the girls weren't going to make it.

He hustled them into the timber and wiped the tears away from the little one's eyes. "Okay, gals. I have to ask, cause I have to know how bad you're hurt, so I know what action to take." They nodded in unison again. Damn! He thought, where was Janice when he needed her. Here goes. "Were you three raped?" The little one started to sob, the other two just looked at him.

"All right, ladies, you head right out through the woods, that way," he pointed with his rifle, "You set the pace, and I'll be right behind."

It took all of his control not to go back and try to kill all five of them.

The littlest one was still sobbing as the three clung together and wobbled along ahead of him. This is really great he thought.

Off to the left maybe a hundred yards something moved, gliding from tree to tree. Joe knew that they were being slowly surrounded, and unless their pursuers showed themselves pretty soon, they were dead.

The one up ahead was getting a little too cocky.

Joe waited until his charges were beside a rotten windfall some four feet in diameter, knelt in the snow, gave a single piercing whistle that he had taught the girls and caused them to go flat on the ground, and then fired. The man he shot at screamed and went down. Joe hit the ground, rolled over four times and came up behind a tree ten feet from where he had been. From there he watched the wounded man crawl back toward the lake.

A covering fire was coming from two directions, but they were shooting at where they thought he was, as opposed to his actual position. He shifted his stance so that he could see the girls. They apparently didn't like being shot at, and had crawled as nearly under the windfall as they could get. He needed to get over to where the girls where. He taken only two, running steps toward them when he realized that he had made a mistake.

A fourth rifle barked, not far off to his right, and that shooter had just been waiting for a clear shot.

The first shot hit his rifle, something he only thought happened in John Wayne movies, spinning him around; the second shot raked him across the rib cage on the left side. His momentum carried him in behind the log where he hit the ground face first, filling the front of his shirt with snow.

Rather than allowing himself the pleasure of dying, or even laying there long enough to let them know he was hit, he crawled down the length of the windfall, some twenty feet, and eased his rifle up over the top. It was then that he discovered that the slug had embedded itself in the trigger mechanism, rendering the rifle worthless. "Well now," Joe told himself, "this is turning into a real bummer of a day, and it's only about nine in the morning."

He shoved the rifle in under the log and covered it with snow. He'd just as soon not have them know he didn't have one. He debated about which of the two guns he had left would be the most effective at any sort of distance. It was still snowing hard enough to make anything over a hundred feet opaque. The most effective from a psychological point would be to off one of them with the silenced .22.

When he went to stand up the pain hit, far worse, he was sure, then when he took several hits in Nam. His knees were shaking, threatening to buckle, when he shooed the girls out ahead of him in the direction of where the one he'd hit had gone down. He found where the man had been crouching when Joe had shot him, the bloody snow angel he'd left, and the blood trail back toward the others, but no dropped weapons.

The least he could have done was to leave his rifle.

Less than hundred yards further they began to climb.

It wasn't going to work. The girls were totally spent and he wasn't much better.

Above them was what appeared to be the unbroken line of rimrock that Joe had hoped to get up against, find a cave and wait it out. But between them and safety was a long open slope covered with six or seven inches of snow.

He had no choice but to turn them south along the tree line. There didn't appear to be any pursuit at the moment. Probably seeing one of their own all shot to hell and having listened to him screaming had taken some of the desire out of the group.

Joe wanted to ask the girls some questions about the men, but so far he hadn't had the time. He had to keep them moving until he found a place he could defend, then he could ask them and form some kind of idea of what and who he was up against.

He could imagine that the boss man, and maybe one other, were having some trouble convincing the others that to pursue and kill was a noble and just cause. Especially since the pursued had the capabilities of fighting back. Probably a new concept to them.

The smallest girl stumbled and fell again. Joe had been mentally steeling himself for the time when he was going to have to carry her.

But it was her friend Susie who helped her up and, putting the smaller girl's arm around her shoulders, helped her along.

He wondered how any human could want to damage and destroy anything as precious as these little gals.

Somehow he had to keep his promise to Sally.

After maybe a hundred yards, or less, they came to a jumbled pile of boulders that had come off the rimrock above. The pile of rock looked inviting, but there was no way for one man to defend it. There was, however, a shallow cave created by the way the boulders had come to rest.

Joe called a halt to their trek and let the girls rest while he cut a piece of wire off of the roll of mechanics wire from his pack, wrapped it around a twig and jammed the twig up in between two rocks about four feet back inside the cave. He then took a cracker box out of his pack and after giving each girl a packet of crackers hung the bright red box from the wire. Next he tore a small square of aluminum foil from the packet of it kept for cooking purposes and hung that on the wire right below the cracker box.

He roused the girls and they continued on until they came to a narrow deep canyon carved out of the hillside.

Sally or The Voice had mentioned a trapper's cabin on the south side of the first creek below the lodge. He had also been told that it was almost impossible to find.

Though Joe was not eager to engage the group again, not having seen anything of them since the earlier exchange bothered him. He could be tracked easily, but there didn't seem to be anyone tailing him. They would most likely opt for an ambush, knowing he couldn't wait them out very long.

Joe turned them downstream toward the lake for a ways until he found a stand of bushy cedar that spanned the narrow canyon. He carefully helped his ragamuffins down into the bottom and as he was lifting them one at a time across the creek, Susie noticed the blood oozing out through his coat. She looked at the blood, looked up at him and raised her eyebrows, something he could see her mother doing. He grinned and shrugged his shoulders.

Once he had them to the top of the far side of the canyon, it was obvious that they had gone as far as they were able, at least for awhile. He wrapped them in the two remaining space blankets and, leaving them devouring a quart bag of trail mix and eating snow, took a hike up toward the rimrock.

They had been almost directly across from the cabin before he had turned them downstream. It was a ten-foot square box, sagging with age and backed up against a rock slide twice as big as the cabin was.

Joe was working his way back down to where he'd left the girls when he saw two of his pursuers across the draw. He eased down beside a tree and watched as the two men came up toward the rimrock on the other side of the canyon. They were about a hundred feet apart, the man furthest from Joe apparently was in visual contact with one still further over.

He couldn't see the girls from where he was, they were well hidden under the cedar tree. He was sure though that they were watching him, as he held a finger to his lips, pointed across the canyon and then gave them the signal to lay low.

Then he turned his attention back to the two men. After he'd shot one of them they must have pulled back to the lake and started a sweep upslope. When they caught his tracks headed northeast they probably spread out and were moving slowly up the slope forcing their prey to climb so that they could trap him and the girls between the timber and the rimrock. When he'd cut back to the south he had managed to get past them. In a very few minutes they would catch tracks headed south, drop back, regroup and come up from the lake again. They knew what shape the little girls were in, and they must know that they had hit him. The cabin wasn't going to do him any good except as a coffin, unless he came up with a plan fairly quickly.

He didn't want a firefight, as he was totally outgunned, and besides, the girls were more or less between him and the two men he could see. Maybe he thought, he could drop them with the .22 and the others wouldn't know for a while. The closest one to him stopped with several trees between himself and Joe. The second man in was moving on upslope, nearly to where Joe and the girls had come down. It was now or never. He took a rest against the tree and aimed for the man's head. As he began to squeeze the trigger, he grinned, not because he was about to shoot a man, but because now he had a plan. He lowered the front sight to rest on the man's belly and squeezed the trigger once, twice, and then a third time.

A look of disbelief on his pursuer's face turned to horror as the pain clamped down. The man threw himself backwards down the slope, a high-pitched scream filling the woods around him. He lay on his back, rolling from side to side, blood seeping out between his fingers as he tried to hold himself together.

The man closest to Joe emptied his rifle into the pile of boulders Joe had rigged to look like someone was in the cave. Joe watched as the man abandoned his fallen partner and ran down toward the lake.

As soon as he started running, Joe motioned the girls up to him. They came like three little ghosts, weaving up through the snow, dragging the blankets behind them. When they got to him, he led them on up to the cabin.

Inside was a rusty single bed frame, a small tabletop supported by crudely-made legs, and a rusty woodstove with a flat top suitable for cooking. A thin rolled-up mattress hung from one of the pole rafters by a frayed rope. Joe cut it down, and unrolled it on the bed frame.

"I can't build a fire yet. They might smell the smoke. But if you kind of scrunch up together under the blankets, you'll get warm."

Joe was reaching for the door latch when the littlest one said, "He was the one."

Joe looked at her and said, "Then you didn't mind that I shot him?"

She shook her head 'no.'   "Cause he kicked me in the crotch."

"He what?"

"He kicked all of us, lots of times in the crotch."

"Why in God's name would he do that?"

"He made us watch movies about girls being hurt--."

"Not hurt Jeani. Raped."

"I know that Susie. I just didn't want to say the word."

"Wait a second. Why did he kick you?"

"In the crotch."

Once she got started, she was going to finish.   Maybe seeing the one who terrorized them go down screaming was good. Hell, he didn't know.

"Okay I understand. But why?"

Susie looked at him a second like maybe he wasn't real bright and then decided to tell him. "They were going to make a movie of us being raped, and they wanted it to hurt real bad. So," she shrugged, "They kicked us."

"That one," the second girl spoke for the first time, "Kicked me in the butt, too."

"They did that to all of us."

Joe was nearly speechless with rage, he managed to say, "I'm going back out and see what they're up to. Will you guys be all right for awhile?"

"Do you have any more to eat?"

"What, didn't they feed you either?"

"No, just water."

He dug the last two bags of trail mix out of his pack and gave them to the girls.

"No, you take one," Susie said as she held the bag out to him. "You need it more than we do."

Joe moved downslope far enough to watch what happened across the draw. Almost absentmindedly he began to eat as he watched three men come up through the storm to their wounded comrade. As Joe had hoped the boss man couldn't afford to leave a second wounded man in the brush to die either, unless he wanted a mutiny on his hands. It would take up their time and energy to deal with the wounded men, where if Joe had killed them outright the man in charge would have left them where they lay with no repercussions from the others.

That part was good, but Joe didn't like what he was seeing. The man who had run off was in between two men who knew what they were doing. He watched, almost proud of how well those two had been taught. They would be decent adversaries, under the right circumstances. Each man moved to a position from where he could cover the other, then that one moved, ever vigilant.

When they got close to where their gut-shot comrade was laying, having dragged himself some fifty or sixty feet downslope, the one in the middle, the bait (though he didn't know it), pointed up at the jumble of rock. The other men nodded and moved up past where the middle man was trying to tend his fallen friend. The furthest one took a rest and peered through his scope for a second before throwing himself flat. He cupped his hands and called over to the one closest to Joe, "I saw him in there. I was lookin' right into the glass of his scope."

"Let's take him out," the other one said. His voice belonged to the one they called the Boss Man.

The other one nodded and they crawled into firing positions. The furthest one was too far away for an accurate pistol shot, but by hitting him, Joe hoped to further the illusion of him being in the cave. Once they began firing, so did Joe. After the fifth shot, his target rolled over behind a log and grabbed his leg.

Once the boss man saw that his partner was hit he stopped firing and worked his way over to him. Soon they started down slope, following the trail of where the gut-shot one was being dragged by his rescuer. Joe watched as the one he'd just hit fell twice, the second time heavily before they were swallowed up in the storm.

On the way back up to the cabin Joe realized that the wind had backed around to the west. That should mean a warm Chinook wind coming into the area, and that it was going to start melting. He knew that these early snowstorms were usually washed away about as fast as they came.

The stovepipe was topped with a coffee can wired to a pole to keep water and birds out. Before he went in Joe lifted the can off and set the lash-up to one side.

When he opened the door he found the three little girls sound asleep.

As the wind was now from the west and smoke couldn't be seen or smelled from the lake, Joe built a fire with wood stored under the eves. He found a gallon kettle upside down under the table, filled it with snow and set it on the stove.

He rested a minute, needing to see how bad he was hit and what he could do about stopping the bleeding while the girls were asleep. He had removed his jacket, shirt, and was pulling the thermal top off over his head when he heard the bed squeak.

Susie was sitting on the edge looking stern.

"Do you have a first aid kit?" she asked.

"I've a trauma kit right here. Know what that is?"

She snorted. "Of course I do. My Mom was a ERN before she married my father. She taught me just about everything."

"Oh, good."

Joe pulled the first aid kit out of his pack and handed it to her. Then watched somewhat skeptically as she checked everything out and announced, "This is not a very complete kit."

"Well, it's what I have. Let's see if we can find enough stuff to stop the bleeding."

"Of course. That's the first thing to do. Is the water hot yet?"

"No. It'll take awhile cause it's just snowmelt--purty cold."

"Do you have any pain pills?"

"Just ibuprofen. Before the other two wake up, can you tell me how bad you're hurt. You know, do I need to take the chance of getting you three past them right now, or can you wait awhile?"

"Jeani is bleeding quite a bit. Glenda and I are mostly just sore. None of us can go to the bathroom though."

"The cops should have been here by now. I imagine that they're having trouble in the snow. But they should be here soon."

"How come you built a fire?"

"The wind shifted around so it's blowin' out of the west. They can't smell the smoke unless they are up in the rimrock, which they aren't. And they won't be able to see the smoke in the dark."

"What were they shooting at?"

"You know that cracker box and foil I hung in the cave? They looked through their rifle scopes and saw that and thought it was us."

"Did you shoot any more of them?"

"One. You know the one with the deep voice? Well it's the other big man, the one with long hair."

"His name is Koto. He's the actor. I hope you killed him."

"I didn't, just hit him in the leg. What's the other one's name?"

"Everyone except Koto calls him 'Sir.' Koto calls him Hoss."

"Koto and Hoss were in the Marines together?" he asked.

"Yeah. That's all they talk about. Killing people. Koto has a friend who acts real funny. He's the one that you shot in the stomach."

"Is he the cook?"

"Uh huh. And the fat bald one is Bailey. He's the one that takes all the pictures. He's real scary."

"He's also real dead. That leaves two. One I shot when I got shot and one I haven't seen."

"I think they are both pilots. Cause they talk about flying planes in someplace called Nam?"

"Yeah. There once was a place called Nam."

She walked over and peered into the kettle, "The water is hot."

By the time Susie finished bandaging Joe's side he was close to passing out.

"Hey kid, I want you to wake the others and fix some hot chocolate; there should be about six packets in my pack. Then watch out the window. If you see anything, and I mean anything, wake me up. I'm sorry, but I am going to have to sleep for a little while."

While Susie got the other two up, Joe went out, took a leak, and checked the slope below them. It had stopped snowing and was already starting to get mushy underfoot.

Down closer to the lake he could hear the snow starting to come off the trees.

When he went back carrying a armload of wood, the little one was crying softly. He dug through his pack until he found a full bottle of ibuprofen. He gave each of them three tablets and then took four.

He went to sleep cradling his Beretta, and woke sometime after dark bathed in sweat. The cabin was cold and dark. He lay for a few seconds listening to the rain pound on the roof, and the sound of the snow coming off the trees. He turned enough to make out the figures of the girls, two slumped in chairs next to the stove and one watching out the window. He didn't have to guess which one was watching. For a kid she was something special.

He sat up and whispered," Susie, how come the fire's out?"

"You didn't say to put more wood in it."

"How long have I been asleep?"

"About four hours. We haven't seen anybody."

"I didn't mean to sleep so long. You three get over here and cover up. I'll go get some more wood and start the fire." And then he sensed or maybe heard something that changed his mind.

"Susie! Get the others awake and get over here."

Joe pulled the mattress off on the floor and ordered the girls to lay down on it. He wanted them as close to the floor as possible. Down below where most killers would aim. As he emerged from pain drugged sleep he became more alert, aware of his surroundings. Now he knew that there was a reason that he had awakened and he'd better figure it out.

He didn't open the door, but crawled to the back wall. He had noticed something there when he came in but had been too preoccupied to examine it. Every animal likes to have an escape route, and man was no different. Knowing this he felt along the wall until his fingers found the rough edge of a short board. When he pulled on it, it came loose along with the two beside it, exposing a narrow dark tunnel.

He took the first girl he came to by the arm and guided her into the tunnel before she had time to rebel, the other two followed dragging their blankets. Joe took his pack and, pulled the kettle off the stove (it had all but boiled dry and he dumped what little water was left in it, out), and followed them into the tunnel.

It was just wide enough that he was able to turn around and pull the trap door back into place behind him.

"You kids all right?"

A faint `yes' was all the reply he got. He felt through his pack until he found a package of food-warming candles , and lit one. Each candle would burn for four hours, a lot longer then he hoped they need one in the tunnel.

The tunnel was dug out of the dirt that lay under the rock slide. It looked like the tunneler had followed a water channel and had actually done very little if any, digging. Already a trickle of water was coursing down the tunnel floor from the snow melt, and disappearing under the cabin's floor.

He handed the candle up to the girls and asked them if they could see where the tunnel went.

"It goes around the corner, and then stops." Panic was beginning to take over one of his crew.

"Quit it, Jeani." He let the sternness of his voice rattle through the darkness then continued in a soft tone, "Listen to me, guys. This is an escape tunnel. It's supposed to look like a dead end. But it isn't. Now crawl up there far enough so I can get around the corner too. And try to stay out of the water."

As they began to move he urged them to pull the blankets with them. When they did, their blanket tails scraped along the tunnel wall and bumped against a gallon jug. When Joe got to where the jug was, he discovered that it was half full of kerosene. Beside it, in a recess, was a lantern and a small canvas-wrapped package. He carefully unwrapped the package to reveal a set of dentures.

While he was examining their find and trying to ascertain some meaning from it, a withering hail of rifle fire raked the cabin. Joe hurried his charges to the end of the tunnel. It was, as they said, solid rock. Susie, who held the candle, was beginning to shake.   Jeani was wailing and Glenda was beginning to sob, as still another barrage hit the cabin. Luckily, none of the rounds had found their way into the tunnel. Joe didn't like the idea of a round ricocheting around in there with them.

Joe took the candle from Susie and sat back against the wall. Then he looked up. A natural chimney led up at an angle, some ten feet to a wooden trap door. The rough rock made natural hand-holds. Joe figured that whoever had built the cabin had found the way through the rock pile first. Then built the cabin to take advantage of the 'back door'.

"Hey crew! There's a way out."

Joe threaded a rope through the lanterns bale, tied it to the kettle bale, and setting the gallon jug in the kettle, left them on the floor of the tunnel. He repackaged and left the dentures where he found them and after tying the free end of the rope to a belt loop, led the way up.

When he reached the trap door he told the girls that he was going to blow the candle out and open the lid, and for them not to panic.

He eased the trap door open to find that they were on the backside of the rock slide from the cabin. From here it was a good hundred and fifty feet up to the rimrock. On the other side of the rock from them, the cabin was starting to burn.

Joe knew they had no choice but to climb.

He got the girls out without mishap and pulled his booty up, then replaced the trapdoor, even though he knew that a escape tunnel without a place to escape from was probably pretty useless.

It was raining hard, and the melting snow was beginning to find its way down the slope in slush-filled rivulets as he roped the girls into a line and adding their newest treasures to his pack, began the climb.

He could hear his adversaries yelling to one another and laughing.

Laughing about having killed three little girls. For that, he vowed, they would pay with their lives.

Somehow they reached their goal, and then worked their way along the base of the rimrock until they found a cave some five feet wide and eight feet deep, with a ceiling height of about six feet. The entrance was blocked by a small rock slide that just allowed them to slip past.

All four of them were soaked to the bone and shaking from exhaustion. Before he allowed himself to sit down Joe hung two of the wet blankets over the entrance, one in from of the other, spacing them about two feet apart so that there was no chance of a stray stream of light getting past, and then filled and lit the lantern. The chimney was dirty, and the wick should have been trimmed, but he wasn't after light as much as he was the heat. Within minutes steam was beginning to rise from their clothes.

Joe had mentally gone over what food he had as they climbed toward the rimrock and had decided that once they found shelter he would feed them most of what he had. A good meal now was more important than trying to make what he had last for several days, and besides, the posse had to get here soon.

He climbed back out with the kettle and scooped it half full of slush then once back in the cave he took a small propane stove out of his pack he set the kettle on it. Once it was lit the tiny stove began to add to the warmth in the cave. It took twenty-two long minutes to heat the two quarts of snow melt to a boil. Joe dumped in two packages of freeze-dried beef stroganoff and stirred it with a stick he'd cut from a bush growing next to the cave's entrance, when he'd gone for the snow-melt.

When it was ready the four of them ate from the pot, handing the two forks he had in his pack back and forth.

After they'd eaten, he scrubbed the kettle clean with snow, heated more water and insisted that they each drink at least one cup of tea and swallow three more ibuprofen. The warm tea and the knowledge that they were safe worked on their bladders.

Joe directed them to the back of the cave and climbed out into the rain and waited until Susie called out to him that they were finished.

He still had one more surprise for them in the way of his over-sized hammock designed for backpacking. Joe had camped often enough in snake country to prefer being up off the ground. Here it would allow him to get them up off the cave floor and near the ceiling where the heat was concentrated. Along with the hammock he always carried four rock wedges, which allowed him to either hang the hammock from a ledge or to do a limited climb. Now, though, he set the wedges and suspended the hammock as near the roof as he could get it, and centered over the lantern.

He peeled the wet coats and shoes off of his crew and lifted them up into the hammock, then covered them with two space blankets. Within minutes they were asleep. But not before he had assured them that they would run no further.

Joe removed his sodden coat, wrapped his only other space blanket around his shoulders, and crawled past the blanket he'd hung over the cave mouth and up onto the rockslide that partially blocked the mouth of the cave to wait for what would come next.

There was no movement on the slope below and the snow was melting too fast for them to have been tracked, except by an expert, and he didn't think any of the three left were. With luck they would believe that they had killed him and the girls in the cabin and quit looking.

He slid back into the cave and picked up the kettle, taking it back out with him, where he filled it about a quarter full with slush. He carried it back into the cave and sat watching while it heated, tiny blue flames shot out from under the kettle when droplets of water slid down the outside and onto the propane burner. When at last it began to boil he threw a handful of coffee grounds into the kettle, gave it a good three-minute boil and shut the stove off. A handful of slush to settle the grounds and it was ready.

"Nectar of the Gods." He told himself as he raised his cup in a salute to the elusive ones.

"May I have a cup, too?"

He looked up into the green eyes she'd inherited from her mother, "How come you're awake Susie?"

"Just cause."

"Yeah you can have some, it's pretty hot. You want me to lift you down, or can you handle it up there?"

"Here's fine. Mom taught me how to lay in bed, lean on my elbows and sip hot chocolate."

"Okay, here you go. Ever drink out of a tin cup before?"

"Nope. Is the rim hot?"

"No. See how it's rolled over? It's hollow inside and keeps the coffee from making the rim of the cup hot, so it won't burn your mouth."

She took a couple tentative sips and said, "This is really strong! My father likes his coffee weak with sugar and cream in it."

He only half listened as she talked about her father, until he realized that she had stopped talking and was waiting for a reply.

"What do you mean, 'he doesn't like you'?"

"I hear him sometimes yelling at Mom about how she's nothing, and I'm no better." She paused awhile, and decided he could be trusted to tell something else, "He shot Mom's dog."

"What?"

"He shot Mom's dog."

"I heard that. How do you know he shot her dog?"

"I saw him."

Apparently he was going to have to ask more detailed questions. Joe wondered if driving humans nuts was a common trait among young teen girls, or if it was just due to the events of the last several days. Probably just the stress.

"When did you see him, where did it happen, and does he know you saw him?"

She squirmed around into what apparently was a more comfortable position for her, though it would have broken Joe's back to lay like that, sipped some more coffee, and said, "My father won't let me drink coffee."

He waited, she didn't continue, it was his turn again. He guessed that only one question was allowed at a time. He refilled his cup, leaned back against the wall of the cave, the Beretta on full cock lying in his lap, and tried again, "Why did he shoot your Mom's dog? Was it sick?"

"No, it wasn't sick. He shot it because Mom loved Rex and it made her cry."

"Rex! The dogs name was Rex?" He realized that his voice had taken on an edge.

"Yeah. Is that a funny name for a dog?"

"No. Not really. What kind of dog was it?"

"A golden Labrador. My father shot him, and left him laying in the driveway, down by the highway, and yelled at Mom when she came home and found him, for letting Rex run around. He said the dog got what it deserved."

Joe kept a tight rein on his emotions and asked the next question. "How did Rex get out?"

"My father put his leash on him and led him down there to where he shot him."

"Did you tell your mother?"

She shook her head `no.' "I was afraid to. If I told and Mom got mad at him . . . he might . . . he might . . . ." She buried her head in her cup and slurped loudly at the cold coffee.

"He might what?"

"Hit her again."

"Figures. You want more?" he asked, holding the kettle up. She gave him a tight little smile and shook her head `no' again.

For something to do while he thought, Joe reheated the coffee and carefully poured it into his cup, leaving as many grounds as possible in the kettle. When he looked up at Susie she was asleep, propped up on her elbows, her shoulder blades protruding up against her shirt like small, folded wings. Joe eased the cup out of her hands and tried to figure out how to get her off her elbows so she could sleep better. It looked too risky so in the end he just left her that way, and went out to sit in the rain and watch, wait for the dawn, and try to see the meaning in what was happening.

He knew that he had been called to this dilemma, by what force he didn't know. He knew that it had begun long before the phone call from Bradley, maybe long before that, maybe even before he was born. So far, everything he knew, everything he trusted and everything he hated had presented itself to be dealt with. He looked back at the entrance to the cave and smiled. Even his fear of being left in charge of teenage girls had materialized, and he made it through that, too.

If this was a test, it was a damn good one.

He hadn't thought much about his Dad recently, but when Susie told him that her Mom had a golden lab named Rex too, it was overwhelming. It all meant something, but he didn't know what.

Twice during the night he refilled the lantern and checked on the little ones. Susie still had her elbows caught in the webbing of the hammock and if anything her 'wings' stuck up higher than ever. She was snoring softly, he hissed at her several times to try and wake her up, but she didn't even stir.

He'd never been a father, never wanted the responsibility. Now for the first time he was beginning to realize what he'd missed.

By ten thirty the rain had let up and a ground fog was beginning to form.

Midnight brought a glow to the fog and the smell of wood smoke in the wet air; Joe figured they'd set the lodge on fire to cover their tracks. As the sky turned pink with the coming dawn four military helicopters came hammering over the ridge. The sound was reminiscent of many finished raids, and Joe met the sight of them with mixed emotions. He waited until they disgorged their human cargo and lifted off to scan the area from the air, before signaling to one of them with his space blanket.

Two of the birds hung back while the other two came in for a closer look, then darted away to hang in a row over the surface of the lake.

It took a mere ten minutes for a squad of Marine-supported police to arrive.

After signaling to the choppers, he had disassembled his twenty-two and packed it in the bottom of his backpack.

The girls were in no shape to walk, and after being examined by two paramedics, one of whom was a woman, were carried down to the lake on stretchers, to be whisked away by chopper.

Joe had far too much pride to allow anyone to help him or to even carry his pack for him.

On the way down Joe, the sheriff, and two marines had fallen behind the stretcher-bearers. After Joe gave them a brief description of what the girls had been subjected to the manhunt for the last of the killers was intensified.

Of the seven, two of them had been found dead on the lakeshore, a third sitting by his dead comrades in shock.

Joe stayed at the upper lake for over two hours, holding a cup of coffee in shaking hands and telling the sheriff and the various deputies and marines exactly what happened. As he described each incident, two marines (who were technically on site only to provide transportation) and a deputy left to find, verify, and photograph evidence at each scene.

Joe had been watching the marines, and after several minutes, had realized why they stood out.

Seals.

But why the hell were bubbleheads up here he wondered.

The fourth man, Bailey, was found just before Joe left, floating among the smoking pilings that had supported the lodge.

They didn't find Jerry's body, but there was a trail of a man using two walking sticks and losing blood that went up to the lodge and then over the ridge east of the lake. Two deputies lost the trail in a jumble of rock and brush after less than a mile.

Two other men had headed due north, carrying heavy packs and moving fast, though one of them also used a walking stick or crutch.

The decision was made not to pursue them, as the sheriff's office was not equipped to handle wilderness pursuits.

The state police would take up the chase the next day, but were presently occupied with a murder-suicide involving a fellow officer.

The sheriff was embarrassed as he explained to Joe how his men had become lost in the blizzard yesterday and ended up at another pothole lake two miles east. By the time they realized their mistake and backtracked it was dark. They tried again to find the right trail, but it started to rain and the snow began to melt and he'd had no choice but to recall the searchers to the lodge.

Sometime during the night the military had offered to fly him and his deputies in and so here they were.

It was understandable, and as Joe knew, typical of rural departments to be unable to respond to the occasional wilderness crime since they lacked adequate funding and training and were encumbered by bureaucracy, county and state lines, as well as petty jealousies.

That was one of the reasons that he could go into a situation and handle it.

Joe was also not surprised to learn that there was no trace of Bob and Sally, nor the plane they left in.

Once the chopper taking him to the lodge was airborne, one of the pilots took off his helmet and came aft. He smiled at Joe and stuck out his hand. "Long time no see, Padre."

Joe didn't shake hands, instead he eased back against the wall and looked at the six young bubbleheads and his old skipper from Nam.

"We're gonna park a while, Padre. Do you mind?"

"Does it matter if I do?"

Max didn't answer; the bird was already loosing altitude.

No one spoke until the rotor quit spinning and relative silence descended on them. Two of the Seals were digging through their packs, looking for food. Joe was glad to see nothing had changed, if they weren't allowed to kill it, they fucked it and if it didn't smell good enough for that, then they ate it.

Which meant that at least half their lives were spent looking for food.

"Joe, we got us a little problem."

Joe wondered about the `us,' but was sure he'd find out soon enough.

"Since you left we had a little thing happen out in the sand."

"Yeah. I read about it. Were you invited?"

"Not officially. The Round House set it. We did all the ground recon, which started a month before you heard anything about it on your high-tech crystal set. The flyboys took the credit. We pulled everyone's nuts out of the fire, and went home."

"Hell, I heard the flyboys did it all."

"You know better then that."

"Why are we having this little tête-à-tête? I've got a date with a steak."

Two of the men looked at Joe's tattered, bloody shirt and thought differently.

"Your old buddy, Mad Dog, was squad leader when they went in to do a S&R on a couple flyboys. Uncle forgot to tell all you armchair warriors that they got shot out of the big blue, and ran into a whole hell of a lot of Republican Guards."

"He sent these here kids back with the flyboys, who incidentally were female, and stayed behind with two of the boys who were already shot up and fought the Guards off long enough to get everyone else out."

Joe was cold inside, the hot anger would come later. Two of the young frogs wiped their eyes as the colonel continued, "The Guards took the three of them prisoner and Hussein has them in a courtyard prison. They're in good shape. We believe that he's going to trade them to us for immunity when his world collapses."

"The Main Man in the Round House don't want the black eye. He wants a precision air strike to take our boys out so Hussein won't have any tradin' stock. We want one chance to go in and get them out. And we want you to lead it."

Joe didn't say anything, his side was hurting and he was hungry. He couldn't think of any possible reason why they would want him to lead a team.

A big blond kid who looked like he ate ground beer bottles for dessert had just pulled a food bar out of his pack; Joe waited until he'd unwrapped it and then reached over and took it away from him. It was akin to kicking a hungry Big Foot in the ass. The other bubbleheads nudged one another, while the one who'd lost his dinner looked hurt.

"Why me?" Joe bit off a piece of the bar and went on, ignoring the puffed-up frog, "There must be a thousand guys better suited."

"Padre, if I thought there was anybody better, you wouldn't have been asked." He looked Joe right in the face and said, "Every so often a person comes along who has the ability to overcome the odds, make the right decisions, and enjoy doing it. I've followed your career with interest. The only time your runnin' on all cylinders is when you're lookin' for some lost kid. You know why you find 'em when one else can?"

"Yeah. I do my homework, and I'm not tied up in all the red tape that police departments have to deal with."

"That's part of it. But mostly its because you are only really alive when you're in-country. It's just that simple. Your knee is somewhat fucked up, but these kids are willing to bet their lives and the lives of their comrades on you."

The Seals all looked at him and nodded. The one from whom he had stolen the food bar even gave him a lopsided grin.

"When we heard that you were in a 'thing' up here we took a run up to see how you did. These guys made the final decision on you after seeing how you handled the 'thing.'"

The other men, all young enough to be his kids, nodded again.

They had seen him, knew he was old, knew he limped and probably had heard stories about him and knew that they weren't true, and they still wanted him.

"Think about it, Padre. I need to know within a month."

"This is a sanctioned thing. Right?"

It was the Skipper's turn to look hurt. "Padre, have I ever asked you to start a mission without the proper paperwork?"

Several of the Seals grinned along with Joe. Joe just wanted to know where they stood. The only paper work they would have would be the six sheets of Navy-issue toilet paper in their packs. Joe assumed that if they pulled it off then the Skipper would ask for the paperwork, backdating it as needed. It also meant that they were on their own. There wouldn't be any backup, but it also meant that there wouldn't be any red tape, which was better than the possible support.

While the chopper unwound in front of the Diamond Lake Lodge, Joe pulled a small packet out of the side pocket of his backpack and took his time unwrapping it. Inside was a of box of cards. He tossed the box on the floor of the chopper when he climbed out. One of the frogs handed him his pack, he said "Thanks," turned and started away, then came back and yelled into the bird as the pilot had already started to wind it up, "I'll need about a case of 'em." Turned and limped toward the assembled newsmen as the chopper lifted off.

The box was picked up and the contents shaken out on the floor. There were seven cards inside, each one was a black ace of spades with a tiny silver seal imprinted in the middle of the spade.

The colonel took off his headset and came back to squat among the frogs. He was smiling, "He just said yes. And just so you know, he was packin' two cases of them when he started up the Perfume River the first time. He never left a card except on personal confirmed kills." He started back to the cockpit and turned to say, "For you math whiz's there are twelve boxes in a case."

The big blond kid, the one they called "Four-Twenty," because he could bench press four hundred twenty, moved to the door of the chopper, intently watching Joe as he walked up the beach, watching to see how he moved, how he carried himself, was he aware of his surroundings, cause Joe was now his main man.   No one had ever challenged him before, he grinned, the Padre had, and took him, that was good.

They were half a click away and going up when Padre turned, his eyes boring into Four-Twenty. The Kid had seen all he needed to, this man they called Padre was the one he would stand beside, come what may.

Joe limped up to be surrounded by the news crews. They asked a lot of questions, took a lot of pictures, and then began to leave one by one, until Joe was left standing alone in front of the lodge.

He was too tired to care about how he was going to get to the hospital, right now he wanted a shower and something to eat. The front door of the lodge was locked so he walked around until he found an unlocked side door and went in. There didn't seem to be anyone in the building except him.

He used the railing to help himself up the stairs, found his room and the bags where he'd left them. Someone had been here before him, a softside attach case stuffed with maps and other information he would need was leaning against his duffel bag. Joe smiled, and while he took his clothes off, he wondered how long he had until someone dressed all in black would glide into his room some night and say, "It's now, Padre."

After shaving and then standing in the shower for twenty minutes he picked up a towel, wondering for the third time if he had enough strength left to get dressed and drive to a hospital.

He looked at himself in the steamed up mirror, and saw what he'd become.

Alone.

He laughed at his image and walked back into the bedroom.

Mrs. Bradley was sitting on his bed.

This was a good time for a good line, but instead he stood there naked except for a towel that he held more or less in front of his crotch, dripping and uncertain as to what to do next.

She didn't say anything, just stood and came over to him, and taking him gently by the arm led him over to the bed, where she laid him on his side, adjusted a goose-neck lamp she'd brought with her, and began to examine his gunshot wound.

His last thought before he passed out was that of how nice she smelled.

Chapter Seventeen

Joe was jolted awake, bathed in sweat and smelling smoke, then he realized that it was the smell from the burning lodge on the upper lake. He tried to wake up enough to get a drink of water, couldn't, and fell back into a troubled sleep.

The second time he awoke it was dark, black dark, and the only sound was of his own making, and that of the lodge as it settled with the cooling night.

He gritted his teeth and forced himself to sit up. It wasn't as bad as he thought it would be; it was worse.

Next he pushed himself off the bed and headed in the general direction of where he thought the bathroom was, hitting the door about two feet off center. His head made an interesting kind of 'bonk' sound when it hit the doorjamb. He made a decision, he would use lights.

Fifteen minutes later Agnes Bradley knocked once and pushed the door open with her foot to find him sitting on the edge of the bed wearing black jeans, moccasins, and trying to re-bandage his gunshot wound with what was left of the trauma kit from his backpack.

"Mr. Greene! What happened?"

"I took a shower and the bandages got a little soggy."

She set a tray laden with food on the table and said, "Here, let me do that."

"That food smells better than my side hurts and I see you got two of everything. How 'bout if we eat first? I'll put a shirt on so I don't offend you," he said as he pulled a quilted flannel shirt out of his duffel bag and pulled it on.

"It would take a whole lot more than that to bother me. Do you feel good enough to sit at the table?"

"You bet." He waited until they were seated and she was dishing up what looked like beef stew to ask, "Why aren't you with your husband and the Kid?"

"The 'Kid' is fine. She's in a hospital just down the road about thirty miles -- we can check her out tomorrow -- and my husband is in California, with his businesses and his friends."

Joe mulled over the 'we' in the check-out thing, and decided to let it pass, if he kept his mouth shut, she'd tell him everything she intended to in her own time. "How are the other two?"

"They're fine. Both were flown to hospitals of their parents' choice yesterday."

"You mean this morning."

"Fraid not, Mr. Greene. You slept the clock around."

"No way. I never sleep more than four hours at a time."

"I take it you've never ridden herd over three young teenage girls for any extended period of time before, have you?"

"No, I haven't."

"Well that explains it. That and having been shot."

"Ever hear any more about Bob and Sally?" He finished a cup of coffee and poured another from the carafe.

"No. They didn't land at any known airstrip, and there is no sign of any wreckage. There are still ten planes searching. At least they were until dark."

"Maybe they didn't land at all. Bob was taking her to her Spirit God."

She watched him eat, her green eyes hooded, not knowing if he was serious or not. Not knowing how she felt about the issue either. The best thing to do was to change the subject. "You were in Vietnam weren't you?"

"I'll tell you the same thing I told the Kid, there once was a place called 'Nam. Let's just leave it at that. You want that last biscuit?"

She waved it toward him and shook her head 'no.' "I'm stuffed. As chief cook I had to taste test all the food. You know the line, `It's a job and so forth."

He nodded, watching as she scraped the last of the stew out of the pan and into his bowl. "You're a damn good cook. But you still haven't told me what you're doin' here. The lodge is empty isn't it, except for you and me? Your kid is in hospital, and your husband is in California." So much for waiting for her to tell him everything.

"You scared?"

"I've been in worse spots and pulled through."

"Eat the rest of your dinner and while I re-bandage your side I'll tell you everything you need to know."

Rather than ask him to move again, she knelt beside him and once she could be busy with her hands and not have to look him in the face, she told him, "Tom and I are quits. Probably have been for a long time and just hadn't gotten around to dealing with it. I guess the last straw was when as soon as we knew that the girls were alive, he had himself flown out of here by chopper to catch a private jet for home."

"You mean that he didn't wait to see Susie?"

"That's exactly what I mean. He told me before he left that he had changed all of the passwords and codes to all of the accounts, and that all of his businesses knew not to accept any orders or requests from me. Not that I have ever asked."

"Pre-nuptial?"

"Of course."

"Gonna fight it?"

"Not a chance. I've done rather well with my painting, and have a very nice stash. Without the freedom being married to Tom gave me, I'd probably never become a painter. Nor would I have my daughter."

"Does he want custody?"

"Not in this lifetime."

"So what are you going to do?"

"Well for starters, I'm going to be your private nurse and bodyguard."

"Bodyguard?"

"Yeah. When Susie sees you she's going to go ballistic hugging on you."

"What!"

"Yeah, that's what I thought. You don't have a clue what you're in for. You need me to protect you."

"I've got to fly back to Portland tomorrow morning." He didn't have to, but he sure as hell needed to be away from the Kid.

"Like hell you do. I've been on and off the phone all day with your Janice, and an attorney by the name of Stu, as well as your mother."

"What do they say?"

"Stu says, `Don't bother to come back.'"    She thought a minute and went on, "Janice says, `Everything is shut down here,' meaning Portland, and that she switched all your calls over to the answering service that leases space from you, like you told her to, and that the last four outstanding accounts paid and she made the deposits into Greene Investigations."

"Then she said that you would be happy to know that she is going to go to into partnership with Stephanie, the woman you recommended to Stu as an investigator. They are going to take over your old office like you told her she should. And last but not least, please call her."

"What does Mom say?" he said, wondering how he could protect Janice and her new partner now that he had inadvertently stuck them on the front line.

"That you are a damn fool, but she's glad you weren't killed."

"She's really glad I didn't get killed?"

Hope was beginning to fill his voice when she went on, "Well she didn't really say so, but her tone of voice softened somewhat when I told her you were alive."

"She say anything else?" Still hopeful.

"Yeah, that she was busy with a customer. That's when she hung up."

Joe moved around a little into a more comfortable position.

"Sit still," she commanded. "By the way, I'm sorry I didn't see that nasty lump on your forehead yesterday. You must have bumped it in the cave. I have some homeopathic ointment that will take the pain and swelling away."

Joe mumbled something about not seeing where he was going, she nodded, made soothing noises while she finished bandaging his wound and then tenderly applied some salve to his forehead.

"Do you use natural medications?" she asked.

"Yeah, in Nam some of the hill tribes would chew up leaves and apply them to cuts and bruises."

"You ever try it?"

"It beats dyin' from infection, or bleeding to death."

"What did they do to stop bleeding?"

"You mean like gunshot wounds?"

She nodded, still fiddling with getting the bandage on his side to suit her, it having creased when he stood up.

"First you stuff the wound with spider webs, making sure the spider isn't in the web, and then you crush up some leaves off a sticky, stinky bush and stuff the gluey mess in, then cover it with a another kind of leaf that grows on a squat tree, not the one with the white berries, the other one."

"Then what?"

"You put on a clean shirt and go into Saigon and buy a gallon of moonshine that you drink. That makes you so sick that you forget about being shot and become stupid and volunteer to go back in-country again."

"You know that you have to have this checked by a doctor."

"Why?"

"It's the law. All gunshot wounds must be inspected and reported."

"Stuffy in here, isn't it?"

"The windows don't open in some of the rooms. I don't know why. The ones in my room do, want to go up there?"

"Will I be safe?"

"You keep asking that. And the answer is still, maybe, maybe not."

Joe slipped out of the flannel shirt, as it had gotten bloody from where his wound leaked on it while he ate and put on a black T-shirt, a process he found painful, picked up his Beretta and the duffel bag and followed her down the hall and up a short flight of stairs to her room.

"Hey this is really nice."

"It's one of four suites."

He looked around for a few seconds and said, "Don't turn the lights on, it's a full moon, let's just sit and talk in its light."

She busied around moving things off of the bed and the room's only chair; when she looked up, he had pushed open the double windows and was standing, leaning with his legs against the window sill at the same angle as the line on her easel. The moonlight played off of the window panes giving a bluish cast to his black outline.

The hair stood up on her arms and the back of her neck as she eased down into a sitting position on the bed. And then she could see the rest of the painting. The window frame with the moonlight on the glass, an area of the rug fading out into black and even the arm of the chair and a little of the red cushion showing.

A work of art. One she would never dare paint. Why she didn't know.

She sat watching him for some minutes until he moved away from the window. "That's one purty lake, isn't it?"

She just smiled.

"You know, I've got a feelin' that maybe we've traveled a lot of different roads with the express purpose that we meet. I know it's pretty soon to be saying this, but somehow I get the feelin' that we are destined to become partners. Is that how you feel?"

She nodded again, still smiling, and said, "There have been signs that indicate that. And Susie told me that I was to leave Tom and live with you."

"She said that!"

"Yes she did. Of course part of it was because she wants you for her father."

"Hey look, I'm--."

"Hey look, you don't have a choice. You saved her life, so now you have to be her father. Haven't you ever read the rules of a teenage girl?"

"I didn't know about them."

"Well, they are very explicit. Based mostly on fantasy, with hope and love thrown in, not to mention emerging emotions."

"Sounds like something I want to steer clear of."

"Well you can't. That's why you need me to protect you."

"It might help if I knew your name."

She laughed and said, "It's Agnes." She spelled it for him.

"I like it. So what's next, partner?"

"We buy the lodge from the bank?" She waited until he turned to look at her and she shrugged, "Bob and Sally were six months behind in payments. The bank foreclosed yesterday. The local bank manager tried to get them to hold off at least until they were found, but to no avail."

"That figures. Buyin' the lodge suits me. How much?"

"The notes are around one seventy. Plus the fees, make it about one eighty."

"The bank will want a little profit, I suppose."

"How much?"

"I bet two ten will buy it."

"Is it worth it? There's only ten rooms, plus the living quarters.

"Yeah, cause we both need a base, and this looks good to me."

Agnes frowned. "I can't come up with half of that right now. I'm having a big show in Reno next month that should generate maybe fifteen thousand--."

"I can front the buy-out."

"Will that leave you any operating capital? I know from the report Tom has on you that you have property, but if that runs you short we can probably buy it on contract."

"I doubt it. We're both self employed, new in the state, and the lodge has obviously not been a good investment."

"Are you sure we want it?"

"Yeah."

"I don't know how we could run it any better than they did."

"How good are you?"

"Painting?"

"That too. Are you good enough to give lessons?"

"Yes, and I can paint too." She smiled at him, "Yes. I'm very much sought after."

"Would students pay -- say twenty-five hundred for ten days all expenses except air fare -- to have you teach them up here?"

"I'm embarrassed to say, yes and maybe more."

"Can you handle ten at a time?"

"No sweat. With one assistant, easy."

"How bout ten days on and then ten days to yourself?"

"Done. And you?"

"I've got a couple things goin,' plus I can run my investigation service out of anyplace."

"We have a lot of things to talk about, if you're serious about this."

"I am. How about if I just lay on the bed while we talk?"

"Sorry, but one of my rules is no laying on the bed with clothes on."

She was about to add that she would make an exception due to his delicate condition, but before she could say anything he had stripped his shirt off, unbuttoned his pants and was stepping out of them. What the hell, she thought, might as well see what I'm getting.

He pulled the covers back and laid down on the sheet.

After her command she couldn't very well sit in a chair next to the bed and she couldn't lay fully clothed on the bed beside him either.

"Well old girl," she told herself, "You have created your own bed, now lie in it."

She slipped out of her clothes and eased into the bed beside him.

"Okay," she said, "You go first."

"I've got a rule too. No discussions unless both parties are lookin' at each other."

"All right," she said, propping herself up on one elbow.

"Not good enough," he said, as he gently pulled her over on top of him and then pushed her up into a sitting position straddling him.

She pretended to be shocked. "My! Don't we work fast?"

"Not at all partner, not at all."

He put his hands on her thighs, and ran them slowly up her legs and over her rib cage to cup her breasts. She arched her back against his hands as she reached down between his legs.

"What's this for?" she asked in her most innocent voice.

She didn't wake up until nearly nine thirty, then showered, dressed and made her way down the stairs humming the same tune that her mother had hummed some mornings.

"God, but I hope she was as happy as I am."

She followed the smell of coffee and ended up in the kitchen where she demanded food from the man she'd shared the night with.

He grinned and guided her, with a sweeping bow, to a small table in the corner that was set with a single place setting featuring a small gnarled rose bud that had survived the snow.

"You slept well?" he asked, as he filled a coffee cup for her.

"Well, yes, after I was finally allowed to go to sleep."

"If I recall, you were on top," he said as he placed a warmed plate containing bacon, two eggs over easy, and wheat toast in front of her.

She pursed her lips and tried to think of a reply that would prove that she had been taken advantage of. Couldn't, and changed the subject. "When will you be ready to go into town?"

"I'm waiting for two more phone calls. One from Portland, and one from Las Vegas."

"What's in Vegas?" she asked around a mouthful of toast that she'd dipped in the egg yolk that was spreading across her plate.

"My accountant. She's pretty good and she's very discreet. When I have an appointment with her, it's always by phone. She scans her office and phones constantly for bugs. During a call if a second phone is picked up, or a bug activated, her line goes dead automatically. Everyone is listed in her computer under a separate code word and is accessed by a password that she has memorized."

"So what happens if she dies?"

"I get a new accountant." He took a drink of coffee and picked several papers up off of the drainboard. "I had my accountant fax an agreement up to us. It concerns the lodge only. All other assets and liabilities are our own. And all checks from the lodge account must be signed by both of us. Most of the rest is just lawyerese."

Agnes spent nearly twenty minutes going over the documents before she looked up at Joe and said, "Give me a pen."

"It looks okay to you?"

"A partnership is built on trust. Either I trust you, or I don't. And vice versa. A handshake is good enough for me, but if something happens to one of us, then the other will need the paper work."

"Yeah, I agree."

He stuck his hand out and she stood up and shook it.

"I intend to treat you a lot better than Bradley did."

"What do you know about how he treated me?"

"Just what I learned it from your daughter."

"Really? How long did you converse with her?"

"Bout an hour." He thought that this was a good time to ask, "Did she complain of having a sore back?"

"Not particularly. Why?"

"Well she was up on her elbows in the hammock drinkin' coffee when she fell asleep, an her elbows were kind of stuck in the webbing of the hammock--" his voice trailed off as the look on Agnes's face became more and more puzzled.

"Yeah, go on."

"With her elbows like that, it kind of pushed her shoulder blades out," he grinned, and went on, "Kinda like wings."

"You left her like that?" Agnes's voice was taking on a edge.

"Hell yes. I tried to figure out how to lift her up and straighten her out, but I've heard so much about men touchin' little girls and gettin' in trouble that I didn't know what to do. I mean, you know, after everything that happened to her, if she woke up and found me tryin' to pick her up--."

"I see. You really don't know anything about kids, do you?"

"Nope, not really. I tried to wake her up, she was sound asleep."

Agnes began to laugh as she said, "You were more worried about being around the girls than fighting with those six bastards, weren't you?"

"At least I knew how to handle them." He paused, wondering if it was relevant, decided it was and said, "There were seven, countin' Jerry. An' I sure as hell count him. As for kids, I don't know much about them."

The phone rang and Joe answered it, talked for twenty minutes and when he hung up he was grinning.

Agnes decided to let the discussion about kids drop, for now, and told him, "I need to change the dressing on your gunshot before we go."

"Don't bother. I've been hurt worse reachin' for the last pork chop at breakfast."

"I'm sure. But we are going to the hospital, and my professional abilities will be judged. How they perceive that I treated you will have a direct relationship as to how I am treated in the community as a wife and mother." She realized what she'd said and added hastily, "I will be perceived as your wife or woman, whichever, whether we are married or not."

I guess I won't be crossing verbal swords with her, he thought.

"Okay. Whatever you think best. I was just trying to save you some trouble."

His second call came in while she worked on him, between sips of coffee.

On the way into town, it was decided that they would stop by the bank first, then go `fetch the Kid.' Joe parked in front and held the door open for Agnes. Once inside he asked the lone teller if they could speak to Mr. Harvey, the bank manager.

Joe introduced first Agnes and then himself to the manager who seated them at the desk in his dingy little office.

"How may I help you folks?" he asked, elbows on the desk, steepling his fingers in front of his mouth. It was a habit he'd picked up as a child when he'd used his hands to hide his broken teeth. Teeth broken by a drunken father on Christmas morning of the year he turned twelve.

Joe looked at Agnes who motioned for him to begin.

"We understand that your bank foreclosed on the Diamond Lake Lodge."

Mr. Harvey winced and spread his hands in an attempt to show his personal displeasure at what had happened.

"We know you tried to forestall the main branch, to no avail. We also know that you have outstanding notes against the lodge for around one sixty-five.

Harvey nodded, wondering where he gotten his information.

Joe went on, "Probably the reason that the main branch jumped the gun is that Pete Higgens Jr. who owns Great Getaways and is the son-in-law of the branch manager in Butte wants to buy the lodge for six cents on the dollar." He let that sink in, then added, as though he'd just thought of it, "If this is allowed and there are no other offers, you'll take the fall."

Harvey's face was ashen and his breathing was becoming very shallow.

"Agnes and I want to buy the lodge, at a price that will cover all debt and make you the fair-haired one at the bank managers' meeting this Friday."

He grinned at Harvey, "We are prepared to offer you two ten cash for it, as is."

"Cash?" Harvey's voice broke, he cleared his throat, swallowed, and tried again. "You will pay two hundred ten thousand cash for the Diamond Lake Lodge?"

"As is," Agnes added.

Harvey leaned back in his chair and grinned for the first time. "How, may I ask did you find out about Higgens Jr.?"

Yeah, Agnes wondered, how did you find out.

"I have a very good investigation service." He smiled back at the manager, pulled a sheet of paper out of the battered attaché case at his feet and handed it across to the banker. "These are the numbers of three Portland accounts that I wish to consider having electronically transferred to your bank. If you would get the balances on them, Agnes and I will decide which one we want to pay for the lodge from." Joe paused, a concerned look on his face, "You do have the authority to sell the lodge, don't you?"

"Yes, of course. If I deem the transaction to be favorable, I can sell it. The only time it would go to committee, would be if the offer was below bank policy concerning profit margins."

Or if you don't sell it before Friday, Joe thought.

"Is our offer within your guidelines?" Joe knew that it was, plus a little.

Harvey smiled and said, "Just."

He excused himself and went out into the lobby with the account numbers, where he gave them to the teller. He returned and struck up a conversation with Agnes regarding her painting, though in reality he was consumed with curiosity about the relationship between the two who sat facing him.

A look of shock came over his face, "Oh, where are my manners? Would either of you care for coffee?"

They both nodded and Agnes asked for cream and sugar. While he was out of the office, the teller came in, nearly tiptoeing, laid a stack of three sticky notes in the center of her boss's desk and glided away.

"Is he on the way back yet?" Joe asked.

"No he's still in the kitchen area. All I can see is his back. Why?

Without answering Joe picked up the sticky notes and used the bank pen he'd picked up earlier to add a two in front of the amount on the bottom sheet.

Good, he thought, it was the same ink as the one the teller used.

In response to her sharp intake of breath he said, "Don't worry Agnes, this is just for show and tell. I won't transfer that account."

Harvey was fairly beaming when he came back into his office carrying a plastic tray with coffee and three Danish on it. He was thankful he'd picked up the danish from the day- old sale bin in Safeway on the way to the bank that morning, intending to eat all three of them himself in a indulgent ritual he allowed himself every Monday morning, a payback for the two hour walk he and his wife made every Sunday, right after church, rain, shine, or snow.

They thanked him and busied themselves with their coffee while he tried not to reach for the sticky notes too soon. When he did, his eyebrows jumped at the first figure, he sucked his lip at the second and nearly choked at the third amount.

He spread them out in front of him and greedily looked from one to another, his pudgy fingers drumming on the desktop. For here was the salvation that he had prayed for in church the day before. Here before him was the influx of capital that would insure his security for the next five and a half years until he retired.

"How do you wish to proceed?" he asked.

Joe leaned forward, as if he wasn't sure what was in each account, "What's in the one under your left hand?"

"Six hundred forty nine thousand two hundred fifty-three and four cents."

"That one okay with you?" he asked Agnes.

"Yes, that one's fine. We can buy the lodge, and leave the rest in there for operating capital and expansion."

Expansion, Joe said to himself, what expansion?

"Mr. Harvey, if you would transfer that one into a joint account for both of us, we'll pay for the lodge out of it today."

"Please, just call me Ben." He wished that he could think of something intelligent to say, but right now it was all he could do to keep from jumping up and dancing. "Now, what about the other two accounts?"

"Let's see," Joe said, reading upside down, "Two million nine . . . let's skip that one for today," he said as he reached over and peeled the sticky note off of Ben's desk and folded it into a small square that he stuck in his jacket pocket, "and transfer the other one, it's what, seven hundred something -- I want to keep that one in a personal account."

"I would also like to transfer an account up here." Agnes gave Ben a deposit slip, "Here's the account number. I want it in a joint account with Joe. It's around," she thumbed through her checkbook, "Forty-six thousand." She looked at Joe and smiled. "I'll be making a deposit next month of about sixteen thousand."

Harvey was disappointed that he didn't get the three million dollar account also, but just slightly.

Agnes winked at Joe. It was time to start step two of the plan they made on the drive from the lodge to town.

"Ben, there isn't a car lot in town is there?" Agnes asked.

"Not any more. The Ford dealership closed two years ago in May."

"Would that be a good location for a used car lot?"

"Yes, it's just down the street, across from the saw shop."

"What kind of shape is it in?"

"It's been well maintained. The building is only, let's see, fifteen hundred square feet. There aren't any liens against it. Franklin is asking forty-one thousand for it. That's with a two-bay shop, both with hoists, and the air compressor is still in it.

Up front it has three small sales offices and a parts room. I think that Franklin might take a little less for it. His wife has had some medical problems, and they could use the cash right now."

"Under those circumstances, offer him full price for it."

"You want me to handle the transaction for you?" Ben asked, sitting up a little straighter.

"Please, and charge accordingly." Joe paused again, as if thinking, "Do you know of anyone who we can trust to run it?"

"Not right off hand." He steepled his fingers in front of his face again, even though he was consciously trying not to, and added, " And there won't be any extra charge, servicing your accounts will pay for my time."

"That's what I thought, but Agnes and I don't want to take advantage of anyone." He and Agnes exchanged glances and smiles.

Joe paused thoughtfully, then said, "How 'bout a veteran? I did a little time in Nam, and I'm partial to guys that did the Nam thing. I don't think most of them ever got a fair shake when they came home." He took a sip of coffee and tried to like it. "There must be someone in town who can run a lot."

"The only Nam vet I know of in town is Gus Fuller. He runs a pack string for hunters in the fall, and raises a few head of beef cattle. I don't know if he could do it, though he sure could use a steady job." Ben went on talking as he thought about Gus and his dilemma, "He has a wife, Phyllis, who works full time at the Safeway, and they have three kids." He shook his head, "Last year a new company came into town and is undercutting Gus's prices on taking hunters up into the national forest."

Ben steepled his fingers again and added, "On second thought he probably wouldn't work out."

"Why?"

"Well, he's crippled. Got all shot to hell in Vietnam, and he's getting so that he can't walk very fast, but most of all, he's too honest."

"Sounds perfect. Will you please hire him, by the hour, whatever's fair." Joe winked at the banker. "I'm sure it was your idea that we buy a golf cart with a surrey top for him to run around the lot in. After you have him and the lot, call Agnes, and she'll help him pick the appropriate paint colors, furniture, fixtures and she'll design the sign."

Agnes spoke up with, "We'll use the account I'm transferring to run the car lot with. So draft the checks concerning the lot out of there. If it starts running short during the startup, we can transfer from the lodge account."

Joe was turning the pen slowly over and over, Agnes was sipping coffee. Ben looked from one to the other and quickly picked up his coffee cup so he had something to do with his hands too.

"By the way, Ben. The company that is underbidding Gus is a subsidiary of Great Getaways. It, too, is owned by Higgens Jr. Also, just for your information, at Friday's bank meeting, a guy named Oberst, a junior bank manager working under Simpson in the Butte branch, will be requested by Simpson (right after Simpson gets you demoted), to take over this branch. Oberst is the brother of Higgens Jr. and changed his name just before going to work for Simpson."

Ben carefully set his cup down. "Can you prove this?"

"There will be a full report on your desk Thursday afternoon, and with your permission, copies will be delivered to the five bank trustees an hour before the meeting. I assume that Simpson will be asked to resign, as the report will show that he has a controlling interest in Great Getaways. You will be offered the Butte bank. I strongly suggest that you refrain from taking it and instead recommend Pete Hastings for the position. That will insure that you are protected until you retire in five and a half years."

Joe didn't push it any further and changed the subject back to the car lot, having let Harvey know that he had his life encapsulated as well.

"When you tell me to, I'll have thirty nearly-new four-by-fours and fifteen decent cars delivered."

"Where will you get them?" Ben asked, still having difficulty concentrating on what was being said to him.

"I have them in storage in Oregon."

Ben swallowed, his Adams apple bobbing wildly, "I see. I'll get the forms so we can fill them out for the transfers." He left the office, stopped to steady himself on the edge of the counter, where he waited until his teller finished with a customer and he could ask her to get the needed forms.

Thank God, he thought, I have Susan working today. She knows what form is used for what, and how to fill them out. He certainly didn't, but had always been going to take the time to learn. Now maybe he wouldn't have to ever worry about which form went to what. Now maybe he'd even have a secretary.

Twenty minutes later Harvey had increased the bank's portfolio by one million four hundred eighty-five thousand one hundred two dollars and eighty cents. He felt very sure that if he played his cards right that he would get the additional three million before long.

Joe slid his chair back and stood to leave, "I trust that our financial concerns won't be bantered about the town."

"No, sir, they won't." He wiped his sweaty hand on his pant leg and shook hands, first with Agnes and then with Joe. "I'll have the paperwork on the lodge ready to sign, late this afternoon. Sometime tomorrow, I should know about the lot and Gus." He stopped them in the doorway, "I will however let it be known that you two are very fine people. We don't get the chance to meet real quality folks very often. Thank you."

Once in the car, Agnes turned to Joe and asked, "What in hell just happened in there?"

"We just bought a banker. Cheaper and smarter than buying a bank."

"If we are going to spend very much time in there, I'm going to buy them a coffee pot. Instant coffee is not my cup of tea."

Joe laughed softly at her play on words and added, "I would imagine that after Friday, the bank will take a long, hard look at how they can make this branch show their support for their new accounts and reward Ben. His name will be on the report submitted to the trustees, not mine."

"How did you find out so much about the bank, Higgens, Ben and come to think of it, you knew about Gus and guided Ben into suggesting him. Didn't you?"

"Yeah, the investigation led to Great Getaways which turned up their desire to control all aspects of tourism in this area, which in turn led to Gus and his plight."

"How did you learn it so fast?"

"My accountant has ties with many different businesses. She doesn't service accounts that don't have something to offer in the way of services to other accounts. In other words, when someone calls and says that a friend has a lost child in Maine, she calls me. When I called and said that I needed a quick fix on this bank, she knew of someone who had done an investigation that had accessed the information that I needed. Whoever got the information, didn't need it for what they were doing, and was willing to sell it."

"Where did it come from?"

"I don't know. Won't know. Don't care. Paid handsomely for it, hoping we will get mega returns on it."

"Oh, I think we will. You just saved his career. But I wish you'd told me a little more of what you had in mind before we went in there."

"You're right. I guess I've been playin' it close to my vest for a long time. And it'll take awhile to get used to trusting someone again."

"Me too. But isn't it strange, how we were thrown together, by events totally out of our control, and emerged trusting one another to the extent that we are?"

"Uh huh. I think a lot of it has to do with us both being pretty sure of ourselves and capable of taking care of ourselves and our own, in any typical situation."

"Or maybe it's the Spirit Gods, and we don't really have a say in it."

Joe smiled at her and asked, "The Kid?"

The hospital was a one-story, pink, cement-block building with a view of a sawmill to the west and the city sewer treatment plant to the north. The south end of the building overlooked the gravel parking lot. A double carport stretched away from a set of double doors painted Chinese red with a flood-lit "EMERGENCY" sign above. They walked down the short sidewalk and into the main waiting room.

"Hospitals always smell the same don't they?"

"I was in one in New Delhi that made me wish for the smell of antiseptic."

"What were you there for?"

"To kill a patient."

She stared at him a moment, than asked, her voice flat, "Did you?"

"Uh huh."

"My God! How can you be so cavalier about it?"

"Remember those four kids and their mother who were tortured and murdered in Houston a couple years ago? The killer disappeared?"

"Yes, I would have gladly killed him myself."

"Well, I did it for you."

"Thanks, I guess," she looked at him, "Why did you tell me?"

"So you'd know that I will protect you and the Kid."

"Some men would have said, 'I'll protect you.'"

"Credentials." He looked around and said, "Where the hell is everyone?"

A perpetually-happy woman with frizzy black hair and too much eyeliner came around the corner, and said, "Oh! Hi! Did you ring the bell?" Not waiting for an answer she went on "I'm sorry, I didn't hear it."

"I, ah, we are here to pick up my daughter, and Mr. Greene has a gunshot wound that needs attention."

The Frizz's eyes popped and her mouth dropped open. She regained her composure and said, "No, shot?! Oh-my-God! I'll call Dr. Pierce." She started away, turned and came back, "Oh! Wait! First come with me, I have to stabilize you."

"It's not a big deal, it happened several days ago. Your doctor just has to check it and make a report to the sheriff."

"The Sheriff! Oh, I have to call him too!"

Thankfully another nurse came into the reception area to see what was happening. She listened to Frizz until Frizz ran out of words, and then turned to Agnes with a smile, and said, "Susie just woke up from a nap and is asking when she can go home." She turned her smile to Joe and stuck out her hand. "May I shake the hand of a hero? We have been hoping you would come in. Dr. Pierce is being notified, as you can hear. The sheriff called yesterday and said that you were sleeping out at the lodge and Mrs. Bradley had said she would probably bring you in."

"Frizz there is going to get the doctor all stirred up."

"No, not really. He knows that you're in good hands, and most importantly, he knows Frizz."

"You call her Frizz?"

"What else? Let's go check on Susie until Dr. Pierce gets here."

Joe had steeled himself for an over-enthusiastic welcome and was not prepared for the somewhat cool reception he got.

It wasn't until after Dr. Pierce had finished examining him and Frizz was pushing the Kid out to the battered lodge station wagon they were driving, that Joe had a chance to talk to Agnes alone.

"What the hell was that all about?"

Agnes smiled, "A teenager's sole responsibility to the world is to drive adults crazy. As long as you remember that, you'll be okay." She thought a minute and added, "Actually you won't be okay, but you'll go crazy in good company."

On the way back to the lodge they stopped at Safeway and stocked up on supplies.

From the way they were treated, it was a sure bet that every one in town knew that they'd bought the lodge. And Joe was pretty sure that everyone knew that they'd paid cash for it too.

On the way back to the lodge Joe asked, "How come the Doc used a tuning fork on my ribs?"

"He was checking to see if any of them were broken. A broken bone will vibrate and hurt like hell."

Joe thought about that for a minute and asked, "Then how come most doctors and hospitals use an X-ray machine?'

"So they can charge you for the X-ray. And with the sue-happy people of the U. S. of A. the doctors have to protect themselves against lawsuits."

"But if a tuning fork works just as well - -"

"There's no record. So let's say that you now go out and fall off a roof this afternoon- -"

"I'm not gettin' up on any roof."

"This is a let's say, not a for real."

Joe grumbled, but didn't really say anything. In the back seat, the Kid grinned, enjoying their banter, though she was careful to sit where Joe couldn't see her face in the rearview mirror.

"So anyway, you get a clean bill of health with the tuning fork, then you fall off of a roof and break those same ribs, and then you go to another emergency room and say, 'He said they weren't broken.'"

"I wouldn't do that."

"This is a what if."

"Okay. I see your point, but I wouldn't fall off the roof."

"I wasn't necessarily talking about a roof."

"Then why did you say that I fell off of a roof if you weren't talking about a roof?"

"The roof was a what if."

"Oh, now I get it."

"If you'd rather we could have a bicycle for the what if."

"A roof is okay for a what if."

"You sure?"

"Yeah, but how come he gave me a prescription for pain pills and antibiotics, even though I said I didn't want them?"

"We can do a what if?"

"With a roof?"

"No, this one would be with a nasty infection from a rusty nail."

"Being a doctor sounds pretty risky."

"Yeah. There are a lot of what ifs involved."

"Mom?"

"Yes, darling?"

"What if" I ask you where we are going?"

"Out to the lodge." She looked over at Joe, and then went on, "Joe and I bought the lodge as partners today."

She thought about it for a bit, than asked, "Do we have to go back to California?'

"No."

"Do I have to go back if he wants me to?"

"No."

"Denise's father has visitation rights, and she has to go to Colorado every summer for two months. She hates him, and her Mom doesn't want her to have to go. But if she doesn't then her father will take Denise's Mom to court and the judge will make Denise live with her father forever."

"Honey, I don't think - -"

"Mom, Denise showed me the letter from her Mom's lawyer. I'm not some dumb little kid you know."

Joe adjusted the rearview mirror so he could make eye contact with the Kid, and said, "If you don't want to go stay with him, then you won't have to."

Agnes started to ask him not to make promises that he might not be able to keep, then she thought of what he'd told her in the hospital, "Credentials" was what he'd said.

For the first time since she could remember, she felt like she was being cared for. Not just used, cared for. She slid over the cracked vinyl seat and snuggled up against him. He smelled a little like a hospital. And a little like a lover. Her lover. And a little like burned engine oil?

No.

Wait. That was the car she was smelling. An old tired Buick station wagon with a sick engine.

"I smell hot engine oil," Agnes said.

"Brilliant, Mom." Susie sighed like the world was on her thin young shoulders, "The car has been just about on fire for like ten miles."

"It's all down hill from here," Joe said, "And next week we'll get a newer rig."

"You know that the ice cream is going to melt before we get there." Susie said. "You should have brought a cooler chest like Bob would have."

Joe was beginning to wonder about the wisdom of the partnership when Susie leaned forward and kissed him on the cheek.

"Thanks." she said.

Joe guessed that maybe it had been a good thing after all.

When they pulled up in front, three women and a man came out of the lodge to help unload.

Joe was forbidden to do anything but sit in front of the fireplace in the main room and drink coffee laced with dark rum and fresh cream.

Agnes came occasionally to ask if he had any suggestions on how to staff and run the lodge. For the most part he didn't; the only thing he asked her to do was advertise the hell out of it and make sure that Exec-Air got the contract to haul all the passengers and freight. Providing that Captain Rori Tomlin was the chief pilot on all flights.

"Friend of yours?" Agnes asked.

"No. It's just that I owe her one. And she's good."

"How good?"

"Not that kind of good."

"Oh. That's good."

The sound of vacuum cleaners and the chirping sounds of women talking and laughing died away, leaving Joe alone with his partner and her Kid. He wandered into the tiny side kitchen to find Agnes dishing up two plates with fried chicken and mashed potatoes.

"Where's the Kid?"

"She asked if it was all right to spend the night with a friend in the village."

"A girl?"

"Joe! For God's sake! She's only twelve."

"In Portland, some of the most sought-after hookers are eleven or twelve and some filmmakers," he paused to let that sink in, "Just love little girls. So I'm probably always going to be over-protective. And it's not that I don't trust her. It's the bastards who prey on little girls who I don't trust."

Agnes nodded. "Okay, we can live with that." She finished loading up the plates and then said, "I can make Susie understand your feelings. But you'll have to give her some slack too. Or at some point she'll rebel." She watched him a bit and then said, "Oh, by the way, I said 'no'. She and her little girlfriend are asleep upstairs."

Joe took a bottle of wine out of the cupboard and while he was looking through drawers in the kitchen for a corkscrew said, "Raising kids is a lot of work, isn't it?"

"It's work, heartbreak, and sometimes just plain hell, but worth every minute of it."

He found a corkscrew in the main kitchen and opened the wine. "Sounds like a football game I played in for the state title."

"Did you win?"

"Nope. I dropped a pass inside the ten-yard line with less than a minute to go. We couldn't quite push it across."

"With Susie, we'll make a touchdown."

They ate in silence for a few minutes until Agnes asked, "I've been thinking about what Susie said about Denise's father demanding visitation rights. Tom would do that just to make me suffer."

"I don't think he will."

"Well, I think he will."

"Agnes, you don't understand. I -- don't -- think -- he-- will."

"Oh."

"By the way, I have to fly to Vegas for a couple of days to see my Mom and check on things. Need anything?"

"My painting equipment from my studio, all of my clothes and all of Susie's things."

She laughed, "But Tom will never let you pick them up. And please don't try. He has like a little army of men who lean on people for him."

"Is that how he buys out other businesses?"

"Probably. I've never been allowed to know anything about his businesses."

Joe nodded and changed the subject, "How would you like to furnish the lodge in antiques?"

"That would be great. But it would cost a fortune. I think that we should make sure that we're turning a profit before we start to remodel, don't you?"

"I've got several containers of antiques -- free and clear -- that I've picked up over the years. How about if I bring several of them up and we go through them?"

"Hey! Why not?"

"Okay."

Four days later a moving van found its way through the snow to the lodge and backed up to the main door. Inside, was the entire contents of Agnes's east LA home as well as the contents of their beach-front condo.

The moving van had no more than pulled out when three flatbed semi's, each pulling a trailer with two steel shipping containers on it, pulled into the parking lot. While the drivers were eating, a boom truck pulled up alongside of the parked rigs.

Several of the men from the village, all loggers and used to working with lines and booms and things that Agnes didn't understand, came up and within two hours all of the huge containers were lined up on the frozen lawn beside the lodge.

Joe pulled in around midnight and found Agnes still up.

"I thought you'd be in bed."

"I'm waiting for you."

"I'm here."

She got him a cup of coffee and then sat down at the table in the corner of the small kitchen, across from him. "How in hell did you get the things from my house?"

"Tom and I had a little chat."

"Tom doesn't chat, and I was hoping to wait until the divorce papers had been signed before I pissed him off."

"Oh, I have them. They're in the front seat of the Suburban I bought us for the lodge." He started to get up, "I'll go get them."

"I'll do it," she said on her way out the door. She was already reading through the papers when she came back in. "I have full custody?" she asked.

"That's what you wanted, isn't it?"

"And he's paying how much? Two thousand dollars a month in child support?"

"That's about as far as he wanted to go."

"My God!"

"What?"

"He's giving me a one hundred fifty thousand dollar settlement!"

"The check's in the other envelope."

"Joe! How did you ever get him---" her voice trailed off, "You hurt him didn't you?"

"Yeah."

"I don't condone that. And therefore I won't accept this."

"He killed your dog."

"He what! No, Rex got out of his kennel because I didn't latch it properly, and someone who was driving by shot him. Tom found Rex and my dog died in his arms."

"Tom put a leash on Rex and led him down the driveway to the road and the tied him to a tree and shot him. The worst part of it was that the Kid saw all of it, and couldn't tell you for fear that you would confront Tom and he's beat you again."

Agnes tried to say something, instead she slid down onto the floor where she sat cross-legged looking at Joe.

"Susie saw him shoot Rex?"

"Yeah. And good ol' Tom knew it too." Joe didn't know that for sure, but what the hell, it couldn't hurt his case any. Especially if she was going to get uptight about the newspaper article in the other envelope.

"What did you do to him?"

"I tried to reason with him. Really, I did." Really, he hadn't.

She nodded.

"He called in a couple of goons, as he called them. But wouldn't you know it, they had been in Seal Teams with me. And wouldn't you know it, they tendered their resignations right then. Well, then Ol' Tom and me had a little discussion and I left."

"That's it?"

"The next day, I was reading the paper and found an article that said that Mr. Tom Bradley had accidentally fallen down the stairs or something. I don't really remember what all he hurt."

"And if I was to want to know what all he hurt?"

"Then I guess you could maybe read the newspaper article that's in the other envelope. Or maybe the police report.'

"The police were involved?"

"Yeah. But only because of Tom being such an upstanding citizen and what-not."

Agnes opened the second manila envelope and dumped the contents out on the floor. She didn't pick the papers up to read them but bent over with her elbows on her knees and rested her chin in her hands. To Joe, the way she was sitting looked like torture. Occasionally she would reach down and poke a paper away from another one so that she could read something else. At one point she used a finger to slide the settlement check off to one side where she left it while she read the police report.

"Did you read this?" She asked.

"Read what?"

"The police report where it says that the investigating officers believe that Good Ol' Tom was set on by a pack of mangy thieves."

"It says that?'

"Well, not in those words. But close. And it goes on to say that my friend Tom did not have a clue as to who attacked him. He was sure that there were at least five of them."

"Why the mangy pack of thieves!"

"And then down here it says that my former friend, Tom, sustained several serious injuries. Such as a badly broken left leg, right in the knee, a broken right elbow, and then it says that he will have to suck soup through a straw for some time to come."

Joe nodded. He didn't like the serious look that was coming over her face, maybe he'd discussed Tom's pattern of behavior with him in a little too much detail.

"The scum bag shot my dog, made my child watch, and this is all you do to him?"

"I thought we'd agreed that it was a pack of mangy thieves that set about robbing him?"

"The mangy thieves were a what if."

"A what if?"

"Uh huh."

"So if maybe, and this is just a what if, I did have something to do with his falling down, it was justified?"

"I'm guessing that he will never play tennis again?"

"What does "multiple fractures of the femur and tibia" mean?"

"It means that he will never play tennis again."

"So are you okay with this?"

"He never gets visitation rights. That's all I care about. The rest is gravy."

"Speaking of food. Is there anything around here to eat?"

"Is this a what if?"

"No, this is an I'm hungry."

"I'll fix you something. What would you like?"

"A steak be a problem?"

"Nothing is a problem for my partner."

"I got something of yours in the Suburban. I'll go get it while you fix dinner."

"Are you sure you should be carrying anything yet?"

"I feel okay. It's not bleeding any more, and it doesn't hurt unless some former tennis player hits me in the side. Then it hurts like hell."

"What!" she said, coming around the corner from the kitchen into the main room, a large chef's knife in her hand.

"I give up."

"No, not yet, you don't. What's this about getting hit?"

"When I was discussing your former friend, Tom's, options with him, he hit me with a golf club."

"Where?"

"Well, I think that now I can sue the Doc."

"He broke your ribs?"

"Maybe. They sure hurt."

"Take your shirt off."

Just as she said that, the Kid came around the side of the fireplace, having come down the stairs when she heard Joe come in.

She snorted and folded her arms across her chest. "Mom, we need to talk."

"About what?"

"You should at least wait until you get him upstairs."

"He got hurt again. Someone hit him with a golf club in the same place he got shot."

Susie looked at Joe with her eyes hooded. "Take your shirt off," she said. And then to her mother, "I'll go get the first aid kit."

Joe took his shirt off and was led over to where Agnes could shine a lamp on his side.

"Where did he hit you?"

"Right here." Joe said.

"Joe! It's on the other side from where you were shot."

"Yeah, so?"

Susie came into the kitchen carrying a suitcase-sized kit.

"This little bruise is where you got hit?'

"Yeah," Joe said, trying for at least a little sympathy.

"You needn't have bothered with the kit," Agnes told Susie. "It's like a little soccer kick."

Susie sighed and shook her head. "Let me see," she examined the bruise and told her mother, "I'd be embarrassed to even show you such a small nick."

"I thought nurses were compassionate?" Joe said with all the hurt he could muster in his voice.

"We are. And we tend to call 'bullshit' on baby bruises."

"It hurts."

"I'm sure it does. Now where was I?'

"You were going to fix me a steak."

"Can I have one too?" Susie asked.

Joe was still grinning when he got to the Suburban. The back door was frozen shut and it took him several minutes to get it open. When he carried the first box into the lodge, Susie met him at the door with a hug and a kiss on the cheek.

"What's that for?" he asked.

"You know," she said.

He carried the box into the kitchen and as he set it down he asked Agnes, "What was that for?"

"You know," she said, pointing at the divorce papers laying on the table.

"You let her read them?"

"Susie's as involved as I am."

She turned toward the stove, then turned back around staring at the box. She dropped the spatula on the floor and her face went white.

"Where did that come from?" she managed to ask.

"Your former friend Tom had some things of yours in a locked room behind his home office."

"How did you know to look there?"

"I'm a pretty good investigator, and when I found a blank wall that shouldn't have been there, I got curious."

"Is there more?"

"Yeah. The back end of the Suburban is pretty much full. I brought your stuff myself instead of letting a moving company see it."

"So you know?"

"I didn't open the two big trunks, but I can guess how you put yourself through school."

"And does that change how you feel about me?"

"Sometime, if you don't mind, I'd like to see your act."

"Really?'

"Yeah."

"Did you go through everything?'

"No. But I imagine that Bradley did."

"You want to call Susie? Dinner is about to be served."

"Sure, where is she?"

"Upstairs someplace. I think she went to call her friend Denise."

"It's one-thirty in the morning."

"So? What, phones don't work after dark where you come from?"

He found her with her feet on a bed and her head twisted to one side against a chair leg chattering away to someone.

"Your Mom says 'Chow.'"

"What?"

"Dinner is ready."

"Gotta go. Call me tomorrow."

As they started down the stairs together, Joe asked her, "Doesn't it hurt to lay like that?"

"Why?"

He shrugged and tried to think of something else to say to her but couldn't.

Chapter Eighteen

T he next morning, Joe and Agnes just 'happened' to walk into the town's main diner while Deputy Charlie Walker was having breakfast.

"Mind if we join you?" Joe asked.

Charlie slid his newspaper out of the way and motioned to the chairs across from him.

He stood and held Agnes's chair for her then made sure that the waitress, who was one of his four kids, saw that service was needed.

Over coffee Joe said, "I understand that the Sheriff is going to retire in two months."

"Yep."

"And we hear that it's either you or Ronnie that's gonna get the nod."

"Yep. But I don't figure to have much chance."

"Why not? You're by far the most qualified," Agnes said.

He looked at her a moment to see if she was just blowin' smoke, decided that she meant it and said, "Thanks, but I don't have the funds to run a campaign, and even if I did, I wouldn't know how."

"Well then, you're in luck," she said smiling. "We have the funds, and I know how to run one hell of a good campaign." (After all, she'd gotten a friend elected as secretary of their PTA.)

He sat back in his chair, wondering what, if anything, they wanted.

"If you're wondering, we don't really want anything," Joe said. "Except the best man in the driver's seat. Ronnie hasn't ever done much except administrative paper shuffling. I wouldn't feel very comfortable with him heading up the Department."

Then Agnes threw in the clincher. "And everyone knows that he doesn't like anyone who isn't white."

Charlie let his lip curl, just a little. "There's a lot of folks like me back in the hills."

"Yeah. But unless they've got a damn good reason, they won't come down to town to vote," she said.

"I figured it up once." Charlie said, and ducked his head, "It'll cost near five grand to run against Ronnie." Letting them know that he had seriously considered running but had dropped the idea for lack of funds.

"We are prepared to do whatever it takes," Agnes said. "To run a fair and honest campaign."

"I gotta talk to my wife," Charlie said, forgetting his breakfast, and starting to stand up.

"By the way," Joe said, "I hear that the State Police called off the search for the other two kidnappers yesterday."

"Yeah," Charlie said, sitting back down, "An I don't much like havin' them two bastards up there." He nodded toward the mountains that rose like notches on a saw blade behind the town.

"What say you and me take a couple, maybe three days and go get 'em?"

Charlie looked at Joe, a smile slowly spreading across his face.

Chapter Nineteen

That night, Joe and Agnes had a dinner party for everyone in the village. As each couple came in, they were given a number between one and eighteen (which was the number of the home owners in the village). After dinner Agnes drew numbers from a bowl and the number holder got to pick a piece of furniture from the lodge. The only things not up for grabs were the things in the kitchen, the wooden Indian by the front door, and the little table used by guests to sign in, the only piece of furniture that Bob had ever built.

Within an hour, pandemonium reigned. People held mock battles over beds, mattresses, and even the large, gaudy, hand-painted flowerpots that Sally had bought for the lodge, "To get some color up," she had been fond of saying.

By eleven that night the last of their guests left carrying their loot out to the various pickup trucks that were scattered around the snow-covered parking lot.

A raw-boned woman, carrying one of the flowerpots, her cheeks hot pink with excitement stopped at the door and called to Agnes, "I feel like an invader who just helped rip off a castle."

The next morning Agnes headed a cleaning crew in preparation for unloading the containers, while Joe packed his backpack and checked his weapons.

"You be careful," she told him before he left, trying hard not to sound like a nagging wife, trying not to cry. "You've got two reasons to come back now."

"I will," he said, and after climbing into a newer four-by-four he'd picked up from the first shipment of rigs from Oregon, he started the engine, then got back out and climbed the steps to the porch.

He gave Agnes a hug, then took a deep breath and, leaning over, gave the Kid a hug too.

As he drove away, she looked up at her mother, "What was that all about?"

"A beginning. That's what it was all about. A beginning."

Chapter Twenty

Following the directions Charlie had given him, Joe drove through town and up a side road until he came to a bright blue mailbox beside a narrow driveway that led him through a stand of fire-scarred pine to a neat white farmhouse.

As he pulled up in front Charlie came out carrying a rifle and a backpack. He nodded to Joe then picked up two sets of snowshoes that had been leaning against the porch railing and set them in the back of the pickup along with the backpack. He opened the door, set the rifle in front, and said, "A minute." Joe watched him as he went back up onto the porch and went through the, "Goodbye--Be careful" routine.

Once under way Charlie relaxed some and asked Joe how he was.

"I'm good for maybe ten miles on snowshoes."

"That's got me beat."

Joe wished he'd said something else. Thoughts of Bradley's boasting crossed his mind.

"I mean, that's my max. I'd rather not go that far in a day, but I can."

"Oh."

"So where are we going?"

"North. Back through town, and then head north on Sawtell Creek Road. We'll pull off this side of the main fork." He paused for a minute while he fiddled with the zipper on his coat. "Damn thing sticks." He gave up on the zipper and rolled his window partway down. "I got the report from the State Police. They checked out five cabins in the Sawtell Creek drainage."

"That's where we're goin,' isn't it?"

"Yeah. You shot that one bastard in the right leg. He wouldn't have climbed for very long before he started sidehillin.' And I don't figure that they would have tried to go over the top of the main range."

"I agree. Even if they did go over the top, there still wouldn't have been any way for them to leave the area."

"You're pretty good at finding people, where do you think they are?"

"I figured that they would be somewhere in the Sawtell Creek drainage. But if the Staters checked all the cabins - -"

"I said they checked five cabins."

"So there are more than five?"

"Yeah. If the uppity bastards had stopped to ask damn near anyone in town, they'd have known that there are seven cabins up there. And three mine shafts that are set up to stay in."

"They dragged a heat sensor through the sky for a couple of days. If Hoss and his buddy Kato holed up, then it's probably in one of the mineshafts. The heat sensor couldn't pick them up and it would be easier to defend - - a hell of a lot easier."

"That's what I'm thinkin' too." He fiddled with his zipper some more, then gave up and rolled the window down the rest of the way, "That's what you call them, Kato and Hoss?

"The girls said those were their nicknames. I suppose they have others."

"Yeah. I suppose. The Staters haven't released them though."

"Why?"

"Who the fuck knows."

"Maybe they don't really know who they are."

Charlie shrugged, he didn't much care who they were, as long they took them in.

"This window bein' down bother you?"

"No, not really." It wasn't a good time to be a smartass, so Joe didn't make one of his stupid remarks. "So how do you want to take them?"

"If they're in a cabin, we'll burn them out."

Joe was a little startled at Charlie's biting hatred.

"And if they're in a mine shaft, I guess we go in after them."

"Burn them out?"

"Yeah. It's a lot better than gettin' shot."

Joe smiled.

"What's so damn funny?" Charlie asked.

"When I first met you, I figured you for a by-the-book sort of guy."

"I am, unless it concerns my people."

"Your people just the Native Americans?"

"I'd rather you didn't use that shit term; we're Indians."

"What's that make me?"

"Whatever the fuck you want," he grinned, "And by the way, my people include everyone in this county." He paused to pour them each a cup of coffee out of the thermos his wife had given him when he went back for the "Be Careful" thing. "You still want to back me for Sheriff?"

"Yeah, more than ever."

"You'll be turning off the road just around the next bend."

They pissed, shrugged into their packs, and after checking their rifles and strapping on their snowshoes, headed uphill.

"Damn, I wish we'd had a mile or so of flat ground to get my knee limbered up," Joe said.

Charlie just grunted, and picked up the pace.

Okay, Joe thought to himself, if that's the way you want to play it.

They spent the rest of the day trying to force each other to call for a halt.

Neither did.

It was nearly dark when Charlie stopped and said, "We might as well stop for the night. No use walkin' off a cliff in the dark."

This allowed them to stop without either one of them losing face.

When Joe didn't respond, Charlie turned to see what he was doing.

Joe had stopped some fifty feet behind and was now walking back the way they'd come, stopping every two steps.

"What do you got?"

"I think I smell wood smoke."

Charlie took a quick look around as he levered a round into the chamber of his rifle and then started back toward Joe. He stopped some twenty feet from him, "Damn if you didn't! An I walked right by."

Joe wet his index finger and held it up. "Comin from over that way, isn't it?"

"Yep." Charlie grinned, "You know what this is going to do to my reputation? Letting a White Man out-Indian me?"

"I won't tell, if you don't."

"Oh I intend to. I've never been one to take credit for something I didn't do."

Joe wondered if Charlie was referring to something he'd done, but didn't ask; instead he said, "What's up there?"

"A cabin. The mine shafts are nearly a day further up the canyon."

"I vote we wait till dark."

"Fine by me. "

They found a rockslide that had cascaded down from a rimrock above them, and squatted among the boulders. They hadn't found any tracks that indicated that anyone had been walking through the area since the last snowfall, but to be safe Charlie kept watch while Joe brewed tea. After they each had a cup in hand, Charlie pulled a sack of homemade cookies out of his pack and shared them with Joe. "I hope you like oatmeal cookies."

He did.

They waited until well past dark to begin moving toward the cabin.

They both hoped that the other didn't notice how bad they were limping for the first hundred yards, until the adrenaline overrode fatigue and allowed their "been there--did that" bodies to put one foot in front of the other without sending shock waves of pain through their systems.

"Colder than the brass dick on the courthouse monkey," Charlie said.

"Yeah," Joe managed through clenched teeth.

The cabin was built against the trunk of a large cedar, its snow-covered limbs draping down over the roof.

"Guess now we know why the planes with the infrared cameras didn't find them."

"Uh huh, I should have remembered about this one bein' under a tree."

"You think they were smart enough to pick this one because of that?"

"Yeah, probably. They were both in the Special Forces. Like you."

"I was in the Seal Teams. Way the fuck better unit than Special Forces."

Charlie grinned, "Yeah, right. Guess I forgot that."

"You do any time wearin' green?"

"Nope. Never left this here part of the world. Got a brother who got himself killed in Vietnam."

"We lost the best over there."

"And we lost some of the not-so-best over there too."

Joe didn't push it, either Charlie meant that his brother was a fuck-up or else he was talking in general.

They spent nearly an hour working their way up to the back of the cabin, which had the only window.

Charlie was for just raising his head up and peering in the window but Joe stopped him and gave him a small mirror attached to a telescoping handle, then he stepped back far enough to cover him if anything went wrong.

After several minutes Charlie backed away and motioned Joe in under an adjoining tree. "Neat," he said as he handed the mirror back.

"It's better than getting your head blown off."

Charlie nodded. "It's them. The one you shot looks to be in bad shape. I'd guess that the other one is fixin' to leave him."

"Soon?"

"Probably tonight. He's putting his pack together now. The one you shot is unconscious. His breathin' is pretty ragged an his leg is all swollen to hell. You did alright with your shootin', he's got two holes in his fuckin' leg."

"Best to wait and take Hoss when he comes out, huh?"

"Damn straight. We won't have to burn the cabin down which is good, cause if we do, then he'll have to help Slim build another one."

"Let's move off a ways and wait for him."

Charlie nodded and led the way down to a trickle stream that ran along the front of the cabin, and then up through the brush that grew along its bank to a point where a faint trail led from the cabin across an open space of maybe thirty feet to the creek. There they crouched down behind boulders and brush and watched the cabin.

Joe dug a bottle of ibuprofen and a tin cup out of his pack and took four of the painkillers, chasing them with a cup of creek water.

"Got any more of them?" Charlie asked.

They took turns watching the cabin while the other stomped up and down along the creek trying to keep the circulation going.

Two hours is a long time under those circumstances, three is even longer. It was nearing nine at night when the cabin door opened and the one Joe knew a Hoss came out. He glanced around as he shrugged into his pack and, seeing nothing that bothered him, set out toward the creek. He took only two strides before he fell flat on his face as the warm soles of his shoes turned the snow under foot to ice.

He got up on his knees, cursing softly, and was reaching for his rifle, which was still laying in the snow, when Charlie kicked him in the side of his head.

He grunted and lunged at whoever it was who had kicked him. Charlie wasn't expecting that; he'd never had the training that instilled the instinct to immediately attack whatever attacked him, nor had he dealt with anyone who had.

The two men went down in a flailing heap.

Joe let it go for a minute or so, just to see who was what.

Joe figured that if Hoss hadn't been encumbered by the pack he would have taken Charlie.

At least at first.

Which, in a real life fight like that one, is usually all there is.

First or dead.

Joe waited until Hoss reached for the knife strapped to his leg before he stepped in, grabbed Hoss by his pack and jerked him backward, almost onto his feet, and threw him on his back some ten feet from Charlie.

Hoss didn't know he was done and started to get up, knife in hand, when he saw the automatic glinting in the moonlight . . . but most of all he saw the smile on the face of the man behind the gun.

It was then that he knew that he was done.

He dropped his knife and waited for what would come, be it a slug or handcuffs.

Once they had Hoss cuffed, searched, and slightly roughed up, courtesy of Charlie, (Charlie was somewhat indignant about having a split lip and snow down the back of his shirt), Charlie said to Joe, "You took your own fuckin' sweet time gittin' around to helping me."

"You know, all my life I've heard about 'Injun fightin' and I thought maybe I was gonna get to see some."

Charlie didn't say anything, just glared at Joe.

It was nearly dark the next day that they got back to Joe's pickup. Hoss wasn't looking forward to where he was going, but he seemed fairly happy to be somewhere that didn't involve dragging a homemade sled with his partner-in-crime on it.

While Joe got the pickup started and warmed up, Charlie tied the two kidnappers into its open bed.

Joe called Agnes from the first house they came to that had a phone, and when they pulled up in front of the Sheriff's office an hour and a half later, having excepted the invitation from the home owner for coffee and home made apple pie, there were ten reporters from various agencies clustered around the front door, seven of them having been flown in by chopper.

"What the hell is this? Charlie asked.

"This is the first day of your campaign for Sheriff. Agnes started setting this up right after we left yesterday."

"You coulda told me."

"You didn't ask. Besides, I'm not your fuckin' campaign manager."

Chapter Twenty-One

Later that night when they were alone -- the Kid was spending the night with her friend in the village -- she still didn't like to be alone -- Agnes told Joe to wait ten minutes and then come upstairs as she had something to show him.

He wound his way through clumps of antiques that were haphazardly grouped throughout the lodge, and followed the sound of recorded drums to an empty room next to their bedroom. Inside was a small curtained stage, lit by candlelight, and a single wooden chair. Joe sat down in the chair and waited. After a few minutes, the curtain opened to expose two women, nude except for negligee and feathered headdresses. Then one of them began to dance around the other. Slowly the dancer stripped the clothes off of the second to reveal not a woman but a bass fiddle, elaborately carved into the shape of a nude woman. Slowly the dancer began to stroke and play the fiddle, then as the tempo increased, her stroking turned to fondling and then as the filmy outer curtain closed, the dancer seemed to be making love to the fiddle.

The second curtain closed, the candles in front of the stage went out, leaving Joe in darkness. He realized that they were electric, probably battery operated.

When Agnes came out from behind the curtain, she was carrying a single candle and wearing a loose-fitting silk robe. Beads of sweat shown like diamonds on her arms and forehead.

"Well?"

"That was downright fantastic!" He stood up and pulled her to him, "I've never seen an exotic dancer who was any better."

"That's how I put myself through school. Two gigs a month usually did it, in private clubs and sometimes in private homes."

"Want to go to bed?"

"Sorry, that's not part of the act."

"Yeah, but . . ."

"I'm still pretty good?"

"I never saw you before, but I sure as hell like what I see now." He paused, "I didn't mean the go-to-bed part as part of your act."

"You didn't?"

"No."

"Okay, then we can go to bed."

An hour later when Joe thought nothing could get any better, Agnes sat up in bed and began drawing designs on the bare skin of his chest with her fingernail. "Joe?"

"Ummm?"

"You're leaving pretty soon, aren't you?"

"What do you mean?"

"There was a guy here last night; he said to tell you that they'd see you in a couple of days."

Joe didn't answer, he was wondering what in hell was going to happen next or if this was still part of the ultimate test. The one where he couldn't win and would fail. The one where failure meant death. He wondered if he wanted to go through with it, and deep down inside he knew it wasn't up to him to decide. He wondered if it ever had been his call, or if for always, what he did was guided by whatever force it was that ran him.

About Dave Mead

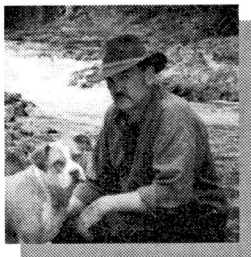

(In His Own Words)

I'm a fifth-generation logger. The West Coast kind who say "cork shoes"
   instead of "calk boots," and drive muddy, battered four-wheel-drive
   pickups as town cars.
Spent three years as a night-shift cop in Portland. (And a damn good one,
   too.)
I've watched a blue heron stalk his breakfast in a mountain lake.
I know what a water buffalo smells like.
Held a newborn baby,
Hunted elk from horseback, and raced cars,
Fought a few fights where second place wore a toe tag.
I can fix a cat (cut the nuts out of one type; rebuild the engine on the other).
Sipped some pretty good wine; drank a few bottles of Mad Dog,
Skied the back-country on white-bright snow, and mucked about in the dark.
I've danced with ladies and bargained with whores,
Built barns and burned bridges.
I can paint a car, but not too well.
I've never been lost, but I've seen those who have.
Dined with the elite, and coffeed up with the down and out.
I don't like being shot at,
But I do like a good fight.
And sometimes when I walk, I limp.
For the past ten years I've been a corporation president. (My office has
   windows that roll down and a steering wheel.)

But mostly, I'm a dreamer.
A watcher of people,
A recorder of almost reality.